CHILD IN THE VALLEY

CHILD
IN THE
VALLEY

GORDY SAUER

HUB CITY PRESS
SPARTANBURG, SC

Cover Illustration: Jeffrey Nguyen
Lead Book design: Kate McMullen
Author photograph © Katie Barnes
Proofreaders: Stephanie Trott, Kendall Owens

Library of Congress
Cataloging-in-Publication Data

Names: Sauer, Gordy, author.
Title: Child in the valley / Gordy Sauer.
Description: Spartanburg, SC: Hub City Press, 2021
Series: Cold Mountain Fund series
Identifiers:
    LCCN 2020047122
    ISBN 9781938235795 (hardcover)
    ISBN 9781938235801 (ebook)
Subjects:
LCSH: Wagon trains—Fiction.
    Overland journeys to the Pacific—Fiction
    California—Gold discoveries—Fiction.
    California—History—1846-1850—Fiction.
GSAFD: Bildingsromans. | Historical fiction.
Classification:
    LCC PS3619.A82295 C48 2021
    DDC 813/.6—dc23
LC record available at https://lccn.loc.gov/2020047122

Hub City Press gratefully acknowledges support from the National Endowment for the Arts, the Amazon Literary Partnership, South Carolina Arts Commission, and Chapman Cultural Center in Spartanburg, South Carolina.

Manufactured in the United States of America
First Edition

HUB CITY PRESS
186 W. Main Street
Spartanburg, SC 29306
864.577.9349 | www.hubcity.org

for Edith, my child
and for Carli

EVERY MAN WHO landed on the island was immediately devoured by these griffins; and although they had had enough, none the less would they seize them and carry them high up in the air, in their flight, and when they were tired of carrying them, would let them fall anywhere as soon as they died.

GARCI RODRÍGUEZ DE MONTALVO, *Las Sergas de Esplandián*

BY THIS SUDDEN discovery of the gold, all my great plans were destroyed.

JOHN SUTTER

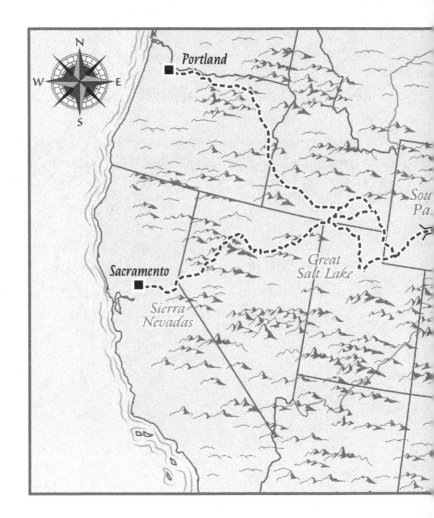

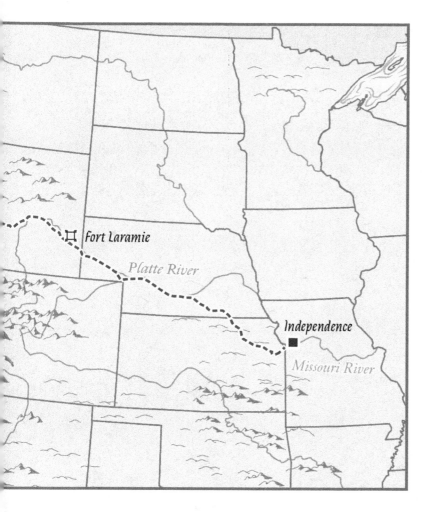

By the 1850 United States census, the non-native population in California had soared from fewer than eight hundred people in 1848 to more than 92,000. Most of those settlers came for the gold, and nine out of ten were men.

PART I

THE CHILD

PRELUDE

If he isn't the youngest boy ever to ride that steamer, he's surely the loudest, contending with those newly inflated infant lungs' chance and circumstance, just as he'll fight those ladies all the way through the rest of his life. He is completely hairless, an errant kind of perfection, and the rain and the river blasts that breach the hull, thin the blood on his body, and begin to clean him, to wash the viscous and coiled remnants of his birthing from the slick main deck. Awestruck passengers snatch the whipping edges of their coats or shawls and pull them tighter. A harsh northerly wind. An aggravated Mississippi licking port then starboard, higher and higher as the boat pitches.

Year of your birth, '32, and the baby boy won't stop crying. He is born into this world bearing the loss of his parents, and in some cosmic way he knows this. So he cries for them, and for his own tragedy that loss bespeaks. And he cries for this torturous moment upon which his birth is marked: a steamer chugging south to St. Louis, in early March, in this tempest that collapses the shoreline and sky in total darkness so that the boat runs now as if enclosed in a giant box. He cries so much that his fresh voice begins to crack, outstretches his arms and legs while he tries to push that angry sky out of sight.

Dr. Gaines frees one hand and wipes his drenched face before he begins to rub circles on the child's stomach.

Shhh, he whispers, though no one, not even the child, can hear him through the storm. Shhh.

Dr. Gaines pauses for a moment, then cuts the umbilical cord with a rude pocketknife a passenger has offered him. The foul stench from the mother shitting herself still lingers and comingles with the blood, but the doctor resumes shoving rags between her legs, his hands, though warm, indistinguishable to him. It's his duty to traffic in the body's cannibalization, and his choice—an inherent source of pride. But it seems he's never seen a woman bleed so profusely. It's as if a hole has opened up inside of her, as if her body is trying to rid itself of blood entirely. She is young, not much more than a child herself, already so pale her new child looks darker beside her. The rain has soaked her dress, thins her with an illusory power, and her arms flop heedlessly beside her like two dying eels.

The doctor has long run out of fresh rags, so he pulls out the old ones, wrings the blood onto the deck, then drapes that rag over his knee to let the rain clean it further while he pressures into her pelvis a rag he's wrung just prior. Pinned between his knees, the child lies atop his coat. He wasn't meant to be birthed out here, but the mother had simply collapsed, no moving her under the hurricane roof after that. And the father? He lost his footing on the deck running to fetch the doctor, tumbled over the side and was consumed in the swallows of that river so quickly that those who saw him fall said he simply disappeared into the black.

Given these circumstances, the doctor has already named this infant child: Joshua, he calls him, without even thinking about it. Joshua Gaines.

Soon, the clustered and rain-spattered passengers give up their spectating, while from the boiler deck still others continue to watch this scene, the hazy jacklights silhouetting and malforming their figures, a party of unwelcome spirits. No one seeks to help. Too much trauma, too much struggle, which plucks too closely at the chords of their own lives and the lives of those they've loved.

Dr. Gaines drags his face with his sleeve. He pinches his monocle with his cheek and eyebrow as he does, the cold and the rain and the fatigue stinging his eyes. There's been no sign of life in the mother for some time now. Still, he tries to stop her bleeding.

Twenty-four stars and those peppermint stripes whip overhead so fiercely the ends of the flag begin to fray. Then a gust tips the steamer even more to its port side. The flag sheet breaks from its pinning and the flag tangles around the sheet and all of it strings out in the direction of the tipping steamer, guiding its way underwater. Dr. Gaines grabs hold the railing with one arm to keep from tumbling across the deck, the other clutching Joshua, the child's toothpick chest pumping rapidly, the heart in all its mystery so new and yet so ready for a world fraught with chaos.

Suddenly freed from the doctor's care, the mother slides effortlessly across the deck and slams into the railing, her spine reforming itself into a right angle.

Dr. Gaines stares at her for a minute. There's nothing good about the way she's died. Perhaps it occurs to him to utter a cursory albeit empty prayer. Perhaps he thinks she's a believer, but as her body slowly lets go the railing, slinks around the smooth edges of it and slips into the river, those thoughts, if they'd been had, are erased. She's the better for such vanishing anyway because no one, regardless of the calluses physical and otherwise that life in this border state renders, wants to see a mother almost one-day dead brought into the port of St. Louis. By then, and with the beating her body has taken in childbirth and after, she'll be hardly recognizable as human, and what good can come of such a memory, even in the minds of strangers?

Cradling the crying child against his chest, the doctor watches her depart. Then he retrieves his drenched coat, grabs the cleanest rag he can find, and walks with heavy footfalls up the whitewashed stairs to the boiler deck. He looks like a man who's climbed out of the river. His black hair stuck in sprigs to his temples; his black suit wearing the shape of his body, convex here, concave there; his monocle fogged, hiding the coal-bit pupil so that it appears as if he has one eye. With his pointed features, the blackness and straightness of his hair, not to mention the beady eyes that carry an air of alertness escaping most Anglo-descendant men, he looks part foreign, too difficult to place. Maybe Indian, maybe Mexican. Such indefinability makes most people uneasy, and so along with his drenched suit and fogged monocle, what Dr. Gaines also wears, regardless of the season, is a kind of cloak of disconcertedness.

He stands at the top of the stairs for a moment in seeming indecision. Several passengers regard this odd pair, looks of detached pity or dismay. Most explicitly avoid them. Not yet twenty-one, unmarried, without a practice to his name, en route to a home he only knows in his dreams, Dr. Gaines finds a seat among the cargo boxes because he can't afford a cabin. The other passengers—some in apparent ill at ease by the way they shift from leg to leg—engage in curt conversations, perfunctories to rein the evening's finality so that they can retire later, sleep away the child and his foreign doctor.

Dr. Gaines loosens his cravat, commences drying Joshua with the rag. Afterward, he pulls the child into his chest to let him settle into the warmth his body exudes: bone, muscle and ligament, tissue, all of operating in sequence, in magnificent collaboration to render a relaxed state. The child's crying fully stopped, the soft rise and fall of his distended stomach, irises like blue sapphire nuggets.

Above the clouds biding a complex space those on the steamer can't see are the Dippers (Big and Little) and Pegasus. Orion is up there somewhere, and brighter still Venus in all her tormented love. Of course, the knowledge of such astronomy isn't a thing on anyone's mind right now. Just to say those stars are there, shining brightly as they always shine night in and night out regardless of the Earth-bound weather, and such unflinching consistency is a fact too easily forgotten when subject to nature's whims. The storm taunting this steamer won't let up for hours, so not until dawn, just before they make port in St. Louis, will those stars suddenly reveal themselves. Then, only then, will that inexplicable glory of heaven be again truly pondered and little Joshua welcomed as a profundity of improvisation.

PART II

THE ORPHAN

CHAPTER ONE

No longer a child not quite a man, Joshua Gaines arrives in Independence, Missouri a week after he fled St. Louis. He staggers across soggy Lexington Street with its barrage of bonneted prairie schooners and droopy-necked oxen, the men and women who guide the beasts enraged by their stubbornness, mule-drawn carts tottering around them with stacks of wooden crates. Gray snow clumps in the lee of the flat-faced storefronts, the town basting in the dankly wet smell of shit and piss on this anomalously cold April day. He sees a white picket fence in front of the white and cupolaed courthouse, a hitching post the same shade of white and nearly the length of the street before the fence and populated by horses, all of whom swish the incessant cloud of flies. Joshua wipes his forehead with the back of his arm. A useless gesture, clammy skin mashed to clammy skin, while he eyes the horses disdainfully.

Their circumstance is a foregone plight, a hardship they can be privy to only through the immediacy and ephemerality of its present. For them there is no future, and how dark and soulless a life like that must be.

The first three hotels he inquires in are full. The fourth is a good distance from the square, tucked in a grove of hardwoods so that it stays perpetually in shadow. After he wipes his dusty boots on the rag rug, he discovers it has one vacancy.

You've got to share it though, says the innkeeper. Not the bed, I mean. Just the room.

Joshua weighs his options while the man stares at him and scratches his cheek and chest apelike as he grows visibly impatient with the silence. The man taps his pen on the ledger, points it at the medical bag.

That yours?

I'm the one carrying it.

The man frowns at this wit, though he lets the slight go as quickly as he'd reacted to it.

So you a doctor then, huh, he says.

The assumption, so simple and so declarative, is to Joshua the very embodiment of possibility, a future of reclamation and self-definition. He is a doctor here because he chooses to be, as he can choose to be anything—not an indebted young man twice orphaned in the span of seventeen years, for instance—and so in turn be that by his choosing.

I've never seen one before myself, the man continues. You look different than I'd expect a doctor to look. More normal, except for that limp you got. What happened to your foot there?

Joshua looks at the innkeeper for a moment without reaction, then shrugs.

The innkeeper frowns.

I see, he says.

Reminding himself that this is the only hotel with a vacancy, Joshua checks his snideness. He turns and regards the bulbous wax figurine on the end of the counter. It looks like nothing more than a gnarled ball, but he's seen enough terrible crafting on the streets of St. Louis to know a terrible crafter will never refrain from talking about his terrible crafts.

Did you make that? Joshua asks.

I did, the innkeeper says proudly. I sculpted that bust out of old candles. It's me, see?

The innkeeper picks it up and holds it beside his face as if to mirror that kinked visage, the nose that angles so severely toward the corner of his mouth someone must've beaten him silly once. Joshua glances from the bust to the man whose jaundiced skin mimics the color and consistency of the wax, rendering an even greater resemblance between the two. A malfunction in the liver, Joshua thinks.

Gives the place a…how is it the Frogs say it? Raisin detra, says the innkeeper.

He nods and sighs, deeply and satisfyingly.

I see it now, Joshua says, and he's not lying.

So.

The innkeeper smiles, pulls the room key off its hook, slaps it on the wooden counter.

You want the bed or not?

For seven dollars a week?

The innkeeper smiles again and shrugs.

There's no supply, but there sure is demand.

And what if I don't stay a whole week? Do I still have to pay the full seven dollars?

If you aren't here by the end of this week, it means you're on your way to the gold fields. So you won't need that seven dollars then. Consider it an offering to those of us less fortunate than yourself.

Joshua frowns. What does this man know about the state of his fortune? And why would someone so presumptuous about the riches to be found in California not abandon his post and strike out west himself? Seven dollars is more than he'd planned for his stay here, but he knows he has no choice. He's tried the other hotels, he's seen the congested streets that seem to birth wagons.

He pulls out a mix of two-dollar notes and coins and hands them to the innkeeper.

Top of the stairs, second room on your right, number three, the innkeeper says, pocketing the money.

As Joshua watches the bills depart, it dawns on him why the innkeeper is staying put when so many, from this country and otherwise, are landing here just to keep going west: This man has already discovered his gold, because only those whose nothingness is the result of someone else's somethingness—the indebted, the destitute, the fathers, the lovers—must mine the earth for its raw and hidden treasures.

Joshua grabs the key, heads upstairs. A brass three hangs horizontally from a loose middle screw, looking like a pair of testicles. The hallway is nearly dark with no window, and there's no light coming from under the room's door.

Joshua puts his ear to the dense wood, hears nothing. Still, he knocks before walking in, but he finds the room empty.

LATER THAT EVENING, the wind turns in a cold front. His roommate, a preacher, returns in silence and falls fast asleep, a woolen blanket pulled over his gigantic body and tucked underneath the white thicket of a beard that disappears his chin. Joshua shivers as he lies in his bed, the wind issuing from the open window and sharp with human stink.

He's staring at the ceiling, at the gobs of cobwebs decorating the black and amorphous water stains that resemble tumors, and he's wondering what this world is he's brought himself into. He had a home in St. Louis, he had a father, which meant he had a sort of love that even now reluctantly clings to him in pieces. But life like the body, he knows, must have no past. It must recalibrate, reformulate, reconstitute to usher forward. Only the mind can wallow in has-been, so Joshua closes his eyes and pictures California, or at least what he imagines California to be. A flat and verdant land glistening like a field after a summer rainstorm, luscious rivers that are so filled with gold the water takes on the color and texture of honey.

Outside his room, scattered mounds of half-melted snow recrystallize, rainbow in the setting sun like diamonds, the wind churning a dust plume that hovers just above the macadam, just above the animals' hooves (the oxen, the mules, the horses) like the whole town is stuck in a kind of low-lying mist and bestowed in an undue mirage. Struggling to hold this precious image of California in his mind while his heart tugs him backward in time to a complex sorrow, Joshua wraps his arms over his body for warmth but refuses to shut the window. The cold will spartan him, bring him clarity and rigor, all of which he believes is the key to his prosperity, was the key to his father's lack of it.

Come nightfall, it begins to pour.

CHAPTER TWO

Joshua is awake before the blue-black sky, bruised from the now-passed storm, succumbs to the sun's glare. He glances at the preacher, but the big man is only a larger, denser shadow among a conflation of them. The sporadic gurgle emanating from the bed is the only indication he's still there, and sleeping. Joshua feels the scratchiness in his throat from the dust that's accumulated in the room overnight, stifles his cough with his sleeve, a cough he knows will only get hackier throughout the day. He dresses quietly and quickly so as not to wake the preacher. He puts his trousers on first, the knee blowing out when he slides his foot in.

Even this early, and because fortune is tireless, the streets are as busy as he's ever seen them. Wagon companies gather in rows in the square and advertise like a flea market. Blue-coated Army veterans with their gold epaulets fresh off the Mexican War or frontier trappers with scant a patch of human skin visible like Neanderthals proclaim their rugged superiority, compound their baseless guarantees of Indian protection, shortcuts, supplies for the hardly meager sum of three hundred dollars to those solitary emigrants looking for a way onto the trail.

Joshua wanders the town, his ragged coat buttoned to his neck. He doesn't have three hundred dollars, not even close, so he hefts his medical bag for credibility and makes his rounds among the companies, volunteering his expertise to subsidize his accommodation. A doctor is as rare in these companies as a woman, he knows, but as the morning wanes, so it seems his opportunity does also.

Several of the wagon leaders are too skeptical of a gimp doctor who sounds grossly ill. The Morris Outfit, the Bandy Voyagers, the American River Brigade look him up and down, laugh while they shoo him away proclaiming, You're too young to be a doctor.

The Charleston Company tells him they have no need for one, even less need for charity. The Boston Company points to Dr. Charles Robinson—A degreed physician, the captain decries.

Still, Joshua keeps on. He circles the square twice over as the sun rises above a symphysis of boned-out trees, exposing him and his deficiencies like his father's operating lamp. Several times his two-toed right foot slips in the mud and he has to correct himself, the trailing tracks he creates odd and disconcerting.

On the northside of the square, a wagon has begun to display motorized gold-digging contraptions that resemble the digestive system with their network of pulleys, belts, and gears. Joshua gathers with the crowd for the demonstration, watches as the handler, half-deaf from the machines' noise, models the contraptions' efficacies with gold coins or rocks painted gold. No one seems to notice the little girl who, awed by the exhibition, reaches her hand through a small slot to feel the precious tumbling metal.

Her father lunges forward from the crowd, snatches the girl back by her dress. Miraculously, her arm is unscathed, and the demonstration continues without pause.

Joshua leaves the wagons entirely, crosses to a clothier he's passed many times today but not yet entered. Mechner's, it's called, so noted by a white canvas awning that advertises the entire world under one roof: Scottish wool sweaters, Mexican serapes, New York frockcoats and dresses, Chinaman's silk, Navajo blankets. Joshua may not have attained passage to California yet, but he can get new trousers.

A clattering of bells sound when he opens the door. Inside is filled with tables stacked high with clothing: hats; brogans and boots; an assortment of cravats, bowties, and neck chains; cuffs and collars; trousers; union suits; any piece of clothing Joshua has ever thought of and even those he hasn't. He stands alone in the doorway for a moment expecting someone to come greet him. When no one does, he approaches the center table full of vibrant serapes. He unfolds one to admire its pattern, its tale of a geography and a people—and of an experience—entirely foreign. This, he thinks, is what waits for me in California.

Suddenly, the door bells sound again. A short man walks into the store talking at a tall man who wears a gaucho. Joshua quickly tosses the serape on the table, takes a step back, but neither of the men seem to notice him.

There isn't a store better if you're looking to get outfitted for your journey, the short man says. Why, I've been outfitting folks going on fifteen years, and, yessir, I've never heard one word of disappointment in all that time. When folks come back through, those folks that come back through that is, they make it a point to stop here and they tell me, 'Mr. Mechner,' they say, 'Mr. Mechner, I couldn't have made it without the chattels you sold me. Not at all. I'd have been trapped up in the mountains stiffer than a tree branch and more lifeless than a stone.'

The short man, Mr. Mechner, laughs while he slaps his thigh.

He says, Lord knows that isn't any way to cut short a life, I tell them. He yours?

The tall man stops and looks out the front window where a black man, also wearing a gaucho and with two red bandanas tied around his trousers just under each knee, stands with his thumb in his waistband. He stares at the two of them with something of a man who knows he's being wronged and knows that the party wronging him harbors a resentment toward him that can never begin to rival his own, so all he can do is smile, which he does, but his eyes swell with anything but pleasure.

That man is nobody's, the tall man says, facing Mr. Mechner again. At least no one who is around to claim him anymore.

That so, Mr. Mechner says smoothing back his oiled hair and wiping the sweat that doubles his upper lip. He just following you then, that it? Just wandering the streets like the damned soul he is?

The tall man smiles teeth as yellow as butter, but to Joshua, that smile doesn't come naturally, as if the tall man has taught himself this gesture after having watched others smile and understands what it's meant to express, logically, but is devoid of emotion.

As I said, he is no one's. And he is not following me. We are going to the same place, so naturally, we are following each other, and we are leading each other.

The tall man turns and looks back at the Black man. He must've done something, made some gesture Joshua couldn't see, because the Black man pivots around and faces the street. When the tall man turns back, he is smiling again at Mr. Mechner, and he puts his hand on the salesman's shoulder.

Now. How about you show me these goods on which you have been bragging?

Mr. Mechner glances back and forth from the tall man to the Black man. Joshua can tell he's disturbed by the Black man's presence, even when the Black man isn't looking at them, but Mr. Mechner soon composes himself, straightens his body.

The sweaters, Mr. Mechner says. You should see the collection I have. A man could flat live in the cold wearing the sweaters I sell. I tell you, the warmest and most durable wool. Scottish wool, matter of fact. I seen a man once buried in a snowbank here after he fell while sweeping a roof. Head and feet entirely. Came out no colder than he was before that fall and not a part of his chest or arms wet. Course he'd done messed up his shoulder pretty good, but that's neither here nor there. That man was wearing one of these sweaters. They may not prevent injuries, but they'll surely keep you warm.

Joshua steps aside as Mr. Mechner and the tall man approach the table with the serapes, and for the first time, both of the men take notice of him. It's the tall man who looks at Joshua first, offering him that same emotionless smile.

He has long, straight red hair tied into a ponytail that hangs past his shoulders, and his face is hairless, not in the sense that he's recently shaved, but in the sense that no hair sees fit to grow on it at all, which gives him a perennially boyish look, cherubic almost, though his eyes, narrow-set with pupils that seem so big and black it's like he has two thin holes in his face, speak of years long gone and never known by the minds of most men. Where his pinky fingers should be when the tall man braces himself on the table and leans to examine the serapes are two nubs, and he reeks of sulfur so pungently that Joshua has to take another step back.

Mr. Mechner frowns at Joshua. He pushes Joshua away while he guides the tall man to the sweaters.

Mr. Renard, Mr. Mechner says reclaiming the tall man's attention. Take a look at this sweater.

He thrusts the sweater into the tall man's chest.

Ain't she the softest, thickest wool you felt? I can't rightly imagine how you'd cross the Rockies without a sweater like this one to stave off that biting cold. Course I ain't never been in them mountains myself. Never even seen them. What I heard...

Renard, the tall man interrupts.

Pardon?

It is Renard. There is no Mister.

Mr. Mechner stalls for a moment before clapping his hands together with an affirmation that aims to erase the glitch in his selling. Then he continues, apparently oblivious to what Joshua has already figured out about Renard: A man who wears such polished clothing, new it appears by how clean it is and unrent, is an oddity in this town, which means he hasn't come to this store for the clothes at all.

Renard watches the squat salesman churn the stale air and speak with his arms as much as his words. He stands rigidly without his hands in his pockets, and his face is smooth and expressionless while he does so, gauging this situation, gauging all situations by logic, in a world driven by emotion, which renders him the misunderstood. He moves his tongue against his cheek, prying at his teeth for some unknown morsel. Joshua can only see one side of Renard's face, but somehow he feels that Renard is watching him too.

Mr. Mechner tugs at Renard's arm. They move across the store to the shelves of hats, Mr. Mechner talking all the while, having redis-covered himself in the course of Renard's silence. Talking about his goods. About the weather in Independence and the weather he speculates about on some imagined trail west he's never taken and will never take. About the usefulness of goods that seem so vari-able, so diverse that anything he sells in this store can be used for anything, so that a hat can keep your legs unscathed by the thorns he imagines gauntlet that imagined trail and a pair of trousers can shade your face from a sun that never has to contend with a cloud in that big blue Western sky.

Renard remains silent, which seems to calm the salesman, so Mr. Mechner pulls goods from the tables and shelves indiscriminately, handing each one to Renard, who takes them all only for a second until he hands each back and Mr. Mechner mindlessly tosses it, whatever it is, back where he pulled it from. Once, out of carelessness or because he's fallen into some kind of routine he can't seem to break free of, Mr. Mechner picks up a dress, unfolds it in a flinging motion like he's dusting a rug.

Well, Mr. Mechner says a bit flustered now that he realizes he's holding a dress.

I don't figure... I ain't never seen... I heard, I mean what they tell me, the ladies I mean, what they tell me is these things is mighty comfortable for walking. Course... Right, right.

He wads the dress into a ball as tight as his little hands can form and tosses it on the floor.

As the two of them near the front of the store again, the wake of messed items routing their path, Mr. Mechner picks up a pair of brogans before he pauses and says: Pardon me, Renard.

He turns to Joshua.

I don't know what you been doing at this table all this time, son, but you go on now. I ain't in the business of decorating you, and you ain't in the business of wasting time.

Wasting whose time?

Hearing Renard's voice, Mr. Mechner spins around so quickly that he drops the brogans.

Pardon me, Renard. Pardon my clumsiness.

He bends and collects the brogans, then faces Renard again.

What was that you said? Mr. Mechner asks.

Whose time is it that he is wasting?

Mr. Mechner stands for a minute with the brogans cradled against his chest and looking from Renard to Joshua, neither of whom move, and both of whom seem to be stealing the salesman's focus so that he's getting increasingly confused.

Why, he says and clears his throat. Our time.

Our time has not been affected by that young man at all. I do not recall his time factoring into our time, or even crossing it for that matter.

Well, stutters the salesman.

It seems to me that time, as a rule, is wholly individual. His and yours and mine, and none of it travels the same plane.

Well, then his time, says Mr. Mechner.

Renard crosses his arms. He tips the gaucho back with his index finger so that his face is more visible, and he squints one eye. Mr. Mechner rocks back on his heels, as if he's being pushed by that look.

Can a man waste his own time? Renard asks. If it is his time, and he chooses what to do with it, then is it ever wasted?

Nothing emerges from Mr. Mechner's open mouth. He looks like someone who's been doused with a cold glass of water. Renard lets that silence hang into an uncomfortable moment before he smiles—first at Mr. Mechner, then at Joshua. He puts a hand on the salesman's shoulder.

He says, Thank you, but I will not be needing any brogans.

Renard smiles again at Joshua before he turns and walks out of the store. Mr. Mechner and Joshua listen to the clang of the door bells and then watch him disappear behind the door before he reappears in the front window talking to the Black man and gesturing over his shoulder. The Black man glances back, looks at Joshua, and Joshua hears Mr. Mechner hiss through his teeth like a cat.

That nice man is gone now, Joshua hears Mr. Mechner says. And I'm not going to be so kind anymore.

But Joshua can't seem to look away from those two. Only when the salesman's forehead breaks his view of the two men outside does Joshua reorient himself, focus on a man who seems so angry at his presence he wants to punch him.

I won't ask you again, son, says the salesman.

*

A FEW HOURS later, Joshua leans against a post outside a milli-
nery and watches the schooners carting west like a troop of giant
ants. He spent the rest of the afternoon soliciting himself a position in a wagon company and, like every attempt prior this one, he
found himself unsuccessful. When it begins to drizzle, many of the
emigrants hustle under the roofs, but Joshua steps into the street.
He lets his clothes soak up the cold rain springing from clouds that
don't gather in the sky but seem instead to have been obscured by
some illusion and there all along. The water pools on his upper
lip and drips from his eyes like tears while the landscape blurs and
shimmers once it truly commences to rain, the water freezing now
and heavy on his skin. He follows his own breath from wagon to
wagon, where only the shaking heads or laughter of those as determined as he is continue greeting him. Determined or stupid, he
thinks, as we are all playing roulette with pneumonia.

Joshua is beyond caring, though. Beyond caring about everything
that isn't the one thing he cares so deeply about it makes him want to
cry: gold. He sleeves the rain that's accumulated on his face, sleeves
it again, gestures that are now exaggerated, thoughtless, instinctual.
The cold has grabbed his heart and mind and squeezed with the
force of too much history again. His father—that's always what that
history is. And bullying that history is a much more potent feeling
he can't escape no matter how much he walks. A feeling of shame.

A phantom smell of charred wood calcified by the pleasantness of
ether that takes his father's shape follows him into a dark and empty
alley, where he leans against an outhouse and vomits into the mud.

Occupied! a voice yells at him.

Joshua wipes his mouth with the wet back of his hand, continues
on. He doesn't know where he's going, he doesn't remember how he
came, the town square somewhere that he isn't now and the crowd
lost, the clatter of the rain on the wooden roofs boxing his ears.

So it is he finds the dead mule, nearly tripping over its body. He stands over it dripping, his right foot sore from so much exertion, and suddenly hungry. The flesh on the animal's cheeks is wilted at the edges, crisp like burnt paper even with all of this rain. A girl steps out of a door he didn't know existed and lights a candled lantern, squints at Joshua while she does. The lantern projects a dull light, and the mule shapes and colors, and there is its rib cage, and there is its femur, and there are its haunches drawn taut and frail like the head of a drum, which birth in this fecund moisture a swarm of maggots that writhe as they squirm toward its stomach and burrow inside its gut and lose themselves in the feast of a half day at the mercy of this spectator who, this very moment, yearns for that version of the man he still isn't.

CHAPTER THREE

Two weeks and a dry spell later, there is dust in the air. Endless dust the heavy winds lift. Into the cluttered streets Joshua goes until evening and then on, pacing furiously like a forgotten sentry. The sun washes out with the solemnity these late days of spring engender, and the street goers are trapped in a reverie that failing light invites, if only because for them darkness forever means one day closer to departure. Cardinals bright as fresh blood wink in and out of the buildings' shadows before they alight in the hardwood trees where it's like that red is brushed clean off them, so quickly do they disappear. Just before dusk, mourning doves sprint the street gaps, their bodies angular and sharp like unstoppable arrowheads when they fly over the roofs and above the crowd before shooting over the buildings on the other side. Were it not for their shadows, Joshua would never see them. As it is, and still pacing, he sees them only for a second, or time immeasurable less than that, and even then he can't be sure if he imagines that sight, or if the light is itself manifesting these creatures in its kaleidoscopic state.

With so much dust, the emigrants bottling the streets incessantly cough. Couple that with the nervous shouting and desperation this collection of unacquainted men give over to this evening, and it seems to Joshua like all of Independence is staging some sort of cruel joke, one that will climax with his and the other emigrants' utter failure, all of which he experiences with a tense and boiling anger.

When a pair of ladies walks by, true ladies with their hooped dresses swiveling inches above the filthy macadam, the emigrants redirect their emotions, hoot and holler while they gather them-selves around the ladies in a circle, and hop about with erotic and frantic gestures like drab birds of paradise, so colorless has the dust and the lack of wash made their clothing.

Joshua joins this circle, hoping it will make his blood the blood of a man so that each day it can birth in him new and inexplicable desires until he is a man apart from himself. He rides the crowd with its stinking clothes and voices too loud for this quaint town as they harry the terrified women. They holler and they yell, he along with them, and when a man comes up behind him and bumps hard into his shoulder, he turns and shoves the man away.

The man stumbles backward into another man, who catches him and then drops him to the ground, where Joshua sees him fighting off the erratic feet of this crowd only for a second before the man vanishes. The crowd pushes Joshua forward and he doesn't turn back, not even in his memory. He howls, and someone shoots a pistol into the air. Then more pistols fire. The air deaf with shots and that black powder smoke burning Joshua's eyes, gone sucking down his throat.

The ladies, moving as fast as that constrictive clothing permits, tuck their heads into their shoulders almost as if they want to harness the escape of turtles, and they duck into the first store they come upon. The crowd chases after them, piling one into the other while they holler and bang on the windows and the wall, the ladies inside already sheltering in the back and the dutiful storeowner perched in his doorway with a broom held crosswise. Much good that broom will do him if the men decided to enter, and his feeble-handedness with that broom, the slow withdrawal he takes while he shuts the windowed door means such an act of bravery is only an act.

The breath of the other men in that crowd and their damp clothes begin to suffocate Joshua, to frighten him. It isn't long before the pistol shots wane and something else equally arbitrary captures attention, and the crowd begins to disperse.

When Joshua is freed, he turns and witnesses the street nearly the same way it was before, save for a few men who are scattered across the ground not far from him, their clothes torn and their heads bleeding in the weak light emitted by the lanterns hung in the storefronts. Frenzy and calm. War and peace. On whims entirely. Schooners lumbering along, their white canvas bonnets soaking up the lanternlight and the moonlight.

Joshua steps back into the street and turns north. He passes a blacksmith's shop, where outside rock chairs moved by floating cigarette tips that smolder orange, then flare, then smolder again. He passes a grocery, on the porch of which sits a girl half-lit by a candleflame and no older than ten, holding a naked boy who looks too old to be naked. Now there is no crowd, and the passion that roiled him not long ago seems a distant memory.

He turns left, or maybe right. He isn't sure. He comes upon a jail he's never seen before. He hears distant moans and the faraway sound of someone yelling. Some time or other, the moon grows thinner in its rising. Then the sky molds over with dense clouds and the night becomes darker still. Everything is silent now. Even the cicadas who've been his unseen companions shut down their wailing as if Joshua isn't fit for such company anymore.

When finally he pauses and takes stock of the street, he's disoriented and disturbed, unsure where the emigrants have gone, unsure even when he left them. He starts walking again. The pain traveling from his gimp right foot all the way up to his right shoulder runs on a current, and it's like he's wandered into a void, like the world has suddenly ended, and though he hasn't felt the quake of the rapture, he's plummeted to the earth's depths and now faces the terrible scrutiny of isolation.

He starts to run. Twice he trips but catches himself before falling. Even when he steps into a pile of horseshit, he keeps on. The street hasn't yet turned to dirt so he knows he's not left the town's limits, but he rounds a corner more frantically now, wondering if he is traveling farther and farther away unbeknownst to him. When he hears the noises of the emigrants again and after several steps sees the many lanterns floating head-high like earth-borne stars, he realizes he's near the courthouse.

He stops, tries to calm himself. His breathing hard. His heart ramming his chest.

THE EMIGRANTS MOVE with deliberation now, weaving around each other while carrying various goods in hand or rattling their wagons over the macadam. Joshua has no idea what time it is, but by the height of the moon and most of the storefronts gone dark, he figures it's late. He feels a hunger both familiar and not deep inside him that he can't quite quantify. He wipes the shit off his boot with a stick, then crosses the street toward the butcher from whose open door, a block away, he swears he can already smell the iron scent of freshly drawn blood. He'll buy some jerky there, get a drink of water because his throat, just like his stomach, perplexes him with its sudden urges. Other men he passes appear stale and labored in their unwashed garments, and though a cool wind blows out of the north and through the street, the weight of all those bodies produces a rancid heat.

Suddenly, he can't stand this crowd, grows angry at their being, and as he nears the sidewalk, someone grabs his shoulder.

He slings around, again ready to combat.

Easy now. I do not mean you any harm.

Renard holds his four-fingered hands in the air in a feigned surrender, hands that are more like claws in the dark. The Black man he came to Mechner's with stands behind him. Joshua can hardly distinguish their gaucho-shadowed faces. But Renard's red hair still holds its color, the sulfur smell his skin seems steeped in thick and unmistakable.

I saw you shove that other man earlier.

Joshua slackens his arms, feels the pain in his foot again.

I didn't see you in that crowd, Joshua says.

I was not in it. I try to avoid such gatherings.

I don't figure it was a gathering. At least not one had by intention.

Renard turns to the Black man, and the Black man says something in a language Joshua doesn't understand. Then the Black man laughs a high-pitched laugh, which doesn't suit him. Renard doesn't laugh with him, nor is he smiling when he faces Joshua again.

Free Ray says that all white men's gatherings are not intentional.

What's that mean?

You would have to ask him.

What's that mean? Joshua says louder, titling his head to see Free Ray straight on.

Though Joshua still can't see his face, Free Ray doesn't move or say anything. Joshua looks back at Renard.

He doesn't speak English?

Renard glances at Free Ray.

He does. But I suppose he speaks whatever language he is in the mood for.

Why didn't he answer me then?

Because he does not have to. He is beholden to no man, white or otherwise. His previous owners were a couple of Frogs down in south Louisiana, but they are not of this world to claim him anymore. Free Ray saw to that. That is why he is called Free Ray.

Free Ray says something else. Renard smiles, pats Free Ray on the shoulder.

Soon, my friend. Soon.

Renard puts his hand on Joshua's shoulder.

You look hungry, he says. And I gather you could use a drink.

I'm all right.

Come on, Renard insists. You are our guest for the night.

Before Joshua can object, Renard squeezes Joshua's shoulder and leads him to a nameless and shanty saloon umbrellaed by a large redcedar tree and tucked behind an armory. The front of the saloon shimmers from the light of a sputtering lamp that seems each second as if it's ready to give up its burning before the flame flares briefly on the wick again. There are no windows. Two broken fence posts are crookedly nailed onto the front door, a prohibition painted on each: NO REDSKINS. NO SQUAREHEADS.

Renard guides Joshua inside and over a floor covered with sawdust. The walls are adorned with animal skulls: cows, horses, deer, coyotes, squirrels, even a bison. The skulls within arms' reach have been transformed into hat racks, which Joshua can see from the only source of light in this place—a huge candelabra in the middle of the ceiling. No one stands under the candelabra, white wax constantly tearing from it and dripping to the floor. The men cluster in groups along the walls and the few tables that border the walls, none of which have vacant chairs. Their bodies push and weave each other while they drink, and a few try their hand at wooing the women perched at the bottom of the stairs, who need no wooing at all. Just a few coins, and an escort to the dank and even darker rooms above. There is no music, a cacophony of voices, an occasional rumbling from the ceiling that always precedes a man's exit from those whoring rooms.

At the bar, a gruff-looking barman approaches them. Renard orders a bottle of whiskey, which the barman, seeming to anticipate the order, simultaneously pulls from underneath the bar and sets beside it two shot glasses he wipes out with a soiled rag.

We are three people, Renard tells the barman. So we will be needing three glasses.

The barman frowns at Renard, eyes Free Ray for a moment while his jaw pulses before he grabs another shot glass, sets it on the bar without wiping it out, and walks away.

Joshua picks up his glass, turns and watches the whores like he would a carnival show, their faces painted like clowns and hair the color of straw, more skin than he's ever seen on a woman before, as none of them cover their corsets with dresses. They bend and gyrate not like people at all, like they have no spine, movements that seem graceful and obscene all at once. From afar these women are indistinct, a part of a whole, the way we gaze a herd of cattle from the roadside, but when Joshua looks closer, he can see the red lipstick smudged in the corner of one mouth, the smeared paint on another one's cheeks.

There is no need to only look, Renard says. If you allow them to escort you up those stairs, you will find yourself in a position to have a much better view anyway.

I'm not interested, says Joshua.

Renard tilts his head, examines Joshua.

Perhaps a man then, he says. Or a boy. I know of a place not too far from here.

Joshua looks down at the floor. His boots are gray with dust and have parted the sawdust where he stands so that he looks slightly mired in this saloon. His father once explained sexuality as the complex web of our desires, limited only by the confines we so impose. But most, he'd warned Joshua, will never understand that.

Ah, says Renard. You are a man of your own convictions. I admire that. I for one am a celibate, and Free Ray polyamorous. But contrary to what you may have been made to think, the sun still rises and sets each day.

Renard holds up his glass of whiskey in a toast, and Joshua and Free Ray drink. Renard sets his full glass back down on the bar.

You're not drinking? Joshua asks.

Renard shakes his head.

Imbibing is a pleasure I do not indulge.

Joshua pours another glass of whiskey, lifts it in a half-baked, too-naïve toast to Free Ray, who nods, and they both drink again. When he finishes his second glass, he pours a third. He's never drank so much whiskey in one sitting, but he's unable to stop. After his third glass, he shakes away the dullness creeping into his head and tries to focus on the whores.

If it is an issue of money, then that does not have to be an issue, says Renard.

Joshua feels his face flush, wonders if he looks as poor as he feels.

It's not that, he says.

Go on then, says Renard.

Joshua pauses. Perhaps it's the whiskey that forces the truth out of him, or the burn that is inching from his gut through his sternum and into his throat. Either way, after he says what he says, he wishes he never said it: I've never done that before.

Free Ray slaps a hand on the bar and laughs that high-pitched laugh of his.

It's not funny, says Joshua.

Do not mind Free Ray, says Renard. He is a man of his own convictions, too, odd as they may be.

Free Ray pours himself another glass of whiskey, sips it as he turns away from the other two to gaze out at the saloon.

Consider this opportunity a recompense then, Renard continues. For the old life you previously led and the new life this moment will grant you.

A what?

Payment for your suffering.

A large woman who keeps pushing her breasts down because they won't be contained by her strained corset smiles a gap-toothed smile at Joshua. She upturns her chalky hand and motions him over with her finger. When he doesn't move, she leans over the banister so that her nipples, the same blood red as her gums, pop out over the edge of the corset like budding roses. She pretends not to notice this display at first, watches Joshua watch her breasts and runs a sharp tongue over her top lip, before she leans back by rolling her shoulders up and pushes her breasts into her corset again.

Joshua wipes his forehead with his palm. He is dizzy and hot. He braces himself on the bar with both hands and spits a thick flume between his feet.

You should eat something, says Renard.

Joshua nods but doesn't look up. His eyes water, his mouth fills with saliva. For a moment, he thinks he'll be sick, so he folds into his stomach, closes his eyes as tightly as he can, and holds his breath. The feeling passes. He stays pitched forward in this position for several minutes, opening and closing his eyes, trying to focus on his boots, which he knows are below him but can't rightly see. His head filled with cotton, his stomach hollowed by that whiskey. Because of this, Joshua doesn't see the barman approach, nor is he listening when Renard orders the food, but when the barman slides the bowl of rice and stew in front him and sets beside it a can of peaches, Joshua smells it and looks up.

He devours the bowl's contents, then drinks the peaches straight from the can. His head has cleared some by the time he finishes, his stomach settled.

How much do I owe?

As I said earlier, says Renard, you are our guest for the night. As our guest, there is no compensation warranted on your behalf.

I have money.

No one is accusing you of poverty.

I don't take charity.

Renard's laugh seems more mocking than reactive.

I suppose we understand the definition of guest differently then, he says.

Joshua can feel the same anger he felt when he first learned of his financial state compress between his shoulder blades. He breathes deeply to calm himself, lets the harsh chatter of the saloon drain the anger from his body, and reminds himself that he can be someone different here. That is, after all, the point.

Guest or not, Joshua says, if it's free for me then somebody else is out money.

Think it a loan then.

A loan?

That is right.

For what?

For your company.

So you pay for my supper and my whiskey, and my standing here and talking to you is what pays you back?

Renard nods.

That doesn't make much sense.

There is no more sense to be made of it than there is to be made of these men in this saloon, or those whores stalking each night from those stairs like rattlesnakes hidden in the underbrush.

Somewhere across the saloon, a man starts yelling. Then the explosion of a pistol shot. Silence after that, the whole saloon gone mute. Everyone turns to look at the man holding his pistol in the air, the barrel smoking and pointing at the ceiling as if he's holding a cigar. Pale splinters of wood rain down around him and around those nearest, gather in their matted hair like snowflakes. The whores have collapsed their bodies on the stairs and still lie there, faces to the wood and hands covering their ears in those cowering poses, the true and only victims of this heedlessness. The man with the pistol doesn't reholster his gun until the man in front of him, his hands in the air and terror on his face, is snatched by two others and carried out the door. Whatever dispute it was it is not a dispute any longer. And when those two return emptyhanded, the shooter holsters his pistol, dusts his hair with a single swipe of his hand, sits down, and commences to drinking.

Joshua grabs the bottle of whiskey to pour himself another glass. His hand is shaking. He lets go the bottle, taps his hand on his thigh to knock out the nerves. He picks the bottle up again and pours his glass, hoping Renard and Free Ray didn't notice his tremor.

Free Ray says something to Renard in that foreign tongue of his and all Renard says back is: It is a shame.

But what shame it is Joshua isn't sure. If it's a shame that man was expelled from this saloon? If it's a shame that other man blew a small hole in the ceiling that appears already too weak to withstand the elements and so will now surely leak at the slightest thought of rain? If it's a shame that man didn't shoot the other man instead of the ceiling and so put to rest the disturbance with the surety and determination all good men settle scores? This is a breed of men Joshua hasn't the vaguest notion of, having witnessed them come into town and yet not privy to their character at all. These are the travelers west. These are his companions, if not literally, then plucked from the crop of those he will eventually travel with. And he fears on some level he refuses to let surface that he is fit for this world after all.

He drinks, and the fourth glass of whiskey does what it is meant to in alleviating that fear, leaving him assured in his own conception of himself all over again. Renard pours his still undrunk whiskey into Joshua's glass, and again Free Ray toasts Joshua, but Joshua shakes his head. He can't drink anymore.

The young man has had enough, says Renard.

Free Ray shrugs and throws back his glass and then fills it again and throws that one back, splitting his lips and sucking the air in through his teeth as he slams the glass on the bar. He stares at Joshua, but Joshua can distinguish nothing in those glassy eyes or smooth skin that tells him what Free Ray is pondering. There seems to be no defect to Free Ray at all. Not a wrinkle on his forehead, nor that stale bodily stench Joshua has become so accustomed to. Not any smell, as if what leaches through Free Ray's skin is clean water, sourceless and pure. Renard is looking at Joshua too. The both of them with those eyes that make him feel like a hive of bees are confined in his chest, hundreds of bees at war with each other in the last great claim for his skeletal cavern.

He tries to look past the two of them, to the loping and drunk souls beyond who fall into each other while they argue. Renard places his hat on the bar, runs a hand down his ponytail.

Do you know why these men are here?

Yes, says Joshua.

Tell me why then.

The whiskey and the women.

That is why they are in this saloon. But do you know why they are in Independence?

They're traveling west.

That is right, says Renard. Every last one of them is bound for California. If not physically, then mentally, for their minds are no longer grounded in this place. They dream of fortunes and prospects. They dream of the kind of wealth even dreams cannot conceive of.

Their reverie then is for a time not of this present. They are celebrating what they believe will happen, and they are spending what money they hope to mine. Is not that why you are here?

Their greed is not his greed, Joshua thinks, because his greed isn't actually greed. His desire for wealth is deserved. He's earned it by his suffering, a suffering that was entirely forced on him. He did not choose for his parents to die, he did not choose for his father to be the weak man that he was, a weakness that pushed him (that pushed them both) into a world of destitution. Every choice that he's made is borne out of a reaction to the choices something (or someone) made for him long before he was even a thought in his mother's mind. So, no, his greed is not their greed, and these men are not him.

I don't care why these others are here, Joshua says. I'm not them.

Renard smiles, combs his eyebrows with his index fingers, almost as if he's communicating to Joshua through some kind of sign language.

I know that, he says. That is why you should come with us.

To California?

Renard nods.

You mean go with you and Free Ray.

And three others. We are members of a party. Organizers is perhaps the more accurate term. You can only venture out west in parties. It is above all for safety that we travel in numbers, but the companionship to be had through such travel is perhaps more essential to the vitalization of the soul. Solitude is a lonely man's want, and lonely men are misfortune's playthings. Besides, Free Ray and I have been there twice before. Successfully, I might add, though need not, as our sitting here with you is proof absolute.

You found gold?

Renard laughs, and Free Ray smiles again.

Come with us, says Renard. Discover for yourself the riches that land affords. After all, that is what you seek—an adventure. The stories I can tell you would make your head swim and your blood squirm, but only once you experience such things for yourself can you truly discover what it is you are seeking.

Renard pauses.

Most importantly, he continues. Your medical expertise will be a great service to our party.

This remark about his medical skill surprises Joshua. Did he mention to Renard that he is a doctor? Has he already sought to join Renard's party without recognizing Renard? Joshua tries to swim his thoughts through his whiskey-drowned brain, but the more the remark sits with him the more its flattery overwhelms the origin of it.

Free Ray leans toward Renard and says something in his ear. Renard glances at Joshua's feet, nodding.

Your limp, says Renard.

Joshua frowns.

What about it?

I do not suppose it slows you down at all. Free Ray is making sure that I ask, and seeing as he and I partners, and have always been in these ventures, I dare not deny him that request.

Joshua hiccups.

I lost three toes to frostbite four years ago, he says and hiccups again. So no, it doesn't.

I did not think so. Our defects do not make us the men we are. We are those men in spite of them.

As if in solidarity, Renard holds his hands palm-out with his fingers spread, exposing the stubs where each pinky finger would go.

Agreed, says Joshua. So when do we leave?

It is as if the satisfaction that Renard and Free Ray exhibit at this answer is a pleasure in watching Joshua come to the decision they've long known he would come to, long before Joshua even knew the proposition, and perhaps long before that proposition existed at all.

They both smile and toast him, Free Ray raising his glass of whiskey and Renard his empty glass. They wait for Joshua to match their toast, then they watch him drink. Gone with that whiskey is any semblance of the life Joshua has previously known.

LATER THAT NIGHT with the moon dragging back toward the horizon and the stars eeking out what light they can before the impending dawn, Joshua sneaks into his room. The sleeping preacher doesn't stir when he enters or removes his boots and climbs into bed fully clothed, a tad dizzy, still with the smell of whiskey and sweat on his skin.

Two weeks until we depart, Renard told him. The first week of June.

He saw no clouds when he stumbled back. He let the moon guide him. But as he lies in his bed and begins to feel those first bouts of weightlessness, it begins to rain, and that rain carts with it a thunderstorm. Lightning flashes in through the shut window and lights the hulking preacher, who slumbers across from him. The thunder that follows claps so close the room quakes. As Joshua sleeps, he dreams of a flood, of riding the street that becomes a river on his bed, and the buildings gone, and the strangers he hobnobbed with hours earlier floating past him naked, gray, and bloated, the whole world a washed-out graveyard that stretches on and on with these plains. That give way to more plains. And then more plains, forever chasing the horizon.

CHAPTER FOUR

Joshua sleeps late in the days that follow, spends the afternoon gathering supplies for his journey, stays out long each night while frequenting the saloon or wandering the streets of Independence with Renard and Free Ray, exploring the nebulous lines of decorum, of ownership, filching liquor bottles or eyeglasses or pocket watches done firstly in jest as his companions instigate him, as all manner of dissent commences, the three of them party to the new world and the new world party to them, a celebration of rebirth, the endless revelry of anticipation.

Renard told Joshua he'd provide a horse and mount with saddle bags, as well as waive his party fee as compensation for his medical expertise and assistance along the way. But among the other supplies Renard compiled on a list for both the journey and for digging gold, he also told Joshua to get a good pistol.

As a rule, Renard said, I never purchase another's ammunitions, for choosing which tool will steal another man's soul is your decision alone.

One Sunday morning—this Sunday morning—Joshua's face is pale, his clothes reeking of whiskey, mud, and sleep. His hair is heavy with sweat and he is sweating all over. He squints his eyes, taking in as little light as his head can manage.

You look awful, son. You sick or something? You need a doctor?

Who is that? Joshua thinks. It's a man speaking. What man? Joshua tries to focus. The man spits, uses his shirt to wipe his chin. Joshua wipes his own chin with his sleeve, a gesture not meant to mime the man but done so simply because his mind can't work enough to conceive of an original action. The whiskey acrid on his tongue, his mouth strip-mined raw. He turns away from the man to hide his breath.

I'm fine, he says.

You don't look fine, says the man. You look like you been drowned and then pumped back to life.

The irony of this remark isn't lost on Joshua as the man spits again. This time the man clears his chin entirely.

Joshua doesn't respond except to nod, then brushes past the man into Mechner's, his head bobbing with each step.

What can I do for…, Mr. Mechner begins until he recognizes Joshua. What you doing in here, son? I've got no business with you.

I need a hat, says Joshua.

You got the money for it?

Swaying slightly, Joshua stares silently at Mr. Mechner.

No money means no shopping. I'd appreciate it then if you kindly exit my premises.

The salesman reaches for Joshua's arm, but Joshua backs away from him. Mr. Mechner's face swells with anger, his eyes and mouth tightening in his resolve. He pushes a finger into Joshua's chest, opens his mouth to unleash whatever insults are burning up his tongue, but Joshua never lets the salesman get that far.

He punches Mr. Mechner in the face. The salesman falls backward as straight as a broom handle and doesn't even get his hands underneath him before the cracking sound of his head hitting the wood floor sends Joshua stumbling out the front door and down the street.

What follows is a rush of excitement and power. So much power that his skin feels hot, like he's been burned by it. He isn't watching where he's going, moving mindlessly as if tethered to some cosmic rope, so frightened is he by this newfound rush and what it suggests he's harbored deep down in some dark region of his soul all along.

Eventually, he finds himself south of town at the edge of the dense woods. He's alone, and the commotion from town, which he can barely hear now, is so tenuously a part of this landscape it's easily forgotten. The lowing sun lows further. The tree shadows stripe one side of him and on the other a great unbroken light rests on his limbs so that he becomes suddenly the keeper of these margins, the transient who ducks between wooded acres and grassland. The walk has sobered him, the pain in his hand, now twice feeling the brunt of another man's face, a gratification.

When he can no longer hear the town, he figures he's walked far enough and long enough for Mr. Mechner to give up any immediate pursuit of him and turns around. He can easily avoid the square on his reentry tonight. And tomorrow he's off to California anyway. He walks for a while longer before he spots a man coming toward him. It's his roommate, the preacher.

Joshua ducks down in the tall grass. The preacher walks straight and assuredly with a bible in one hand. At a giant oak some fifty feet from where Joshua crouches, the preacher turns and enters the forest. Joshua waits a few more minutes before he approaches the oak. A cross no bigger than his hand is carved on this side of its trunk, and leading from it into the forest is a thin trail he missed before.

He takes it for a hundred yards or so before he begins to hear the preacher's resonating voice. After a bit longer, he comes upon

a treeless and lush glen with its soft-soiled grass and its population
of devoted followers. Most adults there are standing and shaking
their hands in the air, children in the very back tiptoed on upturned
crates, other adults kneeling in prayer at the edges of the congregation, still others seated on large rocks that form a semicircle in front
of the preacher, who has his head turned toward the sky, eyes closed,
one hand gripping his bible and the other held outward at the congregation, as if in blessing, while a huge cross made of sectioned
pine trunks and nearly ten feet tall leans against a tree behind him.

You see, I'm not childless. You see, you are all my children. And
you're God's children, whether six or sixty years of age, for we're
all children in the eyes of our Lord. You see, it ain't the years on
this earth that make us fit for the Grace of God, but the state of our
hearts. I once met a man on a lonely dirt road who was self-proclaimed one hundred years old. That's right. One hundred years on
this earth. Mostly blind, deaf in one ear, so crippled he could hardly
stand. He said he was born in the Colonies. Said he fought in the
Revolution and helped make those Colonies this country. I've seen
things no one believes, he told me, things even I don't believe, and
I bore twelve children to my name, all of them dead and buried
before me. That man then asked me: Saunty? Is God punishing me
by making me live so long? Everyone I know and love has already
died and gone, but still I live. Still I walk this road. Why, I looked
at that man, into that face more wrinkled than a bulldog's, and I put
my hand on his shoulder. I said to him, Son, you haven't yet begun
to live. And I took his hands then. And I prayed with him. I prayed,
Father, bless this child. Guide his heart so that he can find his way
home.

The preacher opens his eyes, scans the congregation. When he
catches sight of Joshua standing in the back, he pauses, but only
briefly, before he places his hand on top of his Bible and continues.

It's a privilege to have a family in this world. But we are all members of the Family of Heaven. Lest we ever forget that, lest we ever forget our way turn to your brother beside you, turn to your sister beside you and say, I need your help.

Joshua feels something behind him, and he glances over his shoulder. Renard is coming through the trees, Free Ray following, the both of them walking their own path off-trail, as if guided by an internal compass. They step out of the trees past Joshua and into the glen, stop near the preacher. The preacher stares at Renard and Free Ray, his mouth open as if at a loss for speech, until he steps back, clutching the Bible to his chest. The sunlight whales through the trees, broken into strips by the broad leaves so that the preacher's face falls into shadow. The woods gone silent.

Why, you smell as if you've been washed in brimstone, says the preacher.

Renard glares at the preacher. Then he surveys the congregation, smiling when his eyes fall on Joshua like he expects Joshua to be here. Free Ray stands still while Renard steps into a pier of sunlight toward the preacher, who takes another step back.

All are welcome here, gentlemen, the preacher says, though even he sounds unconvinced by these words. In any manner of attendance, whether standing, or sitting, or kneeling.

Renard laughs, which further unnerves the preacher. He turns and faces the congregation, who seem confused and irritated at the strangers' presence.

Ladies and gentlemen, Renard says. Has this itinerant preached to you the doctrine of fate? Has he bespoke on you the divinity of his tongue, which he himself believes guided by a god and so warranted in these wooded gatherings wherein he fulfills his destiny?

Renard glances around. No one replies.

I once met a preacher in Virginia who told me that my salvation was predetermined. There was nothing I could do to enter the grace of his heaven if his god had no plans for me to be there, and likewise nothing I could do to avoid damnation were that my pre-scribed path. I asked that preacher what his god had in store for me. He said he did not know. He was ignorant of my future, just as he was ignorant of my past, but he stood on his chair and vilified a life not governed by a devotion to christ. For he told me his god sees all; his god knows all; his god governs all. And do you know what I did, ladies and gentlemen?

Renard pauses, holds his hands up with his palms to the crowd and fingers spread. A few of the followers gasp. Several children exclaim their disgust more viscerally. The preacher doesn't make a sound, tightening his grip on his bible as Renard brings his hands around and extends them toward the preacher's face. Renard paces slowly in front of the awe-struck crowd, like a magician on the brink of a trick, or a caged beast, a sort of spectacle, his body winking in and out of shadow though he himself never darkens, almost as if he's lighted by some internal illumination. When he stops pacing, his eyes fall meanly on the preacher, and the voice he speaks with is stained by hatred.

I put my hand at the feet of that preacher while I retrieved my knife, and I cut off the fingers you see absent. First on my right hand. Then on my left. I picked up each severed finger, and I put it in my pocket. Then I looked up at the preacher. I asked him what I am about to ask you. Is it your god who took my fingers?

Renard faces the crowd.

Be not swayed by this unholy man who tries to convince you of destiny, he says. You are who you are, and what you make of your-self, knowingly or otherwise.

The preacher waves his arms with his bible in one hand like he's swatting away some divine pestilence, a swarm of locusts descended from above in a wave of impenetrable proportion.

The Devil! he shouts. Washed in brimstone and those cloven hands! The Devil!

Renard turns, begins walking away. When he reaches Free Ray, he pauses and looks at Joshua and smiles again before they both take their makeshift path back through the trees.

The entire congregation drops to their knees and begins to pray audibly, the children crying and kneeling and holding tight to the arms of their hysterical mothers and fathers. The preacher continues to condemn Renard as the two depart until he gives up that damnation and turns his attention to his congregation, his eyes wild and possessed while he extends the Bible in front of him as a sort of shield and prays along with them. A pleading and ferocious prayer, so loud it chases Joshua as he hurries away through the trees.

THAT NIGHT HE stays in the schooner, his body propped upright against his duffel bag, everything he owns in the world piled beside him. All around the schooner, voices dance and scepter lanterns with their patches of light spawn shadows on the bonnet. Heads and torsos, bodies in fusion and division like replicating cells while there sits Joshua somewhere between the before and the after, his life and life. Isolated in this darkness and with the stasis this liminal moment renders, his thoughts and his heart begin to redirect to a past he could no sooner let go than yesterday.

He lies back on his duffel, breathes heavily. He tries at first to will himself to sleep before he gives up. He pulls his knees into his chest, breathes into them so that he fills his face with the warmth and wetness of his own being. A weight that's twice his size begins to leave him, loosens his mind, untethers it, a muffled voice out in the distance near his hotel, *knock-knock*...

... *KNOCK-KNOCK.*

Joshua opens the old house's door to a snow-bleached, St. Louis landscape, a man standing sturdy as an ox against the winter wind with a gold chain that extends from one of his gold coat buttons and disappears into his breast pocket. Joshua doesn't have to see the gold pocket watch to imagine its luster, and he thinks how silly he must look to this man, wearing a suit too small and too thin for this weather, having just returned from his father's funeral. His father's suit, actually, a kind of warped homage because the truth is he doesn't know how to mourn a grief that is blended with anger.

He crosses his arm as the wind kicks up again, the sleeves riding halfway to his elbows.

You must be the young Mr. Gaines. I am Mr. Greeley. And I take it by your confused expression that Dr. Gaines never spoke of me.

No, he didn't, says Joshua.

That doesn't surprise me. Dr. Gaines was a man of exceptional mental capacity. However, and if I may be frank, he was a very private man, and his business acumen was very lacking.

Another burst of wind, snow dust rushing into the house. Joshua turns away from both the wind and Mr. Greeley's comment. He knows this trait in his father, and what Mr. Greeley says is nothing Joshua hasn't said to himself before. But something about hearing it out loud from a stranger gives it the weight.

If you don't mind, says Mr. Greeley, we could speak inside where it's warmer.

But the old house isn't warmer. Mr. Greeley takes his hat off and then, perhaps feeling the cold on his head, puts it back on. Joshua starts for the living room after shutting the door before he realizes Mr. Greeley isn't following.

I suppose Dr. Gaines spent some time on that sofa, before he succumbed to the cholera, I mean, Mr. Greeley says.

Joshua looks at the sofa. Without the lamp lit, it is half consumed in shadow, the blankets used to cover his then ill, now-dead father piled at the visible end. The secretary desk across from it is still stacked with Dr. Gaines's alphabetically arranged medical books, and surrounding the living room are shelves upon shelves that hold myriad jars wherein disembodied organs and other unfettered components aimlessly float. A waxen heart, a child's hand, vacant eyeballs, a cirrhotic liver, one enlarged testicle, a fetus, a shriveled ear that looks like a mushroom. Joshua looks back at Mr. Greeley, who holds a handkerchief over his mouth like the room and its occupants (past and present) sicken him. Joshua already hates this man.

Right, says Mr. Greeley. We needn't sit down. Our conversation won't take long.

How long did you know my father?

I didn't know the doctor. I'm here merely as a favor to, or rather, at the behest of my employer, who was acquainted with Dr. Gaines. As I said before, he was a good doctor, as good as a doctor can be, that is. And we are sorry to hear of his passing. Certainly, we are. But the fact is that he borrowed a great deal of money from my employer to keep his practice running, which, circumstances being what they are, presents a difficult situation.

Joshua glances at his feet. Even after the cost of the burial, there is still fifty dollars in his father's safe, though the tightness in his stomach tells him that a man like Mr. Greeley doesn't consider fifty dollars a great deal of money. He looks back at Mr. Greeley, who wipes his nose with the handkerchief then glances at the gold pocket watch, and he understands the situation. His father was not a powerful man, that was always his disgrace. But it will not be his.

How much money? asks Joshua.

Nine hundred and eighty-seven dollars, says Mr. Greeley. Over the course of four years, that is. But a sum is a sum, regardless of its initial components.

Mr. Greeley clicks his tongue.

I warned my employer, he continues. I told him about redskins, that they don't have the first idea how to navigate a civilized world.

Though his skin electrifies with a fresh anger, Joshua knows he has to swallow the insult. A man like this won't have it any other way.

I didn't know my father borrowed any money, Joshua says.

That may be, but his debt is your debt regardless.

The house is getting colder, more consumed by shadows as the sun plays out across the brown Mississippi. The shapelessness those shadows initiate begins to fuse Joshua and Mr. Greeley into a kind of malignancy where the ending of one and the beginning of the other is no longer clear.

Well, says Joshua. I plan to take over my father's practice. I can pay you back with the profits from that.

Mr. Greeley smiles again, shakes his head.

There is no more practice. The owner, my employer, is selling it, as he is this house. Though neither will come close to covering the entire debt.

Joshua shrugs. Mr. Greeley sighs frustratingly and frowns.

You are young, he says, but so far as I gather you are not stupid. So don't act stupid now. It's demeaning to both of us.

I'm not my father.

It's a declaration confounding to Joshua in its competing elicitations of pride and regret. Mr. Greeley nods.

To some degree, he continues, we are all constricted by the life our parents give us, in whatever manifestation those parents come by. But if you work hard, it's very possible that you can repay this debt before you are too old. Then you're free to choose whatever life you wish to lead, with whomever you wish to lead it.

The old house is colder still, but Joshua's face grows hot with bitterness. Has he ever been free to choose? Will he ever be? He looks away from Mr. Greeley. Mr. Greeley wipes his nose again with the handkerchief before he pockets it, puts his gloves on.

I'll return in two days, Mr. Greeley says. You may pack a small suitcase if you have one. No medical instruments, of course. You won't need those. For the most part, everything you need will be provided.

The dark full on by the time Mr. Greeley steps back into the cold.

In a halting sort of stupor, Joshua builds a fire, the house thawing slowly and glowing orange like a jack-o'-lantern. He pours himself some water, in which he puts some drops of absinthe and a sugar cube, the steady scraping of the spoon on the rim while he stirs it, waits for the sugar to dissolve. His headache is growing, a dull thick pain just above his nose.

In a single gulp, he drinks the absinthe. Then he walks into the one bedroom he used to share with his father, picks up an envelope from his desk. He takes the envelope back into the living room and over to the fire before he pulls out the letter. He reads the letter by firelight, a second time, a third time, though the words swim and the page bends as the absinthe works his bloodstream.

> *Dear Mr. Gaines:*
> *As we cannot verify your training nor pedigree, and neither can we subsidize the cost of your education, we kindly decline your offer to sit for examination.*
>
> *Horace Penfield, MD, LLD*
> *Provost, and ex-officio President, Department of Medicine*
> *University of Pennsylvania*

Joshua wads up the letter, throws it and the envelope into the fire, where he watches them catalyze into ember and levitate before floating skyward through the chimney while his own mind follows, tracks upward with the same dramatic flair and looms above his body as he stumbles to the very sofa that housed his dying father just four days prior and collapses into a long and dreamless sleep.

Joshua wakes in the old house from two things: stiffness from a night of shivering on the sofa and a thirst he tries to quench by consuming the remaining pitcher water. Still, neither leave him. He's unsure what time it is. From habit, he looks at the cuckoo clock, then remembers it broke some years ago. For a second it occurs to him that the forgotten time the clock now harbors signifies something of something from his past. But the memory of its breaking is lost to him, and the clock seems foreign now, displaced, the encounter with Mr. Greeley and the final thread of his father and his financial state so powerful they've unhinged Joshua's sense of himself. Nothing is ordinary or familiar anymore, his future a great blank slate both terrifying and exhilarating in its possibility. For if a person, like a knife, can be melted down and remade of the same elements and bearing the same features but shedding its history for a fresh purpose, then Joshua thinks this moment is what that must be.

The absinthe bottle is open and upright on the floor where he left it last night. But he knows he needs clarity today. He fits the cork back in, returns the bottle to the doctor's—to my, he reminds himself—medical bag, which he then inventories. Most of the contents are mundane: Epsom salts, tincture of opium, milk of magnesia, castor oil, spirit of lavender, vinegar. The Dover's powder he imagines will be particularly useful as a pain reliever, the calomel for fevers, the blue mass for consumption and toothaches. Then of course there are the tools, all of which he knows, through some macabre medical intuition, that he will use on his westward journey. The scalpels; a bone saw; a fleam; the drill, the trephine, and the lenticular from an antique trepanation kit; a pair of pliers; a small hammer. He leaves the bag, retrieves a small duffel that he packs full of what clothes aren't worn too thin. Lastly, he stuffs in the last fifty dollars he has to his name.

The fireplace is merely ashes when he finally returns to the living room, so he has to rebuild the fire from scratch. With it finally burning, he removes one of the jars from the shelf, pops the lid off. The acrid chemical stench sets his nostrils on fire and floods his eyes with tears. He jerks backward while he drops the jar. The liquid hissing as it spreads across the floor, the black heart it contained now limp and depressed on the wood like a rotten piece of meat.

Jar by jar he sets about dumping the alcohol on the floor, the sofa, splashing the walls while the fetus plops like a sponge and the child's hand waves goodbye and the ear bounces erratically like a rubber ball. The air is so dense with fumes his brain is trapped in a vice, his eyes fevered by screaming veins when he looks in the wavy-glassed mirror, his skin raw and itching.

He's careful not to get his bags wet, otherwise he'll ruin their contents, what he needs for his travels. He picks up his bags, grabs the final jar with his free hand. For a moment he surveys this haphazard collage of a human scattered across the old house. These pieces are not his father, but they are now no more lifeless than him. With his chest paining and his stomach on the verge of unleashing, Joshua chucks the final jar into the fire and runs for the door.

A sound like rushing water. The heat following. Flames that lick and tease and cackle hop room to room with the kind of speed and ferocity only such condensed energy can achieve. Flames that raze his abandoned boyhood home and all prior history along with it. Ashes to ashes, don't turn hither young Joshua, salt of the earth not yet destined for such return.

PART III

THE EMIGRANT

FROM INDEPENDENCE, MISSOURI
TO THE KANSAS RIVER

ours before dawn, in the pregnant dark of early morning, the six of them ride off, following the well-worn trail west by moonlight, no words between them but the steady *clip-clop clip-clop* of the animal's hooves and the drumming wagon wheels, looking like characters in a wood etching, so two dimensional are their silhouettes against the black and formless horizon. Fifteen-hundred miles before them, through prairies and thunderstorms, woodland and ravines, mountains so jagged they seem carved by giants with serrated knives. And sand, and salt, and sand some more before the last of the mountains take them into Sacramento Valley and to the American River where the gold Joshua yearns for will be waiting for him. If they are lucky, they can travel the schooner roughly twenty miles per day with water plentiful, perhaps even a little further, but when the prairie winds blow so hard they can't open their eyes and the wagons stack up along the dusty trail, they won't be lucky.

Though none of that matters now in this incipient moment. Not yet two miles covered and town is already lost to them, and so too is any sound not made by bard owls or by coyotes with their distant howls or by the creaking schooner, which is pulled by mules for speed and soon finds its own rhythm, the horses and mules taking on a vision and direction of their own. Joshua hasn't yet seen the faces of the three men not known to him, two of them driving the schooner behind him, the other in front of him on a horse. His ass is sore as he rides the young Morgan and his legs are already chafed, though he dares not make audible his discomfort. They keep on through timber, Joshua watching the conjoined shadow of horse and rider in front of him so intently it's as if he expects to be left out here in the dark. A nameless wanderer on this trail not far from town, and already he feels so far away.

Soon they break through the trees, ford a shallow stream, and climb a steep rise that brings them into grassland beautiful in the dawning while it brushes Joshua's feet and sends singing clouds of grasshoppers he never sees. The fresh day rises in him a new fear. Maybe he's sleeping. Maybe this pending light will carry away this dream of heading to California, return him to Missouri where all that waits for him is a life governed by other men, poverty deep enough to drown him twice over.

He shivers. He leans forward, hugs his horse's mane, inhales the animal's wildness. Something so tactile and pungent can only be real.

You need to sit up, one of the men on the schooner hollers at him. You can't ride right if you ain't sitting up. Ride like you sitting a highbacked chair.

Come sunrise they cross a glorious field of sunflowers, like the one and true sun rising behind them is suddenly funhoused, and they ride at this moment a plain of tiny suns, the cosmos itself. At the edge of the field, Renard flanks his horse and brings it into the sunflowers where he surveys the party in a slow walk from front to rear, the vague shapes of schooners plodding along in the distance behind him.

All right, he says.

They move on.

A breeze turns to wind and the wind turns to mist and the mist turns to rain. What little light Joshua savored is gone. He and the others pull their coats on and lower their hats for another few timbered miles until they stop to breakfast, soaked and crammed inside the schooner to eat scrambled eggs and sausage they packed in Independence. The wagon drivers are identical twins, their faces round and pudgy with noses that look flattened by a shovel and graced by countenances that seem hard lived, cut and formed, eroded like layers of rock by a force Joshua can only speculate about. The other man, an Englishman, is much taller, thin as a quill pen with large hands, but not scrawny. He has loose hair that caps an angular face busheled by a prominent beard the same shade of brown as his hair, all of it held in place by a long neck. His face has a hardness that, unlike the twins, seems seasoned and earned, something of a man who has seen a vision of this world that justifies not only who he is and what's he done, but also what he plans to do. The Englishman grins at Joshua, a neat rectangle where his top and bottom front teeth are missing.

Presently, Renard stands, and they set off again.

At the state line some fifteen miles from Independence, sunset brings with it no color, no glory. They hobble the horses though leave them saddled should they have to flee an Indian raid. The rain suddenly stops just as they are beginning to make camp. As if pondering the actuality of this abrupt weather change, everyone pauses for a moment, looks at each other. Then Joshua sets off into a grove of softwoods to gather firewood as he's been instructed but returns with little.

The two of us might have more luck, the Englishman with the beard (G. Quillard is his name) says.

G. Quillard wears a loose linen shirt, trousers that have been patched and sewn in so many places they seem more a conglomerate of random textiles than a unified piece of clothing.

It's all that's dry, Joshua says. You can go look yourself if you don't believe me.

I wasn't suggesting... G. Quillard pauses. The subtle hurt on his face immediately following Joshua's remark quickly morphs into indifference, all in the incremental time it takes for Joshua to dump the wood next to the fire pit they've dug. He says, I was simply offering.

Joshua stands back up to face the Englishman. G. Quillard leans with his weight on one hip while he sips whiskey from a tin cup, another cup of whiskey in his other hand, his shirt flapping across his taut stomach in the wind, a loose piece of hair that keeps wiping his eyebrow. So congenial in this world, and Joshua wonders what country could produce such a man and drop him out here.

G. Quillard glances at Joshua's gimp foot, looks back up.

I can do it on my own, says Joshua, if that's what you mean.

I know you can, G. Quillard says.

He hands Joshua the extra cup of whiskey.

He says, But you don't have to.

G. Quillard grins again before turning his attention to building the fire. Renard gives Joshua a cold bowl of rice, which Joshua eats while the Englishman works. Then he retrieves his medical bag to lance the blisters on his palms. Other campfires reflect off the distant trees, more emigrants they'll pass tomorrow given their smaller and more efficient party, and out here is something of a crowded loneliness Joshua feels in his bones though hardly understands while he replaces his scalpel and resituates the medical bag on his horse. Eventually, G. Quillard begins to sing.

What's that you're singing? Clayton asks.

It's an old English ballad called Robin Hood and the Three Squires. A tailor friend of mine in London taught it to me.

Robin Hood? says Klayton.

It is a man's name, says Renard.

G. Quillard looks pleasantly surprised.

You've heard the tale? he asks.

Renard nods.

I suppose I am not so far away from my homeland after all.

Well I've not heard of him, says Clayton.

He's a legend in England, says G. Quillard. A selfless do-gooder. Poor by his own making so that he can help others.

You mean he gives up is own money? asks Klayton.

His money and all other material things.

Why would a man ever give up his own money?

That's a fair question, says G. Quillard. But I never asked it until a year ago. Something about justice and the greater good. Now I think old Robin Hood is just a story to make poor men happy about being poor.

It does sound made up, says Joshua.

I suppose all legends are grounded in some truth.

Maybe, says Joshua. Maybe not. What could be true to some is just fiction to others.

Everyone is silent for a minute. Then Clayton turns to G. Quillard with a mean look.

I don't like it, he says. It makes no sense to me, true or not. The way I figure, that son of a bitch deserves to be gutted and his money took. A man got no business having money if he ain't having it all for hisself.

Clayton stabs his knife into the mud, warms his hands near the fire.

Renard says, The pursuit of wealth is every man's journey. For some that wealth is physical. For others, spiritual. Robin Hood, as I understand him, was interested in the latter.

So they say, says G. Quillard.

Still, says Renard. He takes his eyes off the fire and looks first at the twins, then at G. Quillard, then at Joshua. He says, Only one of those pursuits is truly worth a man's journey.

Much later they wrap themselves in blankets like bunned sausages and sleep in the damp grass.

Joshua dreams his eleven-year-old self, the second Planter's House Hotel in St. Louis bustling with stiff dresses and starched shirt collars, people Joshua hardly recognizes in himself or his father while they walk, as if they are another species entirely and what they've stumbled upon is some alien environment where color and smell and sound and shape are of a substance that appears human but, by every aspect of that word's definition he ascribes to the two of them, can't be his human.

Dr. Gaines holds Joshua's hand, is pulling him forward down the cobblestone road.

Don't think about it, says Dr. Gaines. The mind has a powerful hold on the body, and if you don't think about your hunger, then it will stop being.

Joshua stares at shiny black heels, a gutta-percha cane swinging in front of him. He's thinking about the bakery they passed early, the pillowy smell of bread that tried to tear his empty stomach out of his body—We don't have any money, his father said. I'm sorry—when he sees something glint underneath the man's heel.

Joshua pulls on his father's hand to stop him.

What is it now? Dr. Gaines asks.

Joshua bends down, picks up the silver dollar. He blows the dust off of it before turning it over in his hand, watching the sunlight sheen its surface. He's seen these coins only a handful of times in his young life, and his father has never let him hold one before, trying to engrain in the boy, as Dr. Gaines puts it, that money is nugatory.

Let me have that. Dr. Gaines takes the coin from Joshua. He says, This isn't yours.

It was just lying there, insists Joshua.

Which means that it doesn't belong to us.

Before Joshua can respond, those shiny black shoes he had been watching return, the man with the gutta-percha standing before the two of them, and smiling.

I believe that coin is mine, the man tells Dr. Gaines. I must have dropped it, careless as that seems.

The man glances at Joshua still smiling, his shoulders held back so that his body is straight as a sword and a scowl-faced woman clutching his arm with a white, fox-faced fur framing her shoulders even though it's hot outside.

He didn't drop it, says Joshua to his father. It was just on the ground, and he stepped on it. He didn't even see it.

Quiet, says Dr. Gaines.

The man chuckles, says, The boy is mistaken, of course. I did drop it. Right there in fact.

He points to the ground opposite where Joshua found the coin.

See? says Joshua. I found it over there. It isn't his.

The man frowns now. And the woman huffs. The man leans toward Dr. Gaines, the sharp smell of his cologne nauseating to Joshua in the heat.

You know, doctor, says the man. That boy looks nothing like you.

The man peers down at Joshua, cocks his head to the side, a look that verges on pity sliding across his face now.

He says, You are too thin, no doubt. But you look like you could have been something, if the circumstances were different than they are of course. Now.

The man redirects his attention to Dr. Gaines, extends his palm.

He says, Are you going to give me the coin, or do I need to take it from you?

Joshua looks at his father, who looks at the ground while he hands the coin to the man.

Right, says the man handing the coin to the woman. For something to go on that pretty head of yours.

The man smiles again at Dr. Gaines, glances once more at Joshua and tips his hat before turning away with the woman in tow.

Joshua lets go of his father's hand, crosses his arms, his father's ... difference (because there really is no other word for it) wedging in the most buried and tender part of his heart, where Joshua is beginning to feel that their sharedness begins and ends with a name.

Dr. Gaines puts his hand on Joshua's shoulder.

Hungry or not, he says, we will return the next one, and the next one. To any man who lays claim to that which isn't unequivocally ours.

A FEW HOURS before dawn, they break camp, ride in the line of emigrants until midmorning when they pass a train of three families walking schooners pulled by oxen, a herd of ten pollarded cattle driven in front of them that produce a wide and pale cloud of dust Joshua is forced to take into his lungs, coughing horrendously. He lifts his shirt collar up over his nose, his body ripe. The men nod pleasantly at him while they pass, the women and children (some in their early teens, others too young to fully understand this move) watch him with hard and disillusioned stares. They are headed to whatever destination they imagine so vividly will be the better for them, better than the land and occupations they left behind, if they had any occupations to speak of. Or perhaps they are self-proclaimed wanderers, nomads, some such as this country incites, and so this new journey is one in a succession of journeys, endless and always seeking that new land, that new opportunity, generations of emigrants with eyes forever trained on the road as long as these roads exist to take them.

At the front of the train, a small-boned boy lies strapped to a cot in the wagon bed. He lashes his body side-to-side against ropes that dig at his torso and bind his legs while he wails. From this distance, Joshua can't discern whether what ails the child is a physical malediction or a mental one, but he knows this problem isn't his, and he's glad for that. He turns away, realizes how quickly the wailing is lost in the noise of the driven herd, like such suffering ceases to exist when you simply don't think about it.

Keeping a two-day pace that brings them each night to a distance much akin to what they traveled the day prior and with nothing but the light changing as they ride, they eventually reach the high-banked Wakarusa River. The twins park the schooner in the waist-high brush, set the brake. The others hitch their horses to the rear of the bed.

It's time for a good bath, says G. Quillard.

He stands with his hands on his hips, the dust delineating the creases in his neck, and Joshua realizes that as filthy as G. Quillard already appears, he must look equally filthy.

They walk into the river fully clothed, out to the middle of the limestone bed where the cold water comes up to the top of Clayton and Klayton's chests and to everyone else's stomachs, aside from G. Quillard, who stands only hip-deep. Joshua holds his arms above the water while he sucks in breaths the cold seems to snatch away, a thing painful and invigorating all at once. The current is weak, and they submerge themselves with their hats held up so that at that moment the river looks like an installation of floating hats attached to disembodied hands, the men standing back up and spitting and exclaiming and huffing for air, shaking out their hair and wiping the water from their eyes and faces before they put their hats on again and the water clouded with the dust washed from their clothes and bodies.

Good damn this crick's cold! cries Klayton.

I ain't never expected it to be this cold, says Clayton. You'd think it'd warmed some by now but shit, it ain't warmed one bit.

The twins are holding hands. They look at each other, take a dramatic breath, and go back under a second time with their hats clamped to their heads and still holding hands, moving in sequence through a kind of practiced living, some remnant of a collective childhood spent splashing about in creeks or in the murky shallows of brown lakes that's now executed instinctively, with a mind that has itself grown collective.

Free Ray wades out and undresses. His back is heavily scarred. The body, Joshua thinks, in all its wonderment. Wearing only his gaucho, Free Ray wades back into the middle of the river, where he sinks to his knees. The others follow Free Ray's lead, bodies miscolored with pale torsos and legs set against red necks and red faces, heavily weathered hands. Scars unseen now cleaned like washed out irrigation ditches. No dust in the water. The river running clearer with their newfound cleanliness while they wipe themselves behind their ears, under their arms, and around their groin. Joshua gently rubs the saddle sores on his ass and the inside of his thighs with handfuls of cold water. He lifts each scabbed foot and massages the bottom of it with smooth stones he plucks from the riverbed, inspects broken toenails and what blisters he has, having a mind to lance those blisters later.

He notices the others watching him, waiting for something, which he soon realizes are instructions. He's the doctor, after all, and this possible moment illuminates the trust they have in him, an odd sort of power. He tells them what to do, and they do so.

Afterward, they all wring the water from their clothes and pass around a small cedar branch to perfume everything before redressing, their weight loss, even in such a short span, making them look pitifully thin in these wet garments.

THAT NIGHT, A day or so from the Kansas River crossing, G. Quillard mends Joshua's coat, which Joshua snagged on one of the schooner's nails while pulling out some bacon for supper. As big as the Englishman's hands are, G. Quillard works them deftly and finely in the lamplight, navigating the coat's seams and tear with the same exactitude Joshua always saw his father exhibit during surgeries.

How long were you a tailor? asks Joshua.

As long as I've been alive, says G. Quillard. My father was a tailor, as was his father. It was always my future.

Until you came here.

G. Quillard looks up from his work, smiles.

Right, he says. Like you, like all of us. A new future in a new place with new company.

He glances toward the fire, where on one side Renard and Free Ray sit next to each other, and on the other the twins eat with mirrored rhythm.

Or at least you and I are in new company, says G. Quillard.

The Englishman makes some final adjustments to the coat, hands it back to Joshua.

How many times have you been to California? G. Quillard asks Renard when the two of them join the others at the fire.

Once before, says Renard.

And how many times has he been? G. Quillard points at Free Ray.

Him? says Renard. I believe only once, but I have never truly known the answer to that question.

You're a mysterious man, says G. Quillard. I admire that.

Free Ray is sharpening his Bowie knife on a leather strap, but he stops, looks at G. Quilllard. He wrinkles his eyes like he's trying to figure something about that Englishman's character or intention before he turns his attention back to his knife and begins sharpening it again.

And a fucking mute, adds Klayton.

Oh, he is no mute, says Renard. He chooses not to speak and is free to do so. All men could fare well to make that choice more often. This world would be a more hospitable place because of it.

G. Quillard takes off his socks and sets them on a rock near the fire, puts his boots over his bare feet.

America, he says. I haven't been here long, but the way everyone speaks of freedom, it's as if a man has no choice but to be free.

Why don't you hush now, says Klayton.

You see? G. Quillard says. You want what freedom and representation suppose. But when it bares its teeth and shows its ugly frown, you are the first to look away. I knew a great man in London who understood that. A mulatto, actually. Understood that better than any man I've ever known. He was committed to the fight for true representation, the blood that fight has to shed. But that commitment got him arrested and transported to Tasmania. And it sent me fleeing to New York.

I should think we understand little about freedom, says Renard. If, on the one hand, we set ourselves in comparison to Free Ray.

G. Quillard frowns at Renard. Then he turns to Free Ray.

And why is it you carry that name?

Free Ray examines the knife blade's sharpness against the firelight. Satisfied with its edge, he reholsters it, then looks up at G. Quillard and shrugs.

G. Quillard laughs.

Do not be fooled by his modesty, says Renard. We are lucky to be christened, white men that we are, but never has a man earned his name in the manner Free Ray earned his.

You mean he wasn't born Free Ray? asks Klayton.

I mean he was not born free.

Renard whispers something into Free Ray's ear. Free Ray nods but keeps his eyes on the fire. Renard takes up the rum and holds it in front of him without drinking. He coughs once, spits, clears his throat.

I had ten fingers the summer I met Free Ray.

Ten fingers? interrupts Klayton. So that was before you got your hands caught in those flour mill gears?

Renard grins at Klayton, continues: I was headed north through Arkansas, bound for Missouri from the port town of Natchitoches, Louisiana. St. Louis was a burgeoning city then, and I believed I would try my hand at the apex of the river trade. At the end of a hot, steamy day, I was coming around a bend in the foothills of the Ouachita Mountains. I took a blind corner only to come face-to-face with a man covered, his body entire, in mud, standing square in the middle of the road. Free Ray, though I did not know his name yet, wore no shirt and no shoes. Only trousers. But his trousers were too short for him. They were so tattered as to have been mere rags. We stood there for a few moments like storied adversaries: I fully armed with a knife and a pistol, Free Ray defenseless save for his fists. The shock of having run upon him subsided, I decided I would kill him. It was an easy decision to kill him. One I would not even have to account for were some other traveler to come upon me during the act.

Renard hands Free Ray the rum. He takes a drink.

I took my pistol and aimed it at Free Ray's head. He did not move. He did not even flinch. His eyes were wild as he stared at me, but there was no fright in them. I saw something in those eyes. Something I could not explain then and cannot even explain now. Such a man would do no one any good in death, I thought, and I resolved to take him as my captive and bring him to St. Louis to sell him for a healthy price. I bound his wrists in front of him with some rope I was carrying and hobbled him. In this manner, we walked for two weeks. Free Ray always walked in front of me while I held tight to the rope. From that position, I could see the fresh wounds that painted his back like a maze and scabbed over more each day. When the sun shone on those scabs through the trees, I swear they divulged a sort of script. I was careful not to stay the road whenever possible and never to camp near it. Because I knew that if others happened upon us, Free Ray would be taken from me and I likely killed. Of course, no man would want the proceeds from his lucrative sale of fleshed goods divided more ways than was necessary. Each night I tied Free Ray to a sturdy bole and fed him only a small portion of what I ate to keep his strength and energy down. For six days, he never spoke a word. He was more my shadow than my captive. On the seventh day, we journeyed through the heart of the Ozarks in southern Missouri, a forest rich in white oak and shortleaf pine hundreds of years old that can block out the sun for days. We stopped midday on a downed tree to dinner on wild asparagus and a squirrel I shot off a tree limb. Halfway through his meal, Free Ray looked up at me and spoke in that French tongue of his. I understood him, because I had learned French during my time in Natchitoches. He told me his name was Ray. The only other Black man I had previously known was named Ray, so you can imagine my astonishment and disbelief at that moment. I thought perhaps they were all named Ray. I asked him if that was truly his name, but he said nothing else for the rest of that day or the next. The morning of the ninth day, we passed a trio of boys who sprung from the ferns as if they were making a home there. They were dirty, dim-witted boys. One of them had only one ear, a cluster of skin bubbles where his other ear should have been. The boys jeered and spat at Free Ray. One of the boys kicked him hard in the shins with his boot. I laughed while the boys had their fun. But as their methods of playing grew more violent and their actions more raucous, I scared them off with a threat from my pistol.

Renard waves his pistol in the air to mimic that charade. He laughs heartily at himself, and the others laugh with him. He turns and pats Free Ray on the shoulder, sits there for a moment with his hand still on Free Ray's shoulder like he's sharing that memory with him.

What happened after that? asks Clayton.

Well, says Renard. That evening we camped along Jacks Fork. I burned no fire out of fear of being spotted, and Free Ray, perhaps exhausted by his own silences, began to speak. He told me he had been a slave to a French couple in Hammond, Louisiana, tending their strawberry farm. He never knew how old he was and could not remember where he had originally come from or how he had come to work for that farm. In any case, the farmer and his wife had taken to whipping Free Ray incessantly. By the time Free Ray was a man, he was greatly scarred, but the Frogs, instead of stopping their whipping, only whipped him harder, and longer. One evening, he told me, while he was sharing the bed of another slave, a Haitian woman, the farmer kicked in the door, slipped the whip around Free Ray's neck, and dragged him from the shack into the strawberries. There he lashed Free Ray to the whipping post while he was still naked and set to again. Free Ray closed his eyes, but he said that when he opened them again, his hands had miraculously been freed from the post. The rope that had bound them dangled from one wrist. For a second, he told me, he thought he was dreaming. He was leaning against the lashing post and still being whipped with his blood indistinguishable on the strawberries even though his hands were free. Then he turned around and faced the farmer. The farmer was a slight man, and he dropped the whip in shock when he realized Free Ray had freed himself. How that had happened to his slave the farmer could only wonder. Before he could retrieve the whip, Free Ray rushed the farmer, took the rope in both hands, and wrapped it around the farmer's neck. Free Ray put his bare knees into the farmer's back and pulled so hard he nearly severed that farmer's head completely.

Renard pauses again, his face expressionless. He goes on.

Still naked, Free Ray walked into the farmer's house, his own blood draining from the wounds on his back and the farmer's blood glossing his chest and face. He had to locate the master bedroom in the dark because he had never been in that house before. When he found it, he found the farmer's wife. She was asleep. Free Ray killed her, but only after putting out her eyes. Then he took a pair of trousers from the farmer's bureau and subsequently ran away, heading north, where, of course, I stumbled upon him in Arkansas.

Renard goes quiet. For a long while, no one says anything. Joshua remembers how the scars on Free Ray's back looked that day they bathed in the river, imagines them now hidden beneath Free Ray's shirt and coat. The way the body marks and measures time fascinates him. The way it heals, and what it reveals about relinquishing our past, a sort of reconciliation through a remaking. Like Free Ray's scars, like Renard's missing fingers, like his own missing toes. Living, he thinks, is the accumulation of the body's losses, especially out here, where loss is the de facto state of being.

Klayton finally breaks the heavy silence.

He told you all of that?

Renard nods.

Ain't that the most fascinating truth I ever heard.

Renard says, Free Ray did not speak anymore after that moment. I sat there, contemplating the story he had told me while he lay on his back. I must have fallen asleep thinking about it because the next moment I remember was being awaken late that night with a kick at my foot. Free Ray was standing over me, his wrists unbound, and wearing one of my linen shirts he had evidently taken from my bag.

Renard chuckles.

I believe, gentlemen, that I was more frightened at that moment than any other in my life before or after, he says.

Free Ray takes another drink of rum, hands the gallon back to Renard, who corks it and sets it on the ground.

The mud, Renard continues, which had dried and cracked all over his body those last several days, was completely washed off. I believe he had gone down to the river and bathed himself. There was hardly any moon that night, the forest so dark a man was lucky to see his hands in front of his face. But for all that darkness, and for all the trees that made that darkness even more dense, I could still see Free Ray plain as I had seen him the first day I met him on the road. He looked at me, and I stared up at him for what felt to be ages before he finally bent down and said, I could kill you right now. And believe me, Free Ray was right. He could have killed me. I believe he would have had I not been quick-witted enough to convince him that he should not because I could make him rich, and thereby guarantee his safety. At the end of my argument, I waited, still lying there, still a bit frightened, until he leaned down and said, Let's go then. I said to him, So you are free now. And he nodded. Free Ray, he said. Because you see, gentlemen, Free Ray understands, like all of us do, that a poor life is not a free life. And a free life is the only life worth living.

What happened after that? asks Joshua.

Much happened after that.

You're wrong about that last part, says Clayton. They ain't ever free. They're either a slave to another's vices or a slave to their own.

That may be true in the state we left, says Renard. But out here, you will see what freedom really means.

FROM THE KANSAS RIVER
TO THE PLATTE RIVER

Not long after passing through two Potawatomi villages and trading some iron tools for a bushel of corn, they come upon a line of schooners waiting to be ferried across the Kansas River by two Pawnee for a dollar each. This river is something of a milestone: One hundred miles on the trail bringing them now into the Osage Plains. Their spirits are buoyed by this moment, and the lead Indian who wears an old U.S. cavalry coat, his short mohawk culminating in a long-tail braid and his right ear almost entirely obscured by metal earrings, ferries them into the land beyond, which is smooth and high-rolling with the trail so clogged by the slower-moving parties their own rides alongside in the short grass, the undulating swell of the wagon train ridging the flat landscape like a gaunt man's spine.

After a while, Renard halts their party with the approach of wagons traveling southeast, in the opposite direction. The lead driver is draped in leathers and wearing a beaver hat, has a pile of hides slung over his horse's rear: bison, antelope, wolf, even a few rabbit pelts. The wagons are stamped AMERICAN FUR COMPANY, in which Joshua is sure are many more of those hides stacked to the roof.

The lead driver salutes Renard. It seems a comical, almost satiric gesture, and Renard stifles a laugh while he nods in return.

You traveling alone?

If you are asking whether this is the extent of our party, then the answer is yes, Renard says.

The man squints eyes grayed from too much sun and purses his beard-burdened lips, evidently trying to decide whether to voice his opposition to that decision. Then he relaxes his face.

I seen a man killed and scalped just south of the Big Blue.

He pauses.

Well, he continues, I didn't see it per sey. But I passed a company who said they passed a company who said they seen it, and I'm sure I seen blood on the grass.

We thank you for the warning, says Renard.

The man stares at Renard for a bit, then examines the rest of the party.

Well, he shrugs, good luck to yous.

For the next few hours, Joshua rides with his head shifting side-to-side as he scans for hostile Indians, so much so his neck grows stiff and sore. He swears to himself that the fur trader's warning is gossip, that the Big Blue River is miles off anyway, but it's as if he's been possessed by another more gullible soul, as if he is now living some nightmare that can't possibly be real and yet no physical sensation will wake him. The world around him is soundless. All he hears is his heartbeat in his ears. His eyes water with tears or dust, he isn't sure, and his face feels feverish and swollen. He keeps splashing himself with water from his canteen.

After a while, G. Quillard turns around.

You must stop wasting your drinking water, he says. I don't have enough for the both of us.

Joshua sees G. Quillard talking but he doesn't hear him. He smiles for the sake of reaction, and when G. Quillard frowns at him, he knows that's the wrong response.

Joshua rides with that fear all day, knowing it's a baseless fear, yet he suffers it all the same, perhaps worse each time he aims to convince himself that fear is entirely imagined. But so powerful is the mind that every tree in his periphery, every piece of bluegrass that shakes from the wind is the launching of an attack, and he knows he'd die before he sees the attack play out. He is sure of that. He is sure nothing he can do will save him.

Come evening, the sky deadens with the dark gray of a thunderhead. Joshua, the twins, and G. Quillard hobble and unsaddle the horses while Renard and Free Ray load their rifles and ride off. Preoccupied by his fear, Joshua works mechanically and too slowly until dark, twice being yelled at by the twins for getting in their way. Later, with the sky pitch dark and pulsing with half-blinding bursts of lightning, the rain falls thick as a curtain. Joshua and the others sit crammed into the wagon bed trying to stay dry. The warmth of the others' bodies has calmed him, and Joshua is half-asleep with that fear nearly gone when G. Quillard wakes him with Renard and Free Ray's arrival.

A doe is flung across Renard's soaked shoulders, the blood striping his back. There's no space to clear in the wagon bed, but Renard throws the dead thing into it anyway with the others falling out of the way and back into the rain. She is already gutted, her stomach cavernous, and the blood pasted to those walls like blackened limestone deposits. Her eyes still open, milky and noncommittal in death. Joshua's fear is reignited by the open dark, and staring at those vacant eyes, he swears they divulge a sort of omen.

How'd you get her? asks Klayton.

What? asks Renard, the rain loudly drumming the bonnet.

Klayton cups his hands around his mouth and shouts into the wagon, How'd you get her?

Free Ray shot her, says Renard with a tone that suggests the answer to that question is obvious.

I meant, how'd you find her iffen deer ain't here? I've not seen a single one since we crossed the state line.

Perhaps you have been looking in the wrong places. Or perhaps those deer are better with their eyes than you are.

Klayton ignores this comment, peers into the bed to watch the doe bleed out onto a sack of rice for a moment. He jabs Joshua with his elbow, hoping he will join him in this spectacle, but Joshua refuses. Renard motions Joshua into the wagon to help him clean the doe, but the fear that hangs onto Joshua paralyzes him, as if it will unleash whatever hell is waiting for him in all the darkest parts of this landscape should he move even an inch. Renard stares at Joshua. Joshua feels that Renard can somehow see through him into the heart of that fear, where he will trap it, tame it, harness the essence of it so that on some distant day in some distant place he can replace that old fear inside Joshua with an urge far more powerful, far more transformative in its disruptive possibility. Only when G. Quillard steps into Joshua's vision does Joshua blink and take such a deep breath it's like he'd forgotten to breathe.

G. Quillard looks Joshua in the eyes as if to say I understand before he winks, turns around, and hops into the wagon bed. He and Renard hang the doe with ropes from the backside of the tailgate like a pig on a spit. With the lantern fired, Renard climbs out and processes the animal with his Green River knife, working slowly and deliberately in the manner of a man who's done such processing before. He lets the rain wash each piece of venison while he scrapes it clean before he hands the meat to Free Ray, who dusts it with salt and stacks it in a tin tub. At the doe's shoulder, Renard pauses, stabs the knife point between the rib bones and digs out the one-ounce lead ball. With his thumb and forefinger, he holds the glistening ball in the lamplight for the others to see before he pitches it into the drowning grass.

When he's finished processing, Renard washes the blood from his hands and forearms in the rain, scrapes clean his fingernails with the knife. He returns to the schooner fully soaked again, shaking from the cold, but he doesn't seem to mind. He removes his shirt, puts his unbuttoned coat on over his bare torso. In that outfit and with his long red hair, he looks like a matador, and he smiles with the pride and puffed chest of one freshly victorious.

Afterward, they all huddle beneath the canvas awning staked from the side of the wagon to the ground, and they eat raw offal for supper. The lingering fear has exhausted Joshua, and he falls asleep with his plate half full. Klayton and Clayton take the liberty of finishing his meal in actions that aren't so much eating as devouring.

When Joshua wakes after midnight, his legs are dull from having been crossed. The rain has stopped, the others are sleeping around him, and he sees Clayton sitting picket. He wraps himself into himself, lies with his back to the others. He is calm now. As suddenly as it came, that fear is gone. He is so calm he thinks for a moment he's dead, and he wonders if this is how his father felt in his final moments. Of course not, he reminds himself. Of course he will never forget the pain in his father's wails.

He tries to let go this memory of his father. He listens to the horses snort over and over at the presence of the dead doe, and he allows his mind to shutter with fragmented images of trail violence. All of it retribution, theirs and the Indians, taking for having been taken from and taken from for having taken, so that what passes hands really belongs to no one, including their lives. An odd, arbitrary peace can be found in such balanced affairs, and soon, Joshua is sleeping again.

＊

IN THE PALE of early morning, the twins wash the mules' shoulders with their drinking water to prevent them from soring up. Then they travel on. When their trail merges with the one originating out of Weston, Missouri, and the government road from St. Joseph, the sudden explosion of emigrants forms a steadily pulsing vein in the magnificent heart of this country. They've ridden with water abundant (the wide Vermillion River, the Big Blue, Cove Spring), so that Joshua feels they are want for nothing. He wonders if California will be this way, if the land will offer up to them everything that could make a man content. His mind and belly fulfilled, satisfied.

But nothing is constant—even here. In the upper flint hills, the land redefines itself again, the horses forced to high-step limestone and shale cuestas. Eventually, they enter mixed-grass prairie with monstrous shadows from clouds moving like ships over the tallgrass and subsequently reach the U.S. Army's Fort Kearny, where they repair their wagon's split fifth chain before continuing on to the Platte River's South Fork.

Here, a couple days of rest and recomposition follow. During this time, Joshua passes out poultices and balms, camphor to stymy itchy skin, calomel to relieve the twins' blockage, a tea of willow bark that eases the ague shaking G. Quillard. They aren't for lack of food, but Joshua wanders off to survey some of the other wagons stopped along here until he finds one that smells like cornbread. He waits until the mother preoccupies herself with nursing her baby, then leans in and steals the still-warm pan.

He eats half the loaf without sharing, wraps the other half in an old shirt, hides it in his saddlebag for later. Then he lounges on his back underneath the shade of the canvas awning. When he feels the onset of an intense bilious complaint, he self-medicates on tincture of opium that dulls his faculties, and the image of his father returns.

The notion of his father in such a wild and untethered place grips him with an unexpected and untenable nostalgia, which he washes away with another spoonful of tincture of opium.

Somewhere not far off, two men of another team argue in a language Joshua can't understand, their words sliding together into growly barbaric sounds that make his skin cold and the hair on the back of his neck electrify. He tries to lift his head to see who they are and why they're arguing, to make sure that these men aren't actually beasts, but his body won't let him. His ears sing with their vocalisms (he doesn't consider them voices anymore), he feels their bodies transform into mechanisms of his own terror, which he projects on the canvas awning shivering above him in the gusty plains wind, their eyes now his eyes so that he sees at this moment his own future as a mock-up of his past.

The young men in leathers, that's who they are. They were younger than he is now (not by much), but they will forever be older. Older, bigger, stronger. Young men beside themselves and their bodies baggy and flapping with the store-bought leathers that shaped their arms into prehensile wings, their rank earthen scent like moist fungi steamed Joshua's nostrils, their hands insatiable paws that punched and prodded and unleashed the most deviant parts of himself. And, suddenly, there is the foul smell of the abandoned cannery, the piglet's blood warm on his hands and climbing to his wrists, the butcher that traded the piglet to him for a dull Bowie knife Joshua found on the banks of the Mississippi River.

She's a waste to me anyway since her mother suffocated her earlier this morning, the butcher says, his neck striped with blood as if decorated with war paint. He frowns, laughs, says: Of course not. I don't just give away my goods. Hell son, what's wrong with you? Yeah, that's right. The price is that knife.

Joshua carries away the small bundle of butcher paper. Even through the paper he can feel the jelliness of the piglet's body, the small legs with their small hooves that still retain their flexibility. He avoids the others on this crowded summer day, tacking the street with his head down so that all he sees are his own feet moving in succession. It's the way his father walks, and this mannerism is so much a part of him now it muddles that line between nature and nurture to become inheritance, or something like that. He carries the small parcel with both hands. He's careful not to manipulate the piglet's body too much because he wants more than anything to preserve, as much as possible, the composite of its life.

He finds his way to the abandoned cannery, slides through the ajar door without the use of his hands. In one of the back rooms, he uprights a long wooden table and wipes a section of it off with his frayed sleeve. He can see the brown sludge of the Mississippi slinking along through a half-boarded-up window, a two-man canoe trolling a fishing line. He can almost hear the river's smooth liquid sound.

Joshua lays the piglet on its back on the table. He pokes around its body with two stiff fingers, mimicking exactly what his father has shown him. The stomach, the liver, the sternum, the heart near here, the ilium. The large intestine he traces with his pinky finger, the thoracic vertebrae with his index when he tips the piglet onto its side. He carefully pulls the scalpel from his trouser pocket, makes a slow, clean cut from the larynx to the tail. He will remove the gallbladder, suture the artery. Then he will open the stomach and reclose it. Amputate a front leg, perhaps a back leg by breaking the small bones with a rock chisel he has in his back pocket. All of this to practice his surgery skills.

Deep-throated laughter interrupts him. Joshua thinks at first it's one person laughing, but when he hears the multiple footsteps and the young men talking, he recognizes that it's three of them. He goes still. His fingers are still inside the piglet's body, waiting. Maybe they won't come back here, he thinks. He chose this back room because it was far enough away from the alley that even if someone ventured into the cannery, they might not find him.

He tracks the voices with his head, watching through the walls where he thinks the voices are, and where they're going. He isn't aware how tense his shoulders are until the voices start to recede, and he feels himself relax. They're leaving, he thinks. Then he sees one of them come around the corner, stop, and stand there not far from Joshua. The two of them regard each other for a moment, each as surprised as the other at this discovery. The young man is wearing a thin leather coat that drapes off his body like a curtain. He has a burly face with a bristly beard that makes him look a few years older than his eyes suggest. Joshua has seen him before, coming and going from the school Dr. Gaines has never let Joshua attend, so he can already picture the others who are with him. And when they call out to find the young man, he directs them to this back room, where they now stand beside him, all three wearing odd concomitants of leathers that seem seamless in their composition so that they look like beasts stumbling onto the hiding place of this boy and unsure what to do next.

You're the doctor's kid, the first young man finally says.

Realizing his hands are still inside the piglet, Joshua removes them, wipes the blood on his trousers. He nods.

That's right, says one of the others. I've seen him around.

They're talking around Joshua now.

I've seen the doctor much more, says the third one.

Is that a pig?

Looks like it.

Is that a baby pig?

The first young man is speaking to Joshua again. Joshua nods.

Can't you speak? The third one asks.

Yes, says Joshua.

What the hell are you doing?

Joshua holds up the scalpel, as if that will clarify this mutilated piglet laying in front of him in an abandoned cannery on a summer day. The confused looks on their faces confirm that this gesture doesn't do that.

I'm learning how to perform surgery, Joshua says. We start on animals to develop delicacy.

We? asks the first young man.

My father and I, says Joshua.

The three of them approach the table, put their palms on it so that they can lean in and gaze at Joshua's handiwork. They don't seem appalled or disgusted the way he feared they would be, and a surge of pride moves through him, loosens his nerves some. His incision is precise, straight, and he lets himself admire his own work while the others do.

Is it true he's an Indian? asks one of them without taking his eyes off the piglet. The doctor I mean.

Joshua doesn't respond.

It's true, says the first young man.

He looks at Joshua, smiles. A smile that seems oddly affable and malicious all at once. He pulls out a bottle full of brown liquid, opens it, takes a long drink. The one next to him reaches for the bottle, takes a drink when it's offered him.

What's that?

He points to the liver, and Joshua tells him.

Why's it look like that? the young man asks.

What do you mean? asks Joshua.

It's kind of red.

That's the blood in it, Joshua says. Every organ has blood vessels, which give them a red color.

The first young man takes back the bottle, extends it to Joshua. Joshua shakes his head. The first young man smiles again, shakes his head in return. Joshua wonders if the young man is mimicking him on purpose, or if he's simply declining his own declination.

Turning down a free drink is the same as calling a man a coward, the young man says. And it sounds like we're going to be here for a while so that you can explain what the hell you're talking about. So you might as well have a drink and relax.

Joshua hesitates at first. Then he takes the bottle and drinks from it. He's never had alcohol before, and he closes his eyes against the boil in his throat and mashes his teeth together. The others laugh before one of them snatches back the bottle for a long drink.

Now, says the first young man. What's a liver?

And a blood vessel? says one of the others.

Either from the liquor or their curiosity, Joshua grows increasingly emboldened with his answers, increasingly stimulated by their questions, explaining in long and winding sentences all of the different parts and functions of the body while the young men listen without any sense of disgust or boredom. He's never used his knowledge in this way before. It gives him a new energy, a sudden explosion of excitement and warmth as he connects with others who aren't his father, others who are nearly his age even. How many nights has he dreamed of friends—people formed so abstractly in his mind they are always a composite of his father's features in clunky and horrible ways? How many times has he wondered what it's like to talk without being instructed on what you don't know, or what you should know?

One of the young men asks to borrow Joshua's scalpel before he uses it to stab out the piglet's eye. Joshua is surprised by this act at first, revolted even, but his reaction is soon taken over by the others' contagious laughter, and he follows them in their elatedness, in their juvenile behavior. The young man now makes a long, wending cut down the piglet's side, mangling some of the innards, and Joshua lets go even more, laughs even harder. He doesn't care that his piglet is wasted, his surgery practice ruined. He doesn't care. He laughs, and he drinks some more, and he laughs some more until the room goes askew and he feels his body start to tip backward.

The first young man reaches out, grabs Joshua's shirt with a strong grip to right him. Joshua looks at him, his shirt still bunched by that grip and taut on his sweaty back. Those youthful eyes seem to calm him further, warm him with another sort of warmth that's also stoked by his dreams, and he smiles at the young man, who smiles back, who encloses Joshua in that smile until the young man's other fist collides with Joshua's face.

The room is twirling now, as if Joshua is caught with it in a sort of dance. It flashes with white light when the back of his head slams into the wood floor, the three young men doubled and vibrating with an ethereal quality while they swarm him, two of them pinning his arms and legs, the first young man using the scalpel to slice Joshua's shirt from neck to hip, his trousers from hip to groin while that smile never leaves his face. Joshua is moaning, slowly moving his head side to side while it fills with thick pain, the side of his face that the man punched already rushing with blood and swelling. These young men don't need to pin him. Joshua feels like he couldn't move even if they asked him to, but when he tries to tell them that, his words come out as one jumbled mass of sound that's mixed with the spit dabbling his chin.

Limb by limb they tear the clothes off of his body. He lies there now in the nude, his arms and legs spread, the blood that's running out of his head clumping his hair and licking his neck with its pasty heat. The young men are talking to him, or yelling at him. He can't tell. Their words aren't words but the uttered gutturals of beings not of this world, and with the sweet smell of their leathers—pleasant somehow even in his state—and the only sound in his ears the dull draining of the Mississippi, he transposes himself onto the piglet, sees himself looming over himself while the first young man punches here to check for his liver, punches there to check for his kidney, up and down and side to side all over his body until Joshua throws up.

After that, the young men leave him there alone. He is still naked, his sliced-up clothes wadded into their rough hands only to be dumped in the streets or in the woods or along the riverbank. Joshua cries for a long time, always mindful to hush his crying even with the pains throbbing his body and the cold splinters stabbing his pale butt and thighs. Eventually, he forces himself to stand, slowly enough to avoid getting too dizzy. He retrieves his scalpel, the most valuable item he brought here, and which thankfully they left him. Then he makes his way to the door.

It's early evening, the narrow alley clustered by vagrants who cuss and tease each other with gestures that seem partly in jest, partly malicious. The alley has only one exit. At the other end of it, a tall wooden fence demarcates a chapel. Joshua considers waiting until dark to return home, but the prospect of running through the streets of St. Louis naked and alone after dark strikes him as even more dangerous. He waits until he thinks the vagrants are preoccupied enough. He assures himself that if he sprints, he'll get through the alley before they can register this aberration, grips the scalpel tightly in his hand with the blade of it pointed to the ground in case he trips, rocks back and forth on his toes while he takes a few deep breaths.

He leaps out the door.

As soon as he does, a fresh pain radiates from the bottom of his ribs into his chest, throwing him off balance and face-first into the dirt. Even before he picks himself up, he knows the vagrants are looking at him, watching this spectacle of a something-less-than human running naked from an abandoned cannery into the streets of St. Louis, a lost and bumbling troll.

They shout at him. One heaves a half-empty bottle past Joshua's shoulder. He ignores everything, looks only toward the street he races toward, and then once he reaches that street, toward the next street, and then the next, all the while navigating finely dressed people who gawk in disgust and betrayal. After all, this event is as debasing to their sense of self as it is to his. Joshua doesn't stop, doesn't even notice his foot is cut and bleeding until he reaches his house and crashes through the door.

Jesus, says Dr. Gaines walking over with his medical book still open, his spectacles hanging onto the tip of his nose.

Joshua knows his father isn't a religious man, so this reaction tells him everything. Dr. Gaines helps him up, gathers a blanket to wrap his son's shivering body, then stands there holding Joshua at arms' length and inspecting his injuries from head to toe.

What happened to you? Dr. Gaines asks.

Joshua tries to answer, but his throat is clogged by his own tears.

Where are your clothes?

Joshua still can't answer his father. Instead, he drops the scalpel away from his foot, pushes his father's arm away so that he can lean into the doctor's body.

Later, Joshua lies on the couch while his father examines him more closely for internal injuries and fractures. Dr. Gaines bandages his foot, feeds him a small dose of morphine to ease the pain. Joshua tells his father about the piglet, about the young men and their liquor, about the beating (most of it). Dr. Gaines stares at Joshua with pupils so black Joshua can see his own sadness embodied in there. When Joshua finishes talking, Dr. Gaines looks out the front window, at the world apart from the two of them. He stays silent for a long time until he looks back at Joshua, seeming frightened almost, as if he doesn't expect to see his son in this way or doesn't expect to see a son at all. He sighs, and his expression flattens.

You must take better care of your body, says Dr. Gaines. No one trusts a doctor who doesn't himself look clean and healthy.

Dr. Gaines clears his throat.

And whole, he adds.

It wasn't my fault, says Joshua.

Today maybe, says Dr. Gaines. But your digressive tendencies seem to go much beyond today.

Joshua wonders if Dr. Gaines knows what he himself can barely put words. He feels his face flush, feels a low rumbling in his stomach like hunger, but it isn't hunger. His father's stoic expression doesn't change, and he finds himself thinking again about those young men, almost fondly this time. As if their actions, as vicious and penetrating as they were, are nothing compared to the depthless isolation he feels right now.

Do you understand what I'm saying? asks Dr. Gaines.

Joshua turns his swollen face away, the weight of his father's hands now on his shoulders.

Patients won't bide an unrefined doctor, says his father. But most importantly, women won't bide an unrefined man.

FROM THE PLATTE RIVER
TO FORT LARAMIE

By the third day of their party's resting, the signs of sickness have largely expired. The six of them bathe fully clothed in the brown South Platte and then mount their horses. The trail follows the river for one hundred and fifty miles, a meandering course through the Wildcat Hills that will have them cross the river no fewer than four times, and more if they see fit to wander. They wait on the bank with their arms crossed, as if contemplating whether to proceed. But the truth is each of them is enjoying this moment of respite before they start off again, knowing they won't have such moments in the days to come, for so fleeting is accommodation out here it is worse than luck.

It's Free Ray who commences the journey. He kicks his horse into the river with the others sighing before following, the twins tacking the schooner across the muddy bed to prevent it from tipping in the current. Sixty miles in two days, down a steep hill into Ash Hollow, where they stock up on ash and cedar wood, past Courthouse Rock that Joshua swears resembles the St. Louis Courthouse, the land rising in encroaching bluffs and ravines they have to switchback or, if too wide, cable the schooner down, the pale-sand trail becoming muddy and strewn with mired and abandoned wagons stripped of their goods and ransacked for parts. Tongues and yokes, bonnet canvases torn and flapping in the wind like errant feathers on a dead bird, the jockey boxes gone, the brake blocks missing, the iron tires taken.

This volatile ground makes every bone in Joshua's body sing. He repeats their Latin names in his head, numbers those bones he can't remember given his exhausted state, as if those prior days of refreshment worked against him to eradicate his hardiness and energy. It's the understanding, the certainty that this journey is nowhere near its end that suddenly does him in, so that come each night he sleeps like a dead man through winds and heat and a storm that hurls hail the size of marbles and scatters the horses, who have to be tracked and wrangled come dawn.

On a morning of however many mornings, Joshua surveys his Morgan. The horse looks skinnier for having been pushed so hard and having eaten so little. Its legs shake while it stands, and the afternoon before he noticed the wear on its shoes.

Shit if you're not hurting like I am, he tells his horse.

He pats it, then runs his fingers through the mane trying to untangle the hair. The Morgan doesn't respond to this affection. He leans forward with his elbows on the pommel and pats the horse between its ears. Then, still leaning, he stares into the now-glowing horizon. The stars tacked above coming light are fading, but higher still they are as bright as they were when he watched them fall the night before. He wants the stars to be drowned by sunrise already. There's a sense of discomfort in them, space the only part of the landscape that remains constant, and given that constancy perhaps they haven't traveled so far from what he's always known. This he doesn't want to believe, because engendered by that belief is the notion that the revelatory sunlight might never again find him, and this nomadic world, with all its sickness and hardship and death, will forever trap him in this inchoate and virgin phase where life doesn't yet exist.

G. Quillard walks his horse up beside him.

It's a damn shame, he says.

What is?

The twins. They are hardly ever able to see the sunrise. It's too bloody difficult to turn that schooner around.

Joshua laughs, looks back at the twins. They are seated on the schooner, seem little concerned as to whether they can see the sunrise.

All they'd have to do is jump down and turn around, he says.

Right you are, G. Quillard chuckles. It'd be that easy.

G. Quillard's horse is wheezing, and even in the moonlight Joshua can see its ribs stabbing its coat.

Your horse isn't right, he tells G. Quillard.

I've noticed.

G. Quillard examines each side of the animal, puts his palm on the horse's neck like he might be testing it for a fever. Then he leans forward to better study its face.

She can ride well enough I suppose, he says.

He chuckles again.

She has to. I'm not sure what would happen if she doesn't.

What do you mean? asks Joshua.

We're not a patient party.

Why would we be? The sooner we get to California, the sooner we find gold.

Exactly, says G. Quillard. We've been bloody lucky so far. How many schooners have we seen parlayed for repairs, or Catholic missions overrun with small pox? You remember that man with the broken leg we left to starve.

That man wasn't ours to take care of.

Maybe not. But we've had none of that trouble. And I pray to whatever god there may be that we don't because our leaders are forward-looking men.

Joshua shakes his head in disapproval. He removes his hat, runs a hand through his hair. It is long and matted, bunching over a face that is chapped and scabbed, patched by fuzzy hair on his cheeks and chin.

We're stronger than all that, Joshua says. It's not all luck.

Why are you here?

Joshua looks a G. Quillard, but G. Quillard's back is to the east and his face in shadows, so it's too dark to discern anything about that question from the Englishman's obscured face.

The same reason you are, he says.

Opportunity. Fortune. Adventure. A place for those who have nowhere else to go.

Joshua scoffs at first. Then he laughs.

You make it sound pointless, Joshua says.

Not at all, says G. Quillard. The exact opposite. That is why we're all here. Hell, you'd be daft not to be here for that.

Then of course. I'm here for all those things.

I meant, says G. Quillard. Why are you here with all of us?

Joshua looks again at the inconceivable darkness of the Englishman's face before turning away.

You are not single-minded like the twins, continues G. Quillard. Renard is a nomad, Free Ray a Black man. I don't even have this country to call my own.

So that's why you're with us? says Joshua turning back. Simply because you're not an American? You could be anywhere in this country and still not be an American, you know.

G. Quillard smiles, his teeth illuminated in the lighting sky when he turns his horse sideways

Right, he says. Of course I would then be just another fucking emigrant.

G. Quillard laughs, and Joshua can't help but join him.

You see, says G. Quillard. At least I know why I'm here and what that makes me. Which also means I know what it doesn't make me. And do you know what it doesn't make me tonight?

What? says Joshua.

Happy. Because it's my turn to wash the dishes.

G. Quillard laughs with Joshua again, then leads his horse away. Even now, with such little effort being exerted by that horse, Joshua hears the animal's labored breathing, so he trots over to Renard.

G. Quillard's horse isn't right, Joshua tells him.

Renard is cinching his saddle straps that have been stretched by rain and riding.

So I have noticed, he says.

I can't offer him mine if his collapses.

You are right. You cannot.

It's not like the mules can manage his weight either.

We leave him then.

Leave him?

Renard nods.

He'd likely die if we left him, says Joshua.

Renard finishes cinching his straps, brushes some red ants from his trousers, nods again. Joshua waits, but Renard doesn't say anything else before he walks to the other side of his horse to check those straps.

Do you know what a man without a horse is on this trail? Renard asks.

The red-haired man's face is still so pale even after weeks on the trail that it glows in the nascent light.

No, says Joshua.

Cargo, says Renard.

They head on past Chimney Rock, a sandstone butte tightening upward in a spiral hundreds of feet to lance the sky, which is blood red in the new day. In the blue of the looming bluff behind Mr. Robidoux's log trading post, they rent blacksmithing tools to reshoe their horses, purchase two pounds of flour and three gallons of rum in glass jugs from Mr. Robidoux's half-Sioux children. Their shadows long and thin as posts in the afternoon sun and come evening as grand and festive an atmosphere as can be rendered out here, drinking, dancing man-with-man, to celebrate their progress, country and individual alike.

For days after this celebration, beyond the ridge of the chalky Scotts Bluff, where they stopped to gaze Laramie Peak rising one hundred and fifty miles to their west and signaling the Rocky Mountains, the alluvial fan is fissured like broken skin, the hard wind a constant nuisance until they reach Horse Creek. A train of twenty-five wagons has formed itself into a corral. The cattle are already penned inside, though it's only afternoon, and several of the emigrants are mending split wheels with nails or resetting spokes.

Their own party parks its schooner outside the corral and stakes the horses next to it. Joshua bends down, tears a clump of the brittle grass up, crumbles it in his hand. From dust to dust, its fragility not lost on him.

That evening they're invited to join the other emigrants in the corral for a supper that is more plentiful than one they've had in weeks. The women cook stews of trout and boiled corn, they roast potatoes, they sear salted bison meat. The dishes are passed around and generously taken from, food so good Joshua eats until he can hardly stand.

Supper ended, a boy from one of the other wagons retrieves a guitar, tunes it, and begins to play. He's a good singer, and G. Quillard begins to bounce and jerk like a marionette.

I'm back in a London pub, he calls to Joshua.

He bounces over and waves for Joshua to join him. Many of the other emigrants are watching G. Quillard, certainly their party is, and Joshua's too embarrassed. G. Quillard throws his hands up in a shrug before crossing to an old woman, someone Joshua thinks hardly belongs on this trail. The Englishman helps the woman to her feet, dances in front of her while she sways and laughs as if everything out here isn't anything and life is just this moment. There's purity in that immediacy, an absoluteness G. Quillard embraces that makes each mile of this journey a destination. Joshua wonders if he'll ever feel that way, even after they get to California.

When the boy stops playing and hands his father the guitar, it becomes evident what that boy will one day become. The man looses a songbird's voice that undermines the gruffness in his face and the hard labor his hands seem to have already accomplished in his short lifetime. Joshua finds himself drawn to this man, consumed by the delicate soul that the man's physicality opposes and the imaginative possibilities that form and shape with such an unlikely paradox. His heart is more raw, more open now than it's ever seemed to him, which shames him greatly. And he has to cup his ears to force this man's voice out of his head and focus on the mosquitoes, which, until now, the evening's pleasantries and harmoniousness made him forget. Because if he doesn't do this, then this lust will shred him.

A WOMAN'S WAIL wakes Joshua in the middle of the night. Several men from the other wagons have created torches and surround the woman, who is holding a boy. The boy looks like he could be asleep if not contextualized by the woman's grief and by his small head, which flops freely on his neck. The woman's husband tries to console her, but she is inconsolable, until her grief is interrupted by another woman's wail on the opposite side of the corral. That woman also cradles a boy, younger than the first, who is likewise lifeless.

By now a small crowd is gathered, and Joshua follows Renard and Free Ray over to the first woman, watches the torch-wielding men whose faces grow ever-angrier in that unhallowed light and who speak in harsh and hushed whispers about Indians or sickness, some malady unbeknownst to them. No one knows how the boys died, that much is clear, but killing only children isn't typical of the Sioux, and there are no other signs of Indians in their camp, no livestock stolen or goods lifted, no sound of anyone rustling the grass. Of course, such signs are often looked for in moments of desperation and false hope anyway, because were it that easy to detect the Sioux, there'd be little need for the defensive measures already taken.

There are more torches now. The schooner bonnets simmer a dull orange in the firelight, the corral a kind of medieval stable. Outside the torches' halo, the ground is black and hollow like a pit, heightening the anxiety even more. The remaining children are gathered and taken to one of the wagons where four men bearing carbines stand guard over them. Beyond this, no one seems to know what to do.

Joshua approaches the first dead boy, he kneels and takes the small head into his hands. It feels so light, so fragile, and apart from wondering at this boy's death he finds himself wondering at the continued life in the rest of these children. What sort of childhood is this journey? How can they survive out here?

When the woman begins to protest his presence, Joshua tells her he's a doctor.

You? says a man. A doctor?

Joshua ignores his skepticism.

The whites of the boy's eyes are yellow when Joshua pries his eyelids open. Splotchy rashes discolor his chest and stomach, and even in the boy's expired state Joshua can feel the aberrant warmth of a once-had fever. When he goes to lie the boy's head back down, clumps of the boy's hair peel off into his hands, and he realizes there are more bald spots around the boy's ears. An examination of the second boy presents the same circumstance, in all capacities, and Joshua confirms what this entire train has feared: sickness.

But what sickness? Jaundice and rashes and baldness. Such symptoms he's never seen before, never heard about from his father or read of. It's then, as if the very thought of this disease renders it communicable, that one of the girls in the wagon with the other children collapses and begins to seize, her yellow eyes falling into her head so that she stares at the men who rush to her aid through butter.

The carbines forgotten, the remaining children quickly led from the wagon one-by-one and dispersed throughout the corral. The crowd frantically stirring, the men growing louder and louder as they desperately search for the invisible source of this unknown sickness.

One of the men turns to address someone who's walked past him, bumps into Renard. He looks at Renard with bafflement on his ash-stained face, as if he's seeing this red-haired man for the very first time, but that confusion soon gives way to narrower eyes and a scrunched nose. The man pinches his nose, slowly backs away from Renard, grabs the shirt of a man beside him and whispers something while that man, too, contemplates Renard, then contemplates Free Ray.

Go ready the horses and the wagon, Renard tells Joshua.

What about the children? asks Joshua.

You, interrupts the man. You ride in on the schooner this night, ya?

The others stop talking, stop moving.

You, the man says again stepping toward Renard. And you.

He points at Free Ray.

He says, There is nothing wrong with our children before this night. You ride in, you smell not like a man, two children die. How many more to die? Tell us.

Joshua starts toward the girl, but someone yanks him to the ground by his shirt. The man who has yanked him down, who he doesn't recognize, walks around to face him. Renard puts his palm to the air, as if to stop the mob from advancing, though whatever effect he intends to have with such a gesture the opposite results. Seeing Renard's four-fingered hand, the men gasp. Here is their proof.

The mob pauses then, struck dumb for a moment, before of one mind the men rush Renard.

Renard tries to turn and run. A large man with cartoonishly thick arms reaches out and grabs Renard by the collar, pinning Renard's arms to his sides with his own and lacing his fingers in the middle of Renard's chest like a wrestler. But as quickly as that man binds Renard, his arms go slack. The man lurches into Renard's back, then limply rolls to the ground, landing so hard on his shoulder he bounces, a Bowie knife sticking out the side of his neck.

The mob gapes at the fallen man, gapes at the blood spurting into the brittle grass in short unsequenced bursts, the man twitching, his whole muscular body, until finally he stops moving. Free Ray reaches down and removes the Bowie knife to uncork that blood, so that it drains from the man so black in the darkness, pours over his neck and shoulders like he's being bathed in it. The mob watches Free Ray do this almost nonchalantly, astonished by this scene logic itself is still trying to parse out. They watch him still as Free Ray grabs the front of Renard's shirt and Joshua's hand and pulls them both into a run toward their schooner.

Renard, seemingly as stunned as the other men, keeps glancing back at the man on the ground and stumbling, Joshua a bumbling runner with his gimp foot, though Free Ray holds onto them both, forces them to keep pace. Free Ray says nothing, and it isn't until the three of them have gone thirty feet or so from the crowd that the crowd's senses return to them. The men begin to yell. Soon after, they give chase.

The twins have already whipped the mules into speed on the trail.

After Free Ray, Renard, and Joshua reach the horses, they mount, G. Quillard holding Joshua's reins so that Joshua can steady himself. Renard still looks dazed, frightened even. It is the first time Joshua has seen him scared, and he understands something about the hierarchy between Renard and Free Ray in this moment that never occurred to him before, that probably never occurred to anyone anywhere, given that Free Ray is Black.

The mob moves jerkily and slowly, like drawings in a flipbook, the hopping torches the only indicator of their progress, and the four of them set the horses to gallop before the mob has even crossed through the corral. None of them look back.

They ride in a jagged line strung out horizontally for what seems only seconds before a carbine splits the darkness behind them with a sharp crack. They shift into single file after that, making a thin target that is more difficult to hit. They ride over flat ground that is easy riding even in the dark with Joshua's Morgan goading on G. Quillard's horse as it wheezes more and more and tries to slow its pace. The carbine fires again, and then almost instantaneously another shot, though the shots are both so muffled and distant this time the riders know they are out of range. Klayton is standing, holding onto the bonnet for balance, when the four of them reach the schooner and slow the horses to match pace. Only then does he take his jostling seat, though he keeps poking his head out to the side of the bonnet while he mashes his hat down, glancing back and shouting: I don't see no one coming! I can't be sure but I don't see no one!

No one can hear him, so loud is the blood careening through their bodies and the rattling wheels of the wagon.

They spread the horses out again to keep the dust out of their faces, Joshua grabbing hold of G. Quillard's reins because both he and the Englishman know what separation means. Neither landmark nor formation to distinguish ground from sky save for the dawn-kept stars, the millions of stars puncturing the sky through which they float to become themselves a constellation in this universe. Pediás kaváris, we'll call them, and they'll ride for centuries in the mottled sky just like the fears and dreams that fuel them. They keep on into the afternoon where the temperature climbs to one hundred and five degrees, the animals nearly wilting from the heat and the men covered in sweat. Somewhere in this landscape, at a distance from that camp they aren't sure of, they water the animals at a shallow creek, let them kiss their palms with velvety lips while they feed them grain. Renard washes the dead man's long-dried blood from his neck and face. They all fill their canteens and drink, lie down to rest in the shade of a willow tree, though none can.

Jesus, says Joshua finally.

He gets to his feet, approaches Free Ray.

Jesus, he says again trying to stem the accusation in his voice. You killed that man.

Joshua doesn't know if he expects a response, but Free Ray refuses to grace his statement.

Course he did, says Klayton. You saw that mob. What you expect a mob like that gonna do? They ain't coming at you to talk.

Joshua huffs and turns toward the creek, the water too clear to offer reflection and the creek bed a bevy of gray stones shaped by time and relentless pressure.

Renard walks over.

You should not think of it that way, he says. Free Ray saved me.

Joshua shakes his head.

It was defense, says Renard. Not murder. It was necessary.

G. Quillard laughs, hacks up some dust, spits it into the creek.

How fine a line that is we walk, he says.

Joshua walks further down the stream. There, he bends down to take a drink of water, notices his hands for the first time since they fled the camp. Flecks of dried blood are crusted in the webbing between his fingers. He examines them for scrapes and finds nothing, so he knows this blood isn't his. It can only be that dead man's, and this realization sickens him. He scrubs and scrubs, his broken nails indistinguishable from the dirt that he uses like sandpaper so that that dirt seems a part of his skin now.

In the warped image of himself the roughed creek water creates, his father comes back to him again, but he knows these hands are entirely unlike his father's manicured and clean doctoring hands. Even so far away from St. Louis and already months into a life without his father, in moments of unwanted despair where the overburdened trail sucks Joshua into himself like a vacuum, he still searches his hands for traces of his father, knowing he'll find nothing in them, knowing whatever patterns they draw and ancestry they speak will never reveal Dr. Gaines.

But these hands that he's scrubbing do offer sustenance and progress. They draw him forward, guiding his horse with the purity of action and utility. And therein that fusion of meaning and mechanism he never fails to marvel at the depths of the human body, at the surprises it holds in store for us, at what it can produce, and betray.

FROM FORT LARAMIE
TO SOUTH PASS

For seven days they ride with the daguerreotyped mountains always the size and distance they were when Joshua first spotted them. It's July now—Wednesday, July 4. They're crossing the Black Hills, riding slower each day it seems as G. Quillard's horse continues to weaken.

In the days prior, they forded the Laramie Fork by raising their wagon bed on wooden spacers placed between the axles and the bed, then passed an uninhabited adobe building, which they knew to be Fort Bernard, before reaching Fort Laramie. In that sprawling and turreted adobe structure with walls twelve feet high and almost three feet thick surrounded by Sioux teepees and clotted with prairie schooners and Conestoga wagons, they navigated so many emigrants and as many tongues being spoken, as if they'd arrived at the Tower of Babel, in order to stock up on supplies. They purchased another twenty-gallon cask so that they could double the water they carried in the land beyond. Fifteen pounds of kiln-dried biscuits, a loosely measured amount of bacon, beans, molasses, and vinegar. As much as they could find and afford, as much as the schooner could hold. They knew the thick white clouds that foretold a beautiful and tranquil night as they departed the fort were the only sights of comfort in the pending landscape, one that is fully grazed of its grass and stripped clean of its naturalness, a place where water and flats and time (time most importantly) were soon to become only memories.

Sunset on this seventh day at the North Platte River, ferrying the schooner, swimming the animals. The river then left in the wake of their own dust and the dust they drive through that absorbs the light of the falling sun, as if the whole lot of them (their own schooner and horses and those they follow and those that follow them) ride atop a rim of gilded fog.

What follows is land white as chalk and disrupted by wild sage. The sparse springs are laced with alkali and poisonous, the half-scavenged and desiccated bodies of cattle strewn along the banks like offerings to some Pagan god. A gigantic mud pit in which two abandoned schooners are mired to the hubs, their own schooner splaying on bowed wheels and iron skeins that have come loose in their joints. They lumber past axles and chisels and discarded gold washers and wagon wheels and trunks of lead shot and duffel bags full of clothes and grandfather clocks with the glass shattered and drills and augers and mason jars potted with shriveled plants and cooking stoves broken into pieces where they fell and painted ceramic pottery and wooden barrels, mostly empty but others filled with flour or rice or lard that spills out from the barrels like the innards of a gutted animal, and tattered American flags and bar-iron washers and bellows and saddles and shovels and gold pans and tills and horseshoes and broken jars of mercury that paint the sand silver and tanned bison hides and the relics of wagons that appear so long a part of this landscape you'd hardly guess they are only weeks old and the carcasses of oxen, of mules, of horses, of dogs and countless indefinite gray bones spread in a line like the archeological remains of some ancient monster and graves without headstones formed of mounded rocks, for who can muster the strength to dig in this hellish land, and chests of clothes and cookware and chamber pots and woven baskets leaking wool and tent poles and shredded tent canvas and boots and brogans—children's and adults'—and books. The graveyard of humanity.

Goddamn, says Klayton.

No need, says Renard. I think he already has.

The wind blows a spicy, eye-stinging human stench that makes Joshua wince, though he knows his own odor, even if he can't distinguish it, is equally noxious. Flies spot his hat and shoulders and sleeves to reprint his garments with tiny polka dots.

The debris and the poor travel have created a near standstill with wagons extending in a line beyond the horizon. Impatient, Renard leads their party off the trail and into a defile, where they wend their way past volcanic rock fungal in its shape and nearly blossoming while the sun plays shadow tricks on its surface as they ride. The schooner follows the horses, which ride in twos: Free Ray and Renard in front, then Joshua and G. Quillard. The trail skirts to the left around a tremendous bulge in the rock before it opens in much a wider throat of grass and brush. On the other side of the bulge, as if they are spooked, Free Ray and Renard's horses rear back toward Joshua and G. Quillard. Joshua has to wrench his reins to avoid a collision and takes his Morgan leaping toward the rock wall, where he sees what's spooked the other horses.

The brown bear stands ten feet tall on two legs, and his own horse rears in terror.

His Morgan knocks into the flank of G. Quillard's weak and unreactive horse and spins it. The bear drops onto all fours and rushes the two of them, grabbing hold of G. Quillard's left arm with its teeth so visibly sharp even in the untimeable instant Joshua glances them. In a single synchronous movement, the bear rips G. Quillard from the horse and the horse falls before clamoring up and stumbling back the way it came.

G. Quillard is screaming so hard his voice splits and bubbles. His coat and shirt are shredded around the bear's grip, what portion of his arm Joshua can still see already covered in blood. The bear drags him toward the defile in the direction the horse fled while G. Quillard desperately grabs at whatever slams into his free hand.

Renard and Free Ray fire their pistols at the bear, the shots deafening within the high walls as the guns smoke and the lead buries into the bear's haunches or enormous back. The bullets do nothing, just disappear in the thick fur as if they are formed of air while the bear keeps its pace.

Joshua fumbles for his pistol. His shaking hands drop it. He tries more frantically for his rifle, which, no matter how hard he pulls, won't budge from its scabbard. His hands clam over, and soon he can't even hold onto the butt of the rifle whenever he tries to pull it free. Feeling lost, he looks pleadingly at the twins.

Clayton has already lunged from the schooner. He crawls now underneath it and unlashes the double-barrel shotgun from the reach. The bear reaches the bulge, turns away from the schooner and heads for the defile, G. Quillard on the verge of being lost entirely. Clayton discharges both shotgun barrels at once, a shot so loud the whole scene goes suddenly soundless in Joshua's ears before a distant ringing takes over.

The shot tears through the bear's front left leg. The animal makes a wicked crying sound no one hears in their momentary deafness while it lets go G. Quillard's arm, limps around the bulge and into the gorge, the disembodied paw on that mangled leg swinging from fibrous tendons that glisten in the sunlight.

G. Quillard cries and screams, clutching what's left of his arm to his chest. His eyes are tightly shut, as if his failing to look at his arm will make his injury not real. When he opens his eyes and attempts to stand, Joshua and Free Ray, who have already reached him, push him back down onto his back.

I need to stand! My bloody arm!

He tries again, but Joshua and Free Ray force his shoulders down. Then he passes out.

Oh god, says Joshua staring at G. Quillard's arm.

The forearm looks like it's been turned inside out. Flaps of skin hang over G. Quillard's hand and hide his fingers. His bones are exposed, one broken clean through and the end of it sticking straight up, the muscle shredded and hanging by filaments and of such uselessness now that Free Ray commences a rude debridement, tossing each removed piece behind him as he clears the wound. There is a pool of blood underneath the arm, and the arm itself is a mass of blood. G. Quillard's face is white, even whiter against his brown hair and beard.

Joshua cinches a tourniquet just above G. Quillard's elbow with a bandana, inserting a small stick into the bandana's knot. Without even thinking about it, he is parrotting the work of his father.

Keep twisting this stick to cut off the blood flow, Joshua tells Free Ray.

Free Ray does so until G. Quillard's skin wrinkles around the bandana and the stick won't tighten anymore. Then Joshua finishes the knot. After that, he tries to reset G. Quillard's dislocated shoulder, but when he hears the pop, he can't be sure if he's successfully set it or if he's merely torn the ligaments more.

He stands woozy-legged. He stumbles back a few steps, vomits against the rock. Holding witness is nothing like the actual doing.

I'm sorry, he says to Free Ray.

He's so embarrassed he can't look Free Ray in the eyes.

I'm sorry, he says again.

To Free Ray or G. Quillard this time, Joshua isn't sure. He wipes his mouth, returns to G. Quillard, and kneels back down, trying to turn the stick again. It won't tighten anymore.

Free Ray cuts the remaining pieces of G. Quillard's sleeve off with his Bowie knife so that the cloth won't get caught up inside the wound and infect it. Then he forms a large bandage from pieces of G. Quillard's good sleeve. Joshua retrieves one of the rum jugs from the schooner, uses it to wash the wound. He then tries to bandage the wound, but no sooner has he covered it than the bandage is soaked in blood.

Joshua takes up the rum, drinks three big drinks, and shakes his head, wanting to erase everything he's just seen. But this scene will never leave him.

After he slings G. Quillard's arm with an old shirt, he and Free Ray lift G. Quillard by his legs and arms and carry him to the schooner, where they strap him to a makeshift bed of rice and bean sacks. Then they step back from the wagon and join the other three, who are staring at the Englishman. They can only believe by some miracle G. Quillard won't lose that arm. They don't say anything, just stare with something of remorse and fear and satisfaction all at once. After all, it was him who the bear, who this landscape chose. Not any of them. The sun is already lowing and already the air beginning to cool, but sweat runs down their faces, and if another company rides by, they might mistake that sweat for tears. Of course, tears are superfluous. All five of them understand this.

Finally, Renard turns to Clayton and tells him to go find G. Quillard's horse.

IT'S EVENING BY the time Clayton returns. He hitches the horse to the wagon alongside Joshua's. Joshua watches him work from the bed, where he sits on a sack of beans dabbing, almost instinctually now, at G. Quillard's forehead and neck with a damp rag he made out of a shirt. He's using up his drinking water trying to stave off the fever already smoldering in G. Quillard, but this doesn't concern him yet. If he thought about it, he might find some likeness between this generosity and the generosity he so loathed (still loathes) in his father. But for now, he's consumed with the benevolence tragedy often renders.

He takes up his canteen and soaks the rag once more. Then he puts the canteen to his lips, sucks down the last remaining sips of water that only leave him thirstier as he feels the wagon jolt forward. They're off again.

Will they ever stop moving? Is this endlessness what it takes to choose your own destiny, or to be free to choose? Off his horse and with G. Quillard his only focus, Joshua suddenly has too much time. Those healed faces return to him, sequenced on the canvas like a who's who of deepening poverty and misery. Some of them vagabonds Dr. Gaines knew couldn't afford treatments, but he treated them anyway. Others who swore to Dr. Gaines that they only looked well-off, though Joshua had later followed them to the theater or to the restaurants where money soon flowed with wine and rich meats. And what did his father do when he told him what he witnessed? Nothing. Worse than nothing, actually. He berated Joshua for debasing the ancient Hippocratic Oath. Debasing—that's how his father always said it. Because the value was in your practice, not the comfort of your only forgotten son.

Joshua feels something warm on his thigh. G. Quillard's arm has bled through its bandage, is soaking into Joshua's trousers. After rebandaging the arm with his own shirt, so that he sits in the wagon wearing only his coat, Joshua crawls to the front and asks the twins how far they've traveled.

Quarter mile I'd guess, says Clayton.

A quarter mile?

It feel faster to you or something? We go much faster, and we'll be dragging that Englishman's horse. Besides, says Clayton. Look at that.

Their party isn't back on the trail yet. And Joshua sees that even once they do return to it, they'll return to the very congestion they sought to override when they left the trail in the first place. He crawls back to his makeshift seat careful not to disturb G. Quillard, who sleeps the dense and stiff sleep of an uncertain future.

THEY CAMP ONLY two miles from where G. Quillard was attacked. After Joshua covers G. Quillard with two wool blankets and drips some water onto his lips, he climbs out of the schooner and into the firelight.

I thought that bear did not get you, says Renard pointing to Joshua's trousers.

It's his blood, says Joshua.

No one says anything else for the rest of the night.

By morning, G. Quillard's fever has worsened, but they have no choice except to continue. Soon, they're passed by a banker from Boston and his ragged family. Joshua trades some crackers and bacon for silk gauze and more morphine, some of which he uses that night to doctor G. Quillard. He drips the morphine into G. Quillard's mouth, then treats the gauze with camphor before applying it to the wound. He wraps the bandage methodically and counterclockwise down G. Quillard's arm and over the wound, tying it off with a square knot just above the injury, breaking the strip with his teeth.

How is it you came to be a doctor? Klayton asks.

Klayton has turned around on his wagon seat to watch Joshua work. No one has ever asked Joshua this question before, and he realizes now that it never occurred to him not to be a doctor.

My father was a doctor, he says but this answer is as shallow as it sounds.

Well, says Klayton. Ain't you something valuable.

They plod along so slowly that they make a day's progress over two days. Throughout it all, G. Quillard sleeps restlessly and erratically. He moans and cries whenever he's awake, which haunts their party, weighs on them like bad luck, and none of them are sure whether it's the cold night air that chills their blood now or G. Quillard's agony.

Alone in the wagon bed with the Englishman, Joshua attempts to change the bandage in the lamplight. He grimaces and looks away. G. Quillard's forearm is foul-smelling and oozing viscous puss, the skin on his hand red and ridged like a wattle.

The hour is late. Joshua climbs out of the schooner, approaches the others, who seem well enough aware of the circumstances given Joshua's presence, even though Joshua doesn't say anything. Their party has reached the freezing Sweetwater River. Many more emigrants camp a good distance away from them along the river, positioned with their backs to those six. It's as if their party is a bad omen, or diseased by bad luck, as if by ignoring their plight and putting physical distance between them, the other emigrants will preserve their own companies in a way G. Quillard hasn't been. Understanding the danger inherent to such a journey is one thing, far worse is being physically subjected to the turmoil of it.

I can't keep it, can I, says G. Quillard when Joshua returns to the schooner.

Joshua is unsure whether the Englishman is asking him a question or making a statement.

The arm, you mean? Joshua replies.

G. Quillard nods.

Joshua meets G. Quillard's eyes, thinking this directness might mitigate some of that suffering. He wants to tell him that he knows what it means to lose some of your body. But a few toes are not an arm.

Joshua shakes his head.

G. Quillard begins to whimper. He lays his head on the bag, wipes his eyes with his good hand.

It was your horse that knocked me toward the bear, says G. Quillard.

Joshua's body goes hot with unexpected guilt.

I'm sorry, he says.

But Joshua isn't sorry. All this blame does is weigh him down, and he can't assume that out here. The hubris it takes to believe that circumstance is anything more than the flip of coin makes him angry at G. Quillard. This situation could just as easily have been the other way around, and G. Quillard wouldn't have been sorry now either.

G. Quillard sighs.

Be done with it then, he says without sitting up.

Too weak to stand, G. Quillard has to be carried out of the schooner. He cries out as they move him and cries out again when Joshua takes his bone saw from his medical bag. Joshua buries the blade in the coals, instructs Klayton to bring over the last of the rum, which he gives to G. Quillard to drink. G. Quillard swallows without lifting his head, coughs, opens his mouth for another drink, being catered to like a baby bird. He won't stop crying, he won't stop sniffling, and Joshua draws his hat low to shield himself from this sadness.

After several minutes, enough time to let the saw blade heat, Free Ray positions a wooden ladle between G. Quillard's teeth. G. Quillard bites down hard and tries to nod to signal that he's ready, though when he does, his eyes grow wide with fear. Joshua ties a tourniquet just below the Englishman's shoulder, retrieves the saw from the coals, the blade white and so bright in that nightliness like some kind of sorcerer's weapon. He stretches out G. Quillard's arm, which makes G. Quillard tense and bite down on the stick. Joshua then presses his knee onto G. Quillard's deadening hand. The Englishman winces, a reaction borne more out of instinct than sensation, Joshua knows, and Renard and Clayton brace G. Quillard's shoulders. Joshua starts the blade, slowly, just above the elbow.

G. Quillard lurches up and tries to rip his arm from Joshua's grip, screaming so loudly and so agonizingly Joshua looks away while he forces his knee harder onto the hand. Then, G. Quillard passes out.

Joshua is carefully watching what he's doing, but his mind is sliding, drifting, back to St. Louis two years prior. He sees the ice-packed Mississippi in January slide underneath his raft (an escape is what he'd sought—an escape into something, not to somewhere). That raft slams into an ice floe and the swirl of freezing and muddy water encases his head, the immersion cold overtaking him, the interrogating glare of his father's operating lamp while his eyes drift in and out of focus (how did he get back to the house?), Dr. Gaines positioning the chisel at the base of Joshua's numb pinky toe until the blood that wells from the vacancy, pasty and cold on his foot, replaces it. Then the next toe, then the next toe. Afterward, Dr. Gaines pulls the curtain across the front window and undresses himself. Naked, he slips beside Joshua on the sofa, then covers them both with the wool blanket. Dr. Gaines wraps his arms around Joshua's chest and hugs him tighter than he's ever hugged him. With the heat of his father overwhelming him, Joshua's eyes blink his newly distorted and transmutated life into and out of existence, and once he collapses into his pain and exhaustion, he dreams himself dissected on a table, each part of him puzzled back together like a fossil so that he is at once both human and monster.

When Joshua reaches G. Quillard's bone, the blade stalls. His mind returns to the present moment now, and he repositions himself to finish the amputation. With the arm finally severed, he replaces the blade into the coals and takes the arm up by the hand, pulling it away from G. Quillard's body like he's simply cut a branch from a tree. The others stare at that bodiless arm, seeing and not seeing it all at once, so surreal is it in the dark and on this trail, a trick of the moonlight, a nightmare they'll wake from in the morning and laugh over while drinking coffee.

With the saw blade white hot again, Joshua twice cauterizes the wound before he splashes it with river water to cool it. Then he coats the wound with what remains of the camphor, wraps it with the last strand of gauze, and wets G. Quillard's lips with morphine.

The twins bury the arm somewhere along the bank of the Sweetwater. They hide the grave with rocks and clumps of grass they uproot and then replant. In the morning, G. Quillard will wake without his arm, the amputation done, the grave unknown to him, never subjected to seeing his arm from the perspective he sees another man's. And that is the only gift that Joshua can offer him.

I DON'T BELIEVE it's gone, G. Quillard tells Joshua in the blooming dawn. I can still feel it.

I know, says Joshua.

Could you?

Joshua nods.

Right, says G. Quillard. He coughs a weak cough. Then he says, I'm so thirsty.

Joshua goes out to the river to fill his canteen. Other emigrants prostrate themselves in the shade of willow trees and drink their fill, their chests and heads stabbed by the cold water. Such is the scene here, as if the Sweetwater is in fact the fountain of youth, for as far as Joshua can see men, women, and children drink and drink before they roll onto their backs and stare into the morning through eyes that evidence excitement and rebirth at every bend, so humble are the objects by which one measures the quality of life on this journey.

Joshua returns, but G. Quillard drinks only a little.

We're departing soon, Joshua tells him.

Good, says G. Quillard. You said 'we.'

G. Quillard smiles, frowns in pain, and Joshua spoons him more morphine.

Near this river is Independence Rock, a long slab of granite smooth and bulbous like a breaching whale. Everyone calls it "the great register of the desert," emigrants inscribing their choppy names alongside or over ancient Indian hieroglyphs, painting those names in black or red if they can't find the tools to penetrate the granite. Renard and Free Ray, having written their inscriptions during a previous journey they say, wait by the horses and the schooner as the sun rises and Joshua and the twins join the other emigrants to stake their symbolic claim. Joshua carves the twins' names because the twins can't write. He spells both with a C, not knowing Klayton's name begins with a K. Lastly, he carves G. Quillard's. He has no idea how to spell Quillard, so instead he writes: G.Q.—ENGLISHMAN, 1849

On through the following riparian zone, past Devil's Gate, over land rimmed by oxblood bluffs. They push on for two days, and Joshua thinks at first that G. Quillard is on the mend. The Englishman climbs out of the wagon around midday of the second day to walk alongside, wobbly on his still-weak legs and only lasting a few hundred yards before he's so exhausted and sweating so profusely he has to climb back in.

The six of them stop to wait out the heat of the afternoon. Joshua loosens the bandage to examine G. Quillard's arm. He thinks it's healing, but he admits to himself that he can't really tell.

How do you feel? Joshua asks.

Better before. Worse now.

I expect that.

I'm always hungry, says G. Quillard. But I can't bring myself to eat.

Water's the most important thing. Are you bleeding? Do you notice any puss?

Only a little, which I suppose is a good thing.

Bleeding or puss?

Both, says G. Quillard.

What about your stool? asks Joshua.

G. Quillard looks at him. His face is waxy in the lamplight, and he holds his empty left sleeve with his right hand like he can't keep his own shoulder tucked into his body. He lets go his sleeve, points to a pair of trousers balled up in the corner of the schooner bed. Joshua opens them. The entire seat is stained black from diarrhea, the cloth stiff and still stinking. He tosses them away.

For how long?

I can't remember anymore, says G. Quillard. It doesn't stop coming.

These last two nights they've camped along the Wind River Range, eaten scant suppers of crackers and boiled beans or rice with moldy bread. Joshua's own bowels are painful and rumbling tonight, and earlier the twins experienced a bout of diarrhea that sent them fleeing the camp with their trousers half off before they got ten feet away. Sitting here with the Englishman, Joshua shivers violently and puts his coat on, the weight of the grease and dust making him nauseous. Perhaps it's the food that's making them all sick, G. Quillard included. But of course it can't be because G. Quillard hasn't eaten anything.

I've wanted to go west ever since I got to America, says G. Quillard. That's all I ever wanted. I hated New York, hated the men with their top hats and frockcoats. Hated the narrow and putrid streets. And the rats. The fucking rats. They reminded me of the Liverpool ship I stowed away on, which was the closest thing on this earth to Hell.

I've never seen the ocean, says Joshua. What was it like?

G. Quillard chuckles.

I can't rightly say, he says. I've only ever seen it from the English shore.

He pauses, thinks about it for a moment.

It was wild. It seemed endless, but obviously it does end. Because after six weeks of seeing only shiplap, I was in New York. I suppose you can tell me what you think once we get to California.

G. Quillard smiles. Somehow, the gap in his teeth looks wider to Joshua, as if the Englishman's own body is slowly consuming itself. First the teeth, then the arm, and what's next? Joshua smiles before turning away, thinking about what G. Quillard said, the blood in his stool, the wound still leaking blood and puss, and the hundreds of miles left to travel.

After G. Quillard falls into a heavy and trance-like doze, Joshua returns to the fire with the others.

There will be snow in the mountains, says Renard after a bit. Even in late summer.

I don't expect I can be surprised by much anymore, says Klayton. Though I thank the Lord it was dark during the unfortunates I recently experienced. From the burning of it, I might could've been surprised by what came rushing out of me. And that ain't no kinda surprise a man is wont to have.

The slower we travel the worse it will be, continues Renard. The less time our water and supplies will last as well. After South Pass, we can bypass Fort Bridger and cut through the desert. That route will save us nearly a week's travel, time we cannot afford to lose if we plan to reach the Sierra Nevada range before fall. I believe we have enough water to last the cut-off if we ration.

No one says anything for a moment.

The main trail may be the safer one. But we are not going to California for safety, Renard says.

FROM SOUTH PASS TO
THE SIERRA NEVADAS

One-thousand miles from Independence, they cross South Pass in a constant and unbroken traffic of wagons, ford a trio of river branches (the Sandys) in a rage of white dust that grates their eyes and lips and washes out the wagons that push on relentlessly, and take Sublette's Cut-off.

The unfiltered white sunlight that follows, the rank white sage and broken shapes of white shale eons older than any time Joshua can conceive of, the snow-patched Wind River mountains looming in the blue distance, the white Mormons ferrying them across the Green River, the schooner wheels bleached white rolling beyond an abandoned Bannock village and G. Quillard's colorless face watching only what they've passed while he begins to sleep less often and eat small meals of white rice, the sky so pale and stretched thin you can see the curvature of the Earth. A week after ferrying the Green

River, the trail forks again: continuing via the Hudspeth's Cut-off, or taking the main road to Fort Hall—a long-established fixture in this territory and now primarily used by the American Fur Company.

They know almost nothing about the newly trekked cut-off, so they stop a Shoshone girl who happens to be wandering by. She doesn't speak English, but when Renard points at their party and then down the cut-off, she shakes her head, places the empty pail she's carrying upside down on the ground, circles her hand over the top and then chops straight down along each side. More mountains, and steeper ones, all of which means more wear on the schooner.

Renard looks off down the cut-off. The girl gets his attention again. She points at his canteen, shakes her head. Renard glances at the others, but no one meets his eyes. Everyone knows what no water means, and they also know their faces will betray that.

Still, they decide to ignore the girl's warning and risk the dry mountains. The allure of speed, a kind of comfort in the unequivocal and uncompassionate workings of this natural and scientific world and the fate of the Donner Party, only a blip on their consciousness, and hope dyed gold, which is really the only thing—even now—that they choose to see on the ridged horizon while they head down the cut-off.

Three days later they wend the mountains, unable to find any water. The streambeds are all dried up, and mounds of brown grass are pushed down by humps of snow that still climb the rock or hug the base of evergreens where the sunlight can't reach, the place reeking of petrichor. They pause at midday alongside a stand of pines, trying to conserve their energy. The trees block out the sun, and the shade brings with it that frigid cold again. The barely worn trail veers left up ahead as it rounds a gigantic boulder, is obscured by the trees below, like they are trapped in this liminal moment, their throats as dry and rocky as the streambeds, their hands raw and patched by dry skin.

Joshua's right foot pains him. He removes his boot and sock, lances the blisters with his scalpel, drains the fluid into the dirt. He rubs the wounds with a tallow poultice he's made of wax, melted snow, and bits of finely ground basalt. He massages his foot to ease the pain, and while it soon departs, he knows that pain will never truly leave him. And he welcomes this. There is something about that pain and the permanence it renders of the body that grounds him, makes him understand that he is meant for this world he now inhabits, meant for the life he is on the verge of embracing.

G. Quillard has yet to get out of the schooner today. Joshua puts his boot back on and goes to check on him. The Englishman's fever has returned, and his skin emanates a tang that fills the schooner and burns Joshua's nose. He's seen sickness turn like this before in his father, the body fooled into a fleeting state of healing that only makes it more vulnerable, more exposed so that what follows is a reckoning of its functions and stability. Joshua gathers a handful of snow from nearby. He wraps the snow in a rag, puts the rag on G. Quillard's forehead to help cool his body.

Onward again. Evening and they climb alongside a stand of pines where it's all shadows and shade, darkness now the color of being. When they stop to camp, Renard and Joshua set off down the mountain to find fresh water. A spring, a stream, a puddle on the rocks, anything. They return without water but drag two piles of dry wood behind the horses. They build a small fire over which Joshua boils dirty snow, filters it with his gold-digging sieve, boils it again before distributing. They huddle together like old friends around a low fire to stay warm, though there's no intimacy in their rigid movements. Joshua is aware of each shoulder that brushes his, of all the breath that wind carries and comingles. For all the years he's been alive, he's gauged loneliness by the number of bodies around him, but tonight he realizes loneliness is a state of being. That some men are simply born with loneliness in their blood, with bones that draw strength from skepticism and self-reliance. All his father's love and tenderness that still clings to him erodes the shell of his whole being, strips him of these very qualities. These men he sits with now are not his friends, will never be, and a sudden surge of calm and courage warms him, because he finally understands the recipe for lucrative survival.

At one point, Joshua looks out into darkness, searching every direction for a single something.

There isn't anyone else here, he finally says.

The other four seem as surprised by this fact as he is. They look about for any sign of campfire playing off the rock or the brush.

Nothing. They are alone.

FOR THREE MORE days, they cross mountains polka-dotted by snow packs. Their traveling is much slower again with G. Quillard's worsened state, and any hope of him getting back on his horse recedes with each setting sun. A company of emigrants they passed a day or so ago catches up to them so that they're no longer alone when they camp. Their party eventually rejoins the main trail from Fort Hall at the Raft River, where the Oregon and California trails diverge, and in the miles beyond they pass old beaver dams that parade Fall River before they enter the City of Rocks and cross into ground dry and sun-blanched and, later, a trail surrounded by smoking geothermal springs.

Even now, with G. Quillard's arm buried at the bank of river Joshua can't remember the name of and can't picture anymore, the Englishman wakes some mornings in a panic, forgetting that he's lost his arm and wondering what horror befell him the night before, until the memory, more horrific than what he could ever imagine, comes back to him. Joshua still changes his dressing every few days to keep his wound clean, or something close to that. He reuses strips of shirt that've been washed in what water he can find if their party couldn't trade for gauze, because gauze is, unsurprisingly, not a common item carried by the other emigrants. The twins laugh and make up stories about how funny it'll be to see G. Quillard digging gold with one arm, and Joshua's thankful for these light-hearted reprieves, for these men unburdened by his knowledge and all the ambiguity that knowledge creates.

When they reach the salt desert on the west side of Great Salt Lake City, Joshua wonders, because how can he not, if this whole landscape is in fact real, or if their party perished on some afternoon he's now forgotten, and what he rides through is a kind of purgatory. Lonely wagon tracks impressioning the white ground, dead livestock with their faces and hooves consumed by the sludge like beached sea creatures, the mirage on the horizon making him always think there's a shallow lake at the base of those moonlike mountains, that great magic trick of thirst and desperation. The wind blows hot like a breath here, riles the dust that fogs this stretch and carries with it basaltic sediment from the hills and ash from the ground so that their party appears bathed by some extinguished fire pit, baptized in the hearth of Satan's firey lake. Joshua's lips and cheeks split from the grating. Gnats swarm these fresh cuts, even while he sleeps. Finally, he gives up trying to brush them away. He joins in resignation the so many emigrants traveling with bandanas over their faces and goggles across their eyes so that the lot of them look like a procession of giant insects as they travel one hundred and fifty miles to the Sink of the warm-watered Humboldt River, the pale and humped mountains all the while enveloping them.

At some point, their party comes upon a shirtless emigrant. He's sitting on the ground as if he's prostrating himself to god and sobbing. He tells them that the Shoshones slashed the gastrocnemius muscle on what was left of his cattle herd, then those Indians stole his horse as he tended to the cattle. As he speaks, he stares past their

party and frantically waves his hands in the air to mime his hopelessness. His hands are covered in dried blood, and Joshua watches the
flies that cling to those swarming hands with nothing but curiosity.
Curiosity for the beings that thrive in this wasted landscape, curiosity for the absent emotions that, logically, he thinks he should have
for the emigrant. The emigrant's company, fearing their own danger, left him shortly after they crossed out of the canyon and here,
the emigrant says, he can go no further. He says that man isn't fit
to make such a journey, and he prays for God's mercy and for God's
grace, for he's sure he's already dead and suffering in Hell.

Joshua and the others listen pitilessly, offer him nothing. Not even
sympathy. With the emigrant's crying in their wake, they keep on
across a country where clusters of grass huts are visible in the distance, the trail a broth of carrion, petrifications that are large and
porous and flowering out of the ground like enormous fungi, man
friendly to none other but himself.

Come evening, they stop and dig a well four feet into the ground
to reveal water clear enough and cool enough to drink. Joshua is
the first to sit picket. He hugs his rifle, huddles so close to the fire
his skin begins to feel raw and open, but such pain verifies a life still
being lived. He can hear wolves in the distance, and he realizes it's
been some time since he's heard wolves. A cup of steaming coffee is
his only luxury. His hair hangs over his ears and into his eyes, the
curls matted and greasy. He has a quasi-beard now, too, though the
hair on his face is so blonde and fine you'd hardly notice it unless the
sunlight hit it just right, and even then might mistake it for layers of
dust before realizing it can't be brushed away.

He digs the toe of his boot into the sand, draws a line. Then he
draws a triangle. He erases that triangle with his sole and next draws
a square. Then a circle. He thinks about his missing toes and G.
Quillard's missing arm and Renard's missing fingers and the scars
criss-crossing Free Ray's back, and he ponders whether the soul

mirrors the body. If the soul reshapes and scars also. If parts of what we are born with can be taken away by circumstance, by choice. And if that void can be replaced by a new patch of soul, one not rejuvenated but merely substituted, an otherness fused to the original portion that makes our new soul something else entirely since, with this life, it can never retain its original condition that whatever god or science or cosmic flash intended.

YOU KNOW, SAYS Renard when Joshua climbs out of the schooner and walks underneath the canvas awning. Sometimes a man is stronger than his own body. And sometimes it is the other way around.

Renard sits next to Free Ray on an upturned bucket this midafternoon. A long piece of grass hangs from his lips, a trivial sight Joshua hasn't seen for weeks but that strikes him now as extraordinary. Because at last they've reached mystifying Pyramid Lake and its source the fecund Truckee River, where they're resting and rehydrating for two days. From this point, they can see the Sierra Nevada mountains, the last wall of rock they'll traverse before the gold fields. All this time Joshua has been feeding and watering G. Quillard's horse when he can, amazed at the animal's continued fight for life and wondering if he's a better horse doctor than he is a real doctor. After all, it's the horse that appears to be rebounding.

An arm isn't the same thing as a couple of fingers or a few toes, says Joshua.

No?

Joshua sits down and takes a small drink of water. He drank so much water when they initially arrived at the lake that he threw up. He's since had to moderate his intake even though his body pines for saturation.

A pound of flesh then, is that it? asks Renard.

I don't know, says Joshua. I just don't know anymore. We've come so far already. We're almost there but almost is still weeks away.

Renard laughs.

You think it will get easier once we arrive? he asks. It will be different, certainly.

Different is good, says Joshua.

Different is different. Good or bad does not have anything to do with it. California is full of surprises, and since nothing in this world or in your life prior can prepare you for them, there is nothing you can measure that difference against. So it simply is.

At least I won't be on that damn horse every day.

If you think the horse is bad, you should ask the twins about the schooner seat. Have you seen their asses lately? They are as flat as pancakes.

The three of them laugh. Yesterday, the twins caught a four cut-throat trout in the lake, each nearly two and half feet long, and Free Ray takes two thick pieces of seared trout from the pan and hands one to Joshua. Free Ray nibbles on his while Joshua swallows tiny pieces of the fish whole. The trout is so rich and their stomachs so weak that they can only eat small quantities of it at a time to keep it down.

Where are the twins? Joshua asks.

Renard points to a small outcropping farther down the lake.

He says, Gathering a crateful of grass for the animals. We will dry it and carry it into the last of these mountains now that we have run out of grain. Renard pauses, then he asks, And how is our Englishman?

Resting, says Joshua.

Is he eating?

A little of the trout. Mostly rice mixed with water.

That is good.

Joshua thinks about G. Quillard for a minute, a man largely useless to them in his wounded state, seemingly a drain on resources and speed. He remembers the conversation he had with the Englishman about his sickly horse and its potential demise, about whether that would've stranded him on the trail, and he wonders about that more deeply now. He believes at first he shouldn't bring this conversation up with Renard and Free Ray, that he should let G. Quillard's admonition exist only in his memory because voicing it might give it credence. Maybe abandoning the injured G. Quillard simply hasn't occurred to these two. Or maybe it has, and Joshua asking about it will make up their minds. Still, Renard's concern for the Englishman seems sincere, and Joshua wonders—more potently than he does about G. Quillard's remark—why abandoning G. Quillard has never even seemed like a possibility.

Joshua says, G. Quillard thought we might leave him, you know. Soon after the bear attack.

Renard glances at Joshua, then looks at Free Ray. Nothing about either of their faces changes. No surprise, no confusion, no consternation. Joshua understands then that this possibility was always a possibility. And that it is still one.

He is a savvy man, Renard says casually. Pragmatic in the way of many good Englishmen. We have always hoped for his betterment, but, like you say and like G. Quillard recognizes, we are also pragmatic. You have to be out here.

Why did you decide to keep him with us then?

We did not decide. You did. You put him into the schooner after the attack, you cared for him. He is only here and alive because of you. That is a powerful thing, is it not? To have control over another man's life.

Joshua stops eating and stares at Renard.

I was only doing my duty, he says.

These words leave his mouth before he has a chance to think about them. And hearing them in his own voice feels like a betrayal—to everything he believes he is and everything he believes his father wasn't. Renard smiles again, almost as if he can read the thoughts in Joshua's mind.

Joshua stands as much as he can underneath the awning, walks back to the rear of schooner. The sun is in his eyes, half-blinding when it reflects off the lake water that's so blue it looks dyed. He shields the glare with his hand, squints inside the wagon. G. Quillard is still lying down (always lying down now), and with the fusion of sunlight and shadows manifested by the bonnet, he can't see the Englishman's face. But he can hear him crying, G. Quillard's slack-sleeve of an arm flopping beside him while his chest convulses like there's no vitality left in him at all.

Joshua stands there for a long time, long enough that he has to shift his hand's position to keep blocking the sun from his eyes. He doesn't feel sorry for G. Quillard anymore. Something inside of him has finally hardened, pity not a luxury fit for the world he now inhabits.

WHEN THEY LEAVE the lake and before they reach the mountains, they will have to trudge again through a slough overrun by snakes. On and on with relentless monotony, and they'll use up their fresh water, which will leave Joshua no choice but to drink the brackish sledge. It will make him constipated and sick. He'll break into a cold sweat and his mouth won't stop bleeding, so he'll splash his face with vinegar, feeling cuts burn that he doesn't even know he has. Then he'll lap his lips and chin to help heal his mouth, try to treat the other symptoms with milk of magnesia at first and induce passage before resorting to tincture of opium simply to make himself forget the ills he suffers.

In this dumbed state, Joshua will close his eyes, lace his fingers, and pray for a cool breeze. He won't really know how to pray, and he'll feel silly doing it. Still, part of him will believe it might work. This is the beginning of the world, he'll think, chaos before it was tamed. That scientific thought will remind him of his father, and for a brief moment some cousin of regret will well up inside him while he'll consider the comfort and security his father tried to fashion for seventeen years, though it's a feeling Joshua will refuse to acknowledge. In his mind, he'll see his father's head, the only thing visible on the couch above the tattered blankets. He'll see himself walk over and put the lamp to his father's gray face. His father's cheeks wallowing in craters of bruise-streaked skin, the cheek bones crowned like a cat's shoulders, the white and crusted film on his father's chin like caked flour a remnant of his vomiting. His father's shallow breathing between coughs.

In his mind and in this yet again unceasing slough on the cusp of the final summit, Joshua will cover his own mouth with his hand like he's silencing his horror while he sees himself shine the light on the tin pail beside the sofa. The fresh purge swirling around inside it looks like unstrained rice water. It's then (in the real-time past of this memory) that he does the math between vomitings and assesses his father's lips. The dryness of them and the desiccation they portend inside his father's body frightens him. He picks up a glass of water from the floor, kneels beside the sofa. His clothes, which were always hand-downs from Dr. Gaines, are too small for him, a small hole forming on the knees of the trousers so that his skin grows painful the longer he kneels. He leans into that dreadful and rotten-smelling face, which makes him gag, a reaction that simultaneously fills him with shame and rage.

Only a week before, his father was healthy, their evening filled with a lesson on the exacting methodologies needed for proper drug-mixing. Dr. Gaines was demonstrating how to measure time using the clock candle, stressing that heating the liquid for too long could damage its chemical properties, while heating it for too little wouldn't optimize its efficacy. Then that man was at their door, his wife curled in the belly of the wheelbarrow the way a fetus is inside the womb. She had the same ghastly appearance his father has now.

Please, the man said.

What is his name? Joshua thinks. Did he give a name? Did he have one, or was he a specter?

The man said, You're the only doctor who will help her.

Look at her, Joshua whispered to his father after the woman had been lifted onto their sofa and the man left to return the wheelbarrow outside. He said, She won't live through the night.

Hush, Dr. Gaines said.

Dr. Gaines then turned his attention back to the man, asked him how long his wife had been sick, how many times she'd purged, whether he himself was feeling ill. The man answered with a series of curt responses while Dr. Gaines knelt by the couch (knelt like Joshua kneels in his memory beside his father) and examined her. Joshua focused on his father's work, largely ignoring the man until he heard the front door shut. He turned around, the man was gone.

Don't, Dr. Gaines said as Joshua started to go after him.

I don't think he's coming back.

It doesn't matter.

But we won't get paid.

I won't get paid, corrected Dr. Gaines.

Not four hours after she arrived at their house, the woman died on their dime, and she was buried on their dime as well. Four nights later, his father first fell ill. Now, this night, kneeling beside his sick father and pinching his nose, Joshua lifts his palm so that he can speak underneath it.

You need to drink some water, says Joshua.

Dr. Gaines doesn't reply. Joshua tips the glass against his father's lips. The water sloughs off and drains down the encrusted chin and pools in the pit Dr. Gaines' neck now forms. Joshua tries again, this time prying his father's lips open with one hand while pouring with the other. The doctor coughs, sprays Joshua's face with a mixture of water and foul-smelling mucus.

Joshua claps his hand over his mouth to keep from vomiting and turns away. He rises and gets a rag for his own face and, after waiting for Dr. Gaines to stop coughing, wipes clean his father's chin. He considers feeding his father another spoonful of calomel, but when he opens his father's mouth and peers into it, Dr. Gaines' throat is so red and constricted not even calomel will go down.

It's all right, Joshua says. You'll be all right.

This is a lie, but part of him refuses to acknowledge this even now. He retrieves his father's heavily annotated *Gunn's Domestic Medicine*, begins searching for an answer to a question that can't be answered. Because the body can only handle so much of this world's pummeling before we are forced to let go of our fickle tether lines, when death simply becomes the ceasing of the heart, the hardening of the blood, the curtain closing off the brain.

Joshua slams the book closed. It's then he feels his father's hand on his arm.

You blame her for my sickness, says Dr. Gaines. You shouldn't.

Joshua can see the calm in his father's eyes, as if his father knows at this moment the finality that's approaching and he's surrendering to it. This calm brews in Joshua a grief so deep-seated and pure it feels like hatred. And maybe it is hatred—for his father's nature, for the woman, for her husband, for that city that profited from the two of them without any recompense. All of that now conflated and combined into this singular instance of impending death. Duty or obligation or humanism. Whatever his father wants to call it Joshua only sees as weakness. This didn't have to happen, that woman was always going to die. Joshua knows that, his father knows that. But only one of them chose to sacrifice himself for nothing. And Joshua understands, even at seventeen, that he will never reconcile his hate-fueled grief and, instead, he will let it drive him.

I don't blame her for this, he tells his father while he picks up the tin pail full of his father's vomit. He says, I blame you.

And when Joshua opens his eyes again to reveal this trail and the pending mountains and the entirety of that memory sweeps away, there simply will be the same, hot, dry, stale air.

FROM THE SIERRA NEVADAS
TO SUTTER'S MILL, CALIFORNIA

In the belly of the Sierra Nevadas, anxious and giddy that the rock they're crossing is the very rock shaped by the very river that can no sooner yield them gold, they find springs of snow runoff they scoop with their tin cups and warm with both hands before they drink. The banks of these springs are thick with grass and ferns, and the animals, just like the men, do what they can to remake themselves into unskeletal creatures not on the threads of death.

They supper on greater sage-grouse the twins shoot, though G. Quillard eats nothing. The waxy paleness now the only color of his face and hands, and he won't stop sweating, his body shaking violently. Even his feet shake. No amount of coats or blankets can mitigate it, and the Dover's powder mixed with calomel he's been taking to quell his fevers proves useless. His eyes are glassy, his lips chapped out, his chattering teeth mime crickets. The inside of his mouth is rose red, his tongue plaqued and white. He tucks the stump of his left arm into his chest while he sleeps, but the arm keeps falling away from him, like he is too weak to contain his own severed limb.

Joshua leans over, puts the back of his hand to G. Quillard's forehead. There's no mistaking that raging fever.

I can't feel my face, says G. Quillard. Why can't I feel my face?

Joshua shudders with the implication of this, but he doesn't respond. He heads to the spring to refill G. Quillard's cup. Still in the waning light of twilight, a throat-splitting cough takes hold of G. Quillard. The coughing continues throughout the night, keeps Joshua awake long past exhaustion. It penetrates his tent so that it's as if he's sitting right beside the Englishman, and he knows now he won't sleep tonight.

He wraps a shirt around his head and chin to muffle the sound of that cough. He could leave his tent, gather morphine or something from his medical bag to ease the Englishman's pains and alleviate his cough. But he only lies here, his eyes open, his mind clear, counting the coughs that increase by the minute, until, suddenly, it all stops.

In the morning, Joshua is the first one out of his tent. He stokes a fire out of the embers with mittened hands, has coffee brewing by the time the others emerge. Departure is still a couple of hours off so that the rising sun can burn off the frost and ice that might prove treacherous in so craggy a place. No one speaks. Emigrants camping around them are rising and eating, breaking camp, filling their water supply in the springs. Joshua lets these ambient sounds take him from his own mind and his own words for a moment, finding solace in this cerebral isolation that drifts further west to gold-laced fields shining so brightly in his mind's eye. In the gold fields, he reminds himself, even the weather will become the half-ignored toy of the rich man.

One hour passes. The land grows darker first in shadow while the sun crawls up the eastern peak. When finally it caps the ridge, the whole valley lightens like a magnificent lamp has been flamed. Soon, the valley hazes over by the melting frost, and the party takes this cue to break camp, ritualistic in their manner and duties.

After a bit, Joshua realizes he hasn't heard G. Quillard this morning. Not a cough. Not a moan. Not even crying. He sets his belongings in the wet grass beside his Morgan and goes over to the schooner. He calls first without parting the closed canvas, then calls again. Receiving no response, he enters.

He returns a minute later, and the others are standing just outside. They know without Joshua telling them, and perhaps, with the way they look at Joshua, knew even before he checked on G. Quillard.

Joshua and the twins bury G. Quillard in a grove of pine trees that stand so tall it's likely the ground there never sees the sun and will never see the sun for the thousand more years those pines will bear fruit and die and be replaced by the daughter of the daughter of the daughter of that now sentinel to the Englishman's grave. The twins find a piece of granite that can pass as a headstone and lean it against the trunk. Then the five of them stand over the mound, their hats in their hands and heads to the ground, before Renard looks up.

Like Moses, he says. Unfit to enter the promised land.

With a bandana wrapped across his face to stave off any lingering sickness, Joshua burns G. Quillard's duffel bag and clothes with a kind of distant gaze. In this moment, he feels like he never really knew G. Quillard, or like he only now knows himself, and so he can detach himself from this tragedy. That's what it means to be a survivor. Afterward, Free Ray hitches G. Quillard's horse to Renard's horse with only the guns, shot, powder, and gold-digging tools left strapped to the saddle.

Noon they have crossed so little rock with so much effort that that pleasant valley and the Englishman's death are nothing but a distant memory, a moment just as likely to have never happened as to have happened hours before. Once at the summit they pause, their feet swollen and sore in their boots. But they don't rest. Too much excitement pervades the group as this summit is, knowingly and with anticipation enough to fill a dozen lifetimes preceding it, the last summit they will crest before arriving in gold country.

Late the next morning they come to a small lake that precedes a lush valley, where they water the horses and mules and fill their canteens. They leave it for a stream that borders a bad road, which causes slow travel for their party that is so long overtraveled it seems nearly ridiculous to have to continue such laboring. They slog their way by ropes and by walking, by discarding useless sacks of rancid flour, with nothing but anticipation fueling them. Their faces wear the kind of toll most men absorb after decades. And after a long winding route up a declivity and then along a ridge to circumvent a long canyon, they round a bend where the trees separate, and they all drop their reins and scramble to the edge of the trail to gaze the Sacramento Valley far below them.

An excitement unlike anything he's yet experienced surges through Joshua, makes him weak at the knees and brings tears to his eyes. He understands too fully now that even seeing gold country is a wish beyond his will, and he kneels where he was standing only in part because his legs won't hold him upright anymore. The team behind them, brought to a sudden halt by this act and blocked from passage, begins yelling at their party. But Joshua doesn't care. None of them do. At the bottom of the valley, past the small settlement of Johnston, flows the south fork of the American River through Sutter's Mill. And in that river the mineral that can make them the richest of the rich men.

PART IV

THE FORTY-NINER

CHAPTER FIVE

I t is just past noon. The hot air stings their lungs. The schooner drawn up alongside another on the south side of the American River, land that's been clear-cut for lumber and firewood and lies pegged by wasted stumps, the whole camp reeking of smoke that tears Joshua's eyes and aggravates his throat to no end.

They all dismount and stake a canvas awning from the schooner's bonnet. They place a few wooden chairs underneath so that the shade washes over them while they work.

The first thing they do is slaughter the late G. Quillard's horse for meat. Free Ray puts his Bowie knife to the horse's throat, the animal staring at him so wide-eyed Free Ray can see his own face in that horse's eyes. Free Ray doesn't realize he's smiling until he sees his reflection, and seeing his reflection makes him smile wider. Perhaps for the irony in it. Perhaps for some sadistic inclination that's now becoming unveiled in all of them so far from any kind of civilization previously known.

That smile torments the horse, which tries to buck and heave its head away from Free Ray, but Free Ray is too quick with the knife. In a motion swift and dexterous, he opens a wound dark and glistening with blood. The blood splatters his face when the horse rears. The animal begins to gurgle and choke when it returns to the ground, then wobbles and falls. Free Ray wipes his face with his sleeve, then wipes the knife on his trousers, which are so stiff from unwash he has to wipe the blade three more times to get the blood off.

Renard then butchers the horse with the same care and attention he took while butchering that doe on a day that seems years in the past. He and Free Ray hang the meat, dripping with blood, from the wagon tongue to cure, though so doing spooks the other horses and the mules. Those animals recognize their own scent in that wafting death smell. For fear of the animals breaking their tethers and losing themselves in the hills, the twins lead them away from the schooner, hitch them to tree stumps with their heads pointed away, slap the horses in their throatlatch whenever they try to pull their tied lines.

There's a hurriedness to all of these actions (as time is, quite literally, money out here), and because of this hurriedness Renard slips his knife on the horse's backbone and slices his palm. He drops the knife to the dirt, brings his hand up to his face where his own blood is indistinguishable from the horse's. He sucks in a hard breath.

Never once have I cut my hand while cleaning an animal, he says.

Renard is looking at Free Ray, as if Free Ray will validate that claim, but Free Ray ignores him. Renard presses his palms together to pressure the wound.

He says, But I suppose there are moments enough in this life to do just about anything.

Renard wraps a bandana around his palm while Free Ray takes over the butchering. Holding his hands together in front of him like he's pleading to someone for mercy, Renard walks down to the crowded river and cleans the wound.

Joshua watches Renard squat upstream of two diggers who ignore the blood that runs along the water's surface over their pans. With so many men mining the river, the valley looks like a rotting carcass overrun with flies. There are men from all parts of the world, places Joshua has never heard of: the Sandwich Islands, Sonora, Chile, Peru. These men speak with a woman-like tongue that rolls over vowels so sweetly his own English words sound like pots clanging together. They wear brightly colored clothing, and they bring with them—or at least the Chileans do—great stone wheels that they use to bust up the rock they remove from the river or from the southern hills before they winnow the gravel. Then there are the wooden bateas, and the arrastras the Mexicans use—a primitive machine that requires patience. And then, of course, there are the cradles, the Long Toms formed of hollowed out and halved pine trunks, and the sluices, many of which are still being built.

Renard isn't down at the river long, and when he returns to the schooner, he takes what circuitous route he can at first to avoid all of this bustle. He weaves the wagons lined up in rows along the bank, the tents of recycled mill cloth or bush arbors erected among those wagons, the ditches dug three or four feet into the loose California soil where seekers who sport long and full beards curl themselves into tattered wool blankets and sleep like children, the charcoal pits—approximately fifty-feet long and fifteen-feet wide—that are piled with sod and on which men clamber about using long poles to open holes that leak smoke. Soon, this weaving only makes Renard's path worse. Twice he has to double back and many more times he gets thrown off balance into the very obstructions he aims to avoid and once he steps into a pile of what can only be a man's shit, so he resigns to walking straight toward their camp and stepping on what unsuspecting device or man he might and, in the manner of a magician, trudges through fires still blowing flames until he reaches the schooner.

The twins are almost finished unloading their horses, Free Ray still butchering the horse. Farther downriver is Sutter's Mill. There, the mill wheel churns the water that runs dark with ruffled sediment and the placer miners line out along the sand bar like a human dam. Knee-deep in the cold water they dredge the bed with tin or copper pans scooped toward them, then swirl and tip until they reach black sand (pay dirt, they call it) and, if lucky, find buried in that sand gold enough to cover the costs of their being here. Joshua imagines someone flinging his hand skyward like he's reaching for Heaven and exclaiming what is the greatest music to anyone's ears: Gold! But how piteous the individual that bares his luck, a lesson Joshua will quickly learn.

Joshua turns back to their camp. His hands tremble with the want to grab his gold pan and tear off toward the river. He's surprised by this reaction, and he calms himself, having learned the danger inherent to such rashness so many times already.

He surveys what he can do to help. There's room enough for him to set up only one of their tents. He pulls out the poles and canvas of the best one and gets started. Underneath the canvas, he lays out his wool blanket and Renard's, retrieves his coffee pot and cookware and the utensils he's brought, and piles them in a corner of the wagon bed. He turns around to head back to his Morgan and unload the rest of his goods, but he finds himself standing face to face with Free Ray, who stands with his hands dripping blood onto the dirt near Joshua's feet.

The encounter catches Joshua off guard, if not for the unexpectedness of it than because he can't fully decipher the look in Free Ray's eyes, an amalgamation of fatigue and contentment, the way a drunkard might look right before he draws and shoots you in the gut. Joshua smiles weakly at him. Then he steps aside to let Free Ray return to salting the horse meat.

Gutted and butchered out, the horse's body is cavernous, already sun-rotting. Large black ants bigger than any Joshua has seen before have discovered it and swarm the haunches. Renard, with his bandaged hand, and Clayton attempt to bury the horse beside a large juniper bush, but after Clayton slips and falls into the horse's midsection, his arms sinking into gore up to his shoulders, they give up. The horse's head is still visible, the red stain on the dirt spreading outward equally on all sides like the dirt is being melted by the horse's blood, a hoof or two peeking out of the bush. Buzzards will take care of the rest they figure, or coyotes. Or even a mountain lion.

The five of them strip to their union suits and carry their clothes to the river, where they wash the garments amidst the gold diggers and hastily bathe themselves. Like a main artery, that river is being used for everything: bathing, washing, gold mining, watering animals, even for drinking by those men careless enough to drink from it. When they finish, they wade out of the river with their heads down, scanning for any sign of gold until they reach the bank, then dress without ringing the water from their clothes and return to the schooner dripping but refreshed.

They crouch in the shade of the wagon to rest. They drink coffee, eat a paltry meal of dried fish that is far too many days old and a hunk of hard bread while the sun falls headlong over the hills that look in the coming dark like sand dunes, the sunlight itself refracted and turned gold on the water. The sky stains pink, then gray, then the water eddying along the northern bank is ringed by trout, and so comes nightfall, lanterns hung from posts and lit and the shoreline winking with condensed flames, and the air absent of the chime of cicadas, as if the land grew more silent the farther west they traveled and so out here, where it forms its national edge, there is hardly any sound at all.

I aim to start hunting gold tomorrow, says Klayton in nearly a whisper.

He sniffles and rubs his nose with his sleeve. Then he hacks up something, spits.

Tonight I'll sleep, he says. But I aim to start hunting just as the sun come up so when it dawns, my fortune does as well.

It is no secret that that is the reason we are here, says Renard.

Renard picks up the coffee pot, pours himself another cupful. He holds the cup tenderly with both hands, his sulfuric odor seeming more pungent to Joshua in this valley, like the river grinds it into his skin.

I never said it was a secret, says Klayton. All I'm doing is making audible my intentions.

Plainly heard then, says Renard.

Clayton turns to Klayton and says, With me hunting too we gonna quickly double our fortune.

That may be true, Renard says. But with double the party that fortune must accommodate, the two of you will in fact incur a fortune, once divided, equal to a single man.

Clayton scrunches his face in confusion. There is only a small fire between them, but with so much ambient light in the camp and a half-moon out each of them can clearly see the others' faces.

Two times the fortune is not two times the fortune when it is gained by two men, Renard clarifies.

I never said we'd find only two times the fortune, Clayton says.

Then may god's blessed hand find your shoulder.

Renard makes a mock half-bow as he says this, rolling his hand in front of him with exaggeration and flamboyance the way a stage actor does at the end of a show. Clayton's eyes narrow, almost imperceptibly, but if he takes any other offense to Renard's gesture than what his eyes betray, that offense is conveyed only by silence.

I don't know how you expect to find such a fortune right here, says Joshua.

He is initially talking more to himself than to anyone in particular, but when Clayton asks why not, Joshua doesn't find his reasons hard to come by.

I'd say there are at least a hundred men in that river. And that's counting the ones digging right now, not to mention the scores between us and the bank.

Clayton shrugs.

Imagine how much gold must've been pulled out of that river already, Joshua says. Gone now, like it never existed in the first place. Or washed away by the droves of feet cutting across the bed or the hundreds of pans stirring the gravel.

Joshua leans forward and points to the hills. A sense that he has somehow shifted inside wells itself even more prominently now than it has these past several weeks, and he realizes, at least for the first time conscientiously, that what's driving this discussion and what's driving him in this moment and onward is a raw and inchoate form of greed. How much like a disease greed is, he thinks. Originating as if from the air itself, formed as if from nothing more than the recognition of it only after it has taken hold of the body. Without life, his father once told him, there would be no disease, and yet no life can be lived without being exposed to it. That presents a fine and cosmic balance, if Joshua ever did acknowledge such a thing.

Joshua clears his throat and clears his thoughts. Clayton is still watching him, his mouth tugged at the edges into an almost grin.

Joshua says, Where is it exactly you think that gold comes from? It's not produced in the water, it's carried into it. So ask yourself, what is that river flows through?

That right?

Clayton nudges his brother.

Course you'd know, Clayton says. Being a doctor and all. A scientific mind.

Joshua tosses a stick in the fire, where it slowly births its own flames, and that is science too.

Why don't you go up in them hills yourself then instead of fussing with that river if that be the case? asks Clayton.

Because I'm only one man, says Joshua.

Clayton stares at Klayton, something passing between the twins that Joshua can't make sense of.

He is right, says Renard. Panning is fit for the sole seeker. Any man can work a pan, dredge up some color here and there to meticulously build his fortune. But a pair of men, brothers such as yourselves. Consider the rock you could mine, the wealth to be suddenly unearthed.

The twins smile, as if this kind of mining never occurred to them before.

You should listen to the young doctor, continues Renard. He understands more than that meager beard of his would have you believe.

Renard laughs and Free Ray joins him.

Renard stands, stretches his back with both arms extended above him. He walks a few feet away from their circle, picks up a small rock, which he rubs between his four fingers, then heaves the rock toward the river. None of the others can see the rock more than a few feet after it leaves Renard's hand, but there's a moment of waiting and silence among the group, until they hear a man in the river yell out in pain and start cussing. Renard and Free Ray laugh again. The twins smile at this display, though it's clear they don't really understand it by the way their eyes don't smile along with their mouths. Joshua doesn't know want to make of it either. Renard picks up another rock, again heaves it toward the river. This time, no one yells.

Two rocks, says Renard sitting and crossing his legs. Both heaved by the same arm and for likely equal distance mere seconds apart. One strikes its mark. The other misses. And that probability, gentlemen, is what is in store for you these next couple of months.

✻

JUST BEFORE THE sun caps the hills with the ash dust falling like a snow flurry and the sky the darkest of a dark blue and the moon pinned to that color, the twins emerge from the tent they all share, gather their wares and their horses in jittery fast-talking voices with no modicum of consideration for the others still sleeping, and take to the hills each the other's shadow.

The same day the twins depart Joshua takes up his shiny tin pan and carries it to the river along with a thin-bladed knife he hangs from his belt. He sets to placer mining, teaching himself the technique by watching the others panning around him. The water numbs his hands and feet. His back stiff and sore from bending over, from shivering even with the sun on him, his body still wearing the weakness and suffering of the trail even though he's experienced a sort of rebirth of spirit since they arrived. At its core, he discovers panning isn't a difficult process but one that relies on nuance to distinguish the successful from the unsuccessful, nuances that Joshua must learn through practice, which the redundancy of such a task greatly affords. Much like medicine.

That evening, Joshua wades out of the river, his pockets empty, his pan hanging at his side in defeat, walking stiffly and baby-like with his newly working legs, his gimp right foot difficult to navigate in the loose gravel as he makes his way back to their camp. Word has gotten around that he is a doctor. By supper there's a line of men complaining of ear aches, broken fingers, angry coughs, constipation, chronic sores on their limbs, one with a stabbing pain in his chest, another with a bloated and hardened stomach who can't keep down any food. He treats them mechanically, only half-listening to the descriptions of their ailments as he bleeds them or withdraws bottles from his medical bag he sometimes doesn't look at before doling out the contents. They thank him profusely, which he dismisses, assure him they'll pay richly for his treatment when they strike it rich. He laughs to himself whenever they say this, then, just as quickly, grows dour and angry. How is their unfounded optimism any different from his own?

On and on the digging continues, and each day the gold fever Joshua so often hears about in the valley roots deeper and spreads wider throughout him. His scalp tingles with the blood that wants to jump out of his skin, his breathing so erratic it makes him light-headed. Every river rock is gold in his periphery. He dreams of gold. His food tastes metallic the way he believes gold will. A kind of mania overwhelms him, erasing everything and everyone until it's just him and his strained-out eyes digging until he can hardly stand for the fatigue. Then, exhausted by that fever and his body too welled by anxiety even for thought, he stumbles back to camp and finds Renard and Free Ray newly manifested and preparing sup-per, for these two only exist to Joshua in these brief interludes of their presence. And the nights pass by in frenetic ceremony: *Macbeth* performed under lantern light in the bed of an old and bonnetless schooner, Lady Macbeth an Irishman with a curly red beard that consumes his face, the ugliest man Joshua has ever seen with a grace in his acting that enthralls Joshua. A quartet of men stringing rude instruments that shrill in the dry, chilly air. A horse race, a magic show, a bloody bare-knuckle boxing match between giants who come from some place they proudly call Rossiya!

Joshua refuses every patient now, declares himself no longer the camp's doctor. Eventually, the men stop coming. So many men die of sickness or accident or injury that Joshua counts the days by the number of graves being dug. When individual graves become futile, the bodies are thrown into massive pits that are piled over with worthless dirt and bits of felled trees and rocks and busted wagon parts. Time lost to him. Gold. Hunger lost to him. Gold. Gold. Golden sun on golden days and gold in the piss draining downriver to empty Joshua of anything but this single pursuit.

＊

IT'S A WEEK more before the twins return to camp for the first time, rundown and covered in dust and, like Joshua, with no gold between them. The twins rest for a day with so little said from them it's like such work has rendered them voiceless. They purchase food supplies and water from neighboring miners or from the Nisenan peddlers, who wander about selling various goods: woven baskets; pottery; exotic acorn dishes none of the Americans recognize; an assortment of animal meats; deer and bear hides, some of which have been sewn into coats or blankets. The twins sleep the afternoon away under the schooner while Joshua maintains his digging, and, that evening, they sit in the shadows of their own horses and play a private game of blackjack, a game they can hardly see in the failing light. The day following, they enter the hills again in single file, their pickaxes busted dull from the rock and clanking as they climb the dusty slopesides that still hold the tracks from their initial return.

Joshua pauses his swirling, his own gold pan full of gravel he's just dredged. He can hear the clanking axes, he can see their mirrored physiques with his blistered hand blocking the sun, the solemn procession of the twins playing out before him. When he loses track of the twins, he scoops some water with his hand, gently touches his sunburned neck. He lets himself rest for a moment. Then he picks the larger stones from his pan and drops them in the river. He dips the pan back in the water, washes away more gravel. The more sediment he lets back into the river the more comes that all-too-familiar flutter in his heart, though so second nature now is this panning he doesn't think about it while he does it, and at times he's caught himself panning his plate of supper.

He pulls the pan out of the water, jiggles it to settle the heavier matter in the middle, dips the edge of the pan back into the water to wash out more gravel. He dips the pan again, then still more times until what's left is only pay dirt, a substance so fine he can hardly feel the black grains when he rubs them between his fingertips. The pay dirt swirls counterclockwise nearly hypnotic while he strains to see that miraculous yellow glint. Because he believes that's what finding gold will feel like: a miracle. That thing he has always refused to believe in.

The first two attempts of this morning reveal nothing. Joshua scoops another handful of water into the pan to separate the dirt more, closes his eyes to refocus them while he swirls the pan to work the pay dirt. He opens his eyes and still nothing, the dirt whorling in front of him beautiful if it weren't worthless. His shadow looms over the dirt, so he tilts the pan into the sunlight while he continues swirling.

So fleeting is the golden glint before the dirt swallows the tiny nugget again that Joshua thinks at first he's only imagined it, just as he has hundreds of times before this one. He pauses. He begins to swirl the pan slower, clockwise now. The nugget tumbles out of the dirt a blessed offering, no bigger than the fingernail on his pinky, but unmistakable.

Joshua gasps. The man panning a few feet away throws his head in Joshua's direction, glares at him with a mean and curious look. Joshua glances at the man, then splashes his face with the river water while he holds his pan casually, though carefully, in dissemblance. The man goes back to his own panning, and Joshua quickly pulls the nugget out with two fingers, rinses it clean in the water, then sticks it in a small leather pouch he's tied to his belt. All of this without any inspection of the gold to shield his good prospect from those surrounding him.

Joshua's heart hammers his chest, his breathing coming so fast he feels like he'll pass out from the excitement. This is the beginning, the moment he will be forever transformed from a poor seeker to a rich man. He can feel it in his gut. He believes it using all of the logic he's been reared to use.

He tries to dredge again from exactly the same spot he just pulled that gold, but even with his eyes hawked, seeing things he would never have seen seconds ago, he doesn't find anymore gold or flakes of color by the time he finishes washing the next pan. Or the next pan. Or the next. His excitement recedes as his pouch, which seemed on the verge of overflowing just an hour ago, feels even emptier containing just the one tiny nugget.

Joshua slaps his pan on the water.

What'd you think? says the man beside him. That she was simply going to offer up her treasure?

Joshua could pummel that man, target all of the anger and frustration he has for each empty pan on that indistinct weathered face. But that pummeling isn't worth the energy it will cost him. So he keeps panning. He keeps panning. He keeps panning. He pans on.

The sun lowing, the river turning dark and viscous like oil. Joshua finally stops when he can no longer distinguish the pay dirt from the other dirt. He looks up, waits for his eyes to adjust to a distant perspective, and scans the dimmed valley. Farther away from here, diggers dig the Bear, Feather, or Yuba Rivers; others dry mine across the hills and some seventy Chinese men methodically construct a wing dam at Willow Creek; and yet still farther, over one hundred miles distant, a stamp mill pounds ore from the Mariposa Mine that does the work of thirty men. But every man is the same to Joshua—those he both can and can't see. They are, in his mind, all componented of a singularity: the gold seeker. No more had been or was but only am. This is a world proportioned by freedom and ambition and a determination so narrow and vile it sucks out the lives left behind and the charted past world to render here the very microcosm of frontier. Each to his own. Each for his own.

Joshua hates these men, those already here and those yet to come, a hatred that swells inside of him from something he's never known and feels he'll never need understand. Like a tumor this hate is

steadily growing, and soon it might well encompass Renard, Free
Ray, and the twins, and as much as he can't put words to it, he knows
this hate is a part of him now. The trail did this to him. Or the grace-
less digging. Or the hardship. Or the greed. In truth, he's wrecked
by all of it, detached from his soul like a dead man, but with the way
he incessantly sweats and the thirst that daily sings in his throat, he
can be nothing else but alive.

So it is he feels entirely alone in this world, liberated by this loneliness, hardened by it. And when the other four in his party prove no
longer useful or pose a danger to his own prosperity, they will have
to be abandoned, chucked away like the very belongings strung out
from California to Missouri across this country that prides itself on
growth and expansion and signs its declarations in blood.

CHAPTER SIX

On the tenth of October, a Wednesday, a cold front blows into the valley. Joshua has been panning a little over a month and has found ten ounces of gold, which will fetch him more than two hundred dollars once he carries his find to San Francisco, to an establishment everyone says is owned by a Mormon named Sam Brannan. Brannan makes more money on the miners in a day than most miners make in a month. Some call Brannan a cheat; others a swindler; others the face of the rush; and others simply that Mormon. He owns one of the few stores between the valley and San Francisco, where he'll sell you a gold pan for at least a six-thousand percent profit, for his is the ingenious scheme of riches obtained toil-free.

Joshua knows little about Brannan save for what people rumor, but he has no plans to meet the man of San Francisco anytime soon.

Ten ounces of gold, regardless of what it will bring him now, is not enough for him to consider pausing his digging, is not even close to the sudden wealth he expected. This disillusionment is mirrored in the hearts of so many men, so that the camp wells with a hostility and anger that lingers at every misspoken word, at every unkind gesture, makes itself evident in the nightly cock fights or dog fights that kick up such a pervasive cloud of dust it's like the whole place has been banished to some more unearthly world.

The twins return from the hills for good this tenth day of the month. Renard, Free Ray, and Joshua are tinkering about camp when they spot the twins and their horses stumbling half-dead into the valley.

Blood runs down the horses' front legs, large sores cover their entire bodies as if they have been chewed to bits by bugs. They can't bear to walk any further, but the twins kick at the horses with boot heels worn to the leather and push them forward. Klayton's horse foams at the mouth and gags on its own ragged breath, nearly falling every time Klayton jams his heels into its ribs. He rides with a leather bag pinched at his crotch. Joshua figures that's their gold, as it's the one thing the twins carry that isn't so carelessly lashed onto the saddle as to be easily lost or stolen.

After the twins dismount at the camp, the horses collapse. Clayton doesn't bother to stay on his feet either. He simply sits in the dirt, and Klayton, who clutches the leather bag tightly in one hand, walks over and pulls his brother up by the shirt.

You found success in the hills after all, says Renard.

Klayton tucks the bag into his chest in a kind of defensive maneuver and skeptically looks at Renard. He's forgotten he is among acquaintances now, or perhaps he's come to learn that latent law all men abide by out here: When digging for gold, the only true acquaintance you have is yourself.

A little more than three ounces, Klayton says.

He still holds onto Clayton's shirt, nearly dragging his brother behind him. Clayton doesn't even look at the others, his scabbed head kept down, eyes closed.

Klayton stops in front of Renard, and Clayton falls back onto his butt.

It ain't even enough to cover the expense of our prolonged stay up in them deviled hills, says Klayton.

He shakes his head, starts coughing. His cough grows more violent, and he doubles over with his hands on his knees until it sounds like he's choking, then he goes silent for a moment, sucks in the longest breath Joshua has ever seen him take.

Goddamn dust, says Klayton. My lungs is full of it. I reckon I could fill an hourglass if I had no cause to preserve my throat.

He looks at Joshua.

You got anything for a cough such as this? he asks.

Joshua shakes his head. His medicine bag is long empty, but this response is as much about what he wouldn't offer even if he had it as it is about what he doesn't have to offer.

Klayton sighs. He looks off at the river. He turns back to the others.

That river yield much?

Renard and Free Ray shrug. Klayton looks at Joshua.

For a second, Joshua doesn't know what to say. He's never told Renard or Free Ray how much gold he's found, nor have they told him. In fact, he's never actually considered telling any of them, innately holding this fact close to his chest as if he's always understood the value in secrecy when it comes to prosperity. He sidesteps Klayton's question.

There's gold to be found in it after all, he says.

That answer seems satisfactory enough for Klayton, who forces a smile and bares his rotted teeth. Given how raccooned the twins' eyes are and how withered and emaciated their faces appear, Joshua wonders if they'll have the opportunity to pan at all or if chance will play its spade and the twins, just like G. Quillard, will succumb to the rush.

Klayton opens the leather bag, holds it up to his eye. He closes it, makes like he's going to store it away somewhere, before he opens it again and again peers inside, as if the gold can simply be there one instant and disappear the next. Content enough with this second look, he shoves the bag in his waistband. He lifts his brother by the shirt again and the two of them lumber under the tent, where they collapse to the ground with their backs braced against each other in exhaustion and are quickly sleeping.

The twins sleep through the afternoon and evening, unrustled when the other three climb under the tent around midnight. Joshua, Renard, and Free Ray lie there for about ten minutes before the intolerable stench of the twins drives them out with their blankets to sleep in the cold.

Come dawn, Joshua is in the river. When finally he straightens himself and stretches out his shoulders hours later, his entire body aches from the monotonous rhythm. The cold front has vacated, the heat returned, and he cusses the weather, even knowing while cussing that it's a wasted breath. The sunlight glaring off of the water has whitened his vision so he can hardly see more than twenty feet in front of him while he hobbles to the bank in his spongy leather boots.

He passes a group of heavily bearded men working a cradle. The bottom tin tray of it is filled with mercury, the men digging their thick fingers into the quicksilver in search of the gold that will adhere to it, drawing those silvered fingers out while the viscous liquid works down their palms and to their wrists like an alien organism consuming their bodies. If they find any gold, they check its density with their teeth, which paints their lips silver, then wash the mercury from the nugget in the river, where it drains away in tendrils. There are more cradles being used in the valley now. More sluices and long toms being built. Some parties have even packed in and installed immense gold washers purchased back East that are adorned with plaques proclaiming those devices are GUARAN-TEED TO FIND THE GOLD THAT PANNING SIMPLY CAN-NOT ATTAIN!

It's all false hope, Joshua thinks. The air reeks of smoke from the charcoal pits, and the sound of crushing rocks and yelling men drown out any sense of what Joshua thinks this place might have been in some more tranquil time, the land before it was ravaged by greed.

Back at the camp the twins are still sleeping. Free Ray sits bare-chested on the wagon tongue while he hems his linen shirt. He glances up when Joshua enters.

Is Renard in the river? Joshua asks.

Free Ray shakes his head.

The twins' horses died not long after they returned from the hills, so Joshua glances over at the remaining animals. Renard's horse is gone.

He walks over to his Morgan, shoves his tin pan in his duffel bag. Then he runs his palm down the horse's muzzle. The Morgan huffs while he does so, and Joshua whispers to it about his frustration with the digging and how hot it is even in October. His Morgan is the only being he divulges the circumstances of his digging to, so he's grown accustomed to petting it each midday while he ruminates on what has happened and how, if at all, he can remedy his bad luck. The Morgan is thin, the weight it lost on the trail never recovered, and its eyes aren't very sharp anymore. Some days Joshua thinks his talking to it might be the last time he ever will. With hardly any grass in the valley, he has been feeding the horse what grain he can find at deserted camps or what he can barter away from the other miners or Indian peddlers. Twice he took his Morgan shallowly into the hills to let it graze on bushes or berries, but he was so concerned about mountain lions each time that he decided not to risk the endeavor anymore.

Joshua pulls out his canteen, splashes some water down the back of his neck. He drinks. He cups his hand and lets the Morgan drink a bit before he offers some water to Free Ray's horse. He's exhausted from sleeping on the open ground the night before. Three times he woke from dreams of failure and poverty that cast his body in a cold sweat and made him frantic, though he could never remember the exact circumstances of those dreams, retained only vague images of a past and future life that don't make sense, that seem to conflate both time periods, that he feels more than anything else, and these images spur in him a kind of restlessness he doesn't know how to quell and wonders if he'll ever shake.

He closes his eyes and rests his forehead on his saddle, the sun on his neck soon unbearable. He lifts his head, the oily imprint of it dark like blood on the leather. He tucks the canteen back into his duffel, removes his gold pan. He can only grow poorer the longer he stands here, so he returns to the river without eating and pans until dusk, at which point, scotched by misfortune and his stomach sunken with hunger, he returns to camp.

Bats no larger than his hand swoop and dart the shallow riverbank to feed in his wake. He swats at one of them with his pan but misses by a margin so large he feels silly at the attempt.

RENARD RETURNS AFTER supper in the dark. The others sitting around a wind-bent fire hear his horse before they see it. He shuffles around an unseen entity before his footsteps approach them, his body welling in the ring of that hallowed firelight. He wears his pistol. His shirt is covered in blood. More blood streaks across his neck and still more is dried and cracked on the backs of his hands. He carries something wrapped in a bandana that appears heavy by the way his hand doesn't swing as he walks. Free Ray stands and takes the item from Renard and walks over to the schooner, returning empty handed.

Renard sits down, removes his shirt, throws it into the fire. His shirt catches fire quickly and flares the wondering faces of the others who have too many questions for words. The night is cool and getting cooler, but Renard doesn't bother to put another shirt on. He just sits there, his body as white as cotton and aggravating the dancing light with its warped reflection the way wet leather does.

Jesus, says Klayton finally. You injured?

Renard spits onto the backs of his hands several times, wipes away what blood he can.

No, he says.

He unholsters the pistol, sets it in his lap with the barrel extending down his thigh and pointing across the fire between the twins and Joshua. Klayton scoots closer to his brother to widen the gap that that pistol, should it fire, can send a bullet through unimpeded.

We still got some of that jerkied horse meat, says Clayton. If you've a mind to eat anything, I mean.

Thank you, says Renard. I am not hungry.

Clayton nods and looks back at the fire, then glances back at Renard, where his eyes briefly meet the pistol's hollow eye, before he looks at the fire more intensely, trying to let the flames melt any anxiety or discontent he might presently have. No one speaks for a while.

Then Clayton turns to his brother and says, I figure we ought to hike downriver tomorrow morning, go on past the mill and try our hand at panning down there. The way I figure it, all that activity along the sandbar gonna kick up some sediment and loose some rocks that might bring gold down thataway.

I imagine you right, says Klayton, sucking on a piece of jerky.

I know I'm right. It ain't a question of that. It's a question of how hard we willing to work.

Klayton stops sucking his jerky. He looks spitefully at his brother.

I ain't never once scoffed at a single bead of sweat, he says.

That ain't what I meant, says Clayton. This gold digging ain't easy is all. I ain't expected this sort of hardship.

Holstering his pistol, Renard says, Naturally, and as you so indicate, opportunity is a result of fortitude. But it is also a result of creativity. Free Ray and I have yet to tilt a pan between us, though we have currently obtained a total of five hundred ounces of gold.

The jerky drops from Klayton's hand, and Clayton nearly falls forward into the fire. Joshua is stunned. Never has it occurred to him that Renard or Free Ray haven't been panning, and he feels fooled somehow, a child left out of an adult conversation.

Five hundred ounces? Klayton says. Why that's damn near…that's damn near…

Ten thousand dollars, says Joshua.

I ain't never heard of such money! hisses Clayton.

There are vast riches to be made, says Renard. So long as you have the ambition to make them.

You was up in them hills too then? Clayton jabs his brother. I told you we shouldn't've given up on them hills.

They weren't up in the hills, says Joshua.

A gold washer then? asks Clayton. How is it you come into a gold washer if you didn't bring one stashed in the schooner?

Renard shakes his head.

No such contraption was used in the acquisition of this gold.

He pauses, spits into his palm and wipes his neck, brings his hand around in front of his face to see if he got rid of any of the blood, then wipes again. Down in the river, diggers continue to splash around in their endless searching.

These men are either dreamers or fools, Renard says. The dreamers will never unearth enough gold to cover the expense of their toil out here. In a year or two, they will venture back east broken men and be made to vocalize their failures, which will break them further. The men who strike it rich are the fools. They are marginally smarter, or simply blessed by ample luck, but they know not what to do with their fortunes. So they buy whores, whiskey, arid land too difficult to farm, more tools to find more gold, and all the while that gold is being taken from them by men even smarter than they are. Men with the forethought to know that digging for gold is the surest way to die a pauper. For the true path to wealth is the history of theft. And like all great thieves who preceded him, President Taylor will soon take this land, along with the gold that can be found in it.

Goddamn Washington and its goddamn politics, spits Clayton. Ain't a soul in Georgia who don't think a Washington politician is more dangerous than a cottonmouth.

Renard walks over to the schooner, returns with the bandana-wrapped object he earlier brought in. He unwraps it, then with one hand lifts the gold nugget, which is only slightly smaller than his hand, and drops it into his other hand. His hand bounces under the weight, and given the way the nugget traps the firelight, Joshua thinks nothing less than a plucked star can look so bright and so beautiful in the dark.

Taken from a fool's hand this afternoon, Renard says.

How? asks Joshua.

Renard smiles, and in that instant Joshua sees the enigmatic man that months ago walked into Mechner's suddenly unveiled and made transparent. That depthless smile its own weapon of ruthlessness. Eyes that wear murder and opportunism like the white in their sclera, as if in those eyes is a map detailing the whole history of this country, one of violence, of transience, of oppression, of theft, vision forever and always trained outward so that never revealed is the cruelty that manifests it all. Joshua knows the answer to his question, perhaps even before he asked it, but what shocks him most isn't that Renard, and possibly Free Ray, killed and stole for the gold they've acquired. What shocks him is the fact that he isn't shocked at all. Instead, such an endeavor excites him, greed having steeled his heart entirely and that duplicitous soul of a once-ago child birthed and orphaned on torrid waters now sitting with him father to the man.

Yes, says Renard still looking at Joshua.

Clayton screws up his face and looks at his brother.

We ain't following what you yessing about, says Clayton.

Renard rewraps the gold nugget in the bandana.

He says, No living man willingly relinquishes the gold he has worked so hard to obtain, nor would he ever stop searching for it once it has been taken from him. And no man is searching for this gold.

CHAPTER SEVEN

Two days later the five of them charge their guns, ready their horses, and mount with sunrise still hours below the horizon, Joshua and the twins shifty and skittish with anticipation and looking so much like the marauders they believe they are now, or at least an image of what they think marauders should look like, with their hits drawn low on their foreheads and their bandanas tied around their necks and brought up over their mouths and their pistols worn tightly around their waists while they keep fingering the butts in the want for combat. The twins sit together atop a lean and long-legged saddled horse, which they bought for the price of the meager gold they found in the hills. Klayton in front and Clayton's arms wrapped around his brother's waist, the stirrups too long for Klayton's short legs so they just hang there. All of the horses snort short bursts of fog in the cool morning, stomp their shoes onto the hard dirt to heat the blood in their tired and worn-out bodies. Instinctually, these animals know today is something novel, and it won't be long before the men spur the reluctance from them. Free Ray holds the double-barrel shotgun in one hand with the barrel pointed into the air like a rebel, or a freedom fighter, and the five of them sit still for a moment, no gesture or word passing between them, until, as if by circumstance alone, they simultaneously bring the horses into a trot to the road, then strike them out loping downriver.

Joshua has no idea where they're going. He and the twins blindly follow Renard and Free Ray along the road until the sun dawns on these riders the darkest day of rebirth then they cut off the road to wind through a dense growth of pine and cross the river to be received later at the tributary of Weber Creek. They stop briefly to water the horses among the steep gulches and cataracts shaping the rock. Several more miles across streams and ravines of various depth and width, and finally they enter a mining camp beset by hills that seems a mirror image of their camp.

Some of them men in camp shuffle about with stale bread or bowls of cold rice. Some are in the river. The riders lead the horses around tents that still hum with the sounds of waking, through oily campfire smoke so thick it makes their eyes water. Renard eventually stops on a patch of barren ground between a three-wheeled schooner, which appears to be abandoned, and a tent that's little more than rags of canvas held together by rope and arthritic wooden poles. Three Mexicans sleep underneath the tent, all of them beneath a single, vibrantly colored blanket.

Renard turns his horse to face the others. They draw near him.

What now? asks Klayton.

We wait here, says Renard.

We wait?

You do not plan to draw war against an entire mining camp, do you?

Klayton smiles coyly. Renard chuckles. Clayton leans and spits toward the Mexicans' tent.

We ain't got to wait near these greasers though, he says. Shit, I can smell them even sitting this horse, even with my nose pressed to my not-so-rosy brother.

Renard says, Five men ride into a mining camp one morning well-armed and with no digging tools among them. They stay for the duration of the sun's trajectory before they depart. Later, a miner, or a few miners, is found to be killed. Who do you think it is will be suspected?

No one offers any answer.

You cannot underestimate the power of suspicion, says Renard. But not a white man among us will take a greaser at his word.

They all dismount, hitch their horses to the bed of the abandoned schooner, then huddle around it as if it's their own. Renard explains how to go about scouting for the right miner to rob. He tells Joshua to look for any men not digging, as it's quite possible those men have a gold stash that affords them the luxury of rest, and to listen for the chatter, as he puts it. He tells the twins to walk the riverbank, to watch and listen for any digger that exclaims about his find or rushes from the water. He says that meanwhile he will stand guard over the guns and horses.

When the three of them turn to leave, Joshua notices Free Ray is gone. He glances around. There are but a few Black men in camp. The ones he spots aren't Free Ray. But it doesn't matter anyway where Free Ray went, at least not until evening comes. Joshua is determined to prove to both him and Renard that he brings value to this rogue band of plunderers, and not just as a tool for violence, as he believes the twins are.

Still, he isn't really sure what it means to listen to the chatter. He walks into the heart of the camp. Around one smoldering fire sit five white women on upturned wooden crates with their hands on their knees and their knees spread like they are shitting. It's been weeks since he last saw a woman, and initially he sees them with that vague recollection of knowing what they are without fully comprehending it. The women wear loose-fitting dresses, all of them with dirty faces too rapidly aged for their youth, and they stare at him as he passes with a begrudging acknowledgment. He nods, and one woman grins a hollow gap-toothed grin that's oddly frightening in the still soft morning light. He passes Indian miners who deftly work a sluice, then a pair of trappers that have descended a squat hill, a mountain lion strung across the back of one of their mules. The mule looks jittery and displeased carrying that creature even though it's dead, and the trappers themselves appear half wild adorned from head to toe in furs and skins.

Joshua crests the hill the trappers came down from. On the other side is a narrow ravine. He spots seven men in the ravine, some shouldering pickaxes as they disappear into a manufactured tunnel, some emerging with wheelbarrows full of gravel that they dump into a sluice worked by others who wield shovels or pitchforks, a large wooden sign planted beside the sluice that reads: WE, THE UNDERSIGNED, DO HERE LAY CLAIM TO 300 FEET SQ. COMMENCING AT THIS SLUICE AND EXTENDING UP THIS RAVINE TO THE OAK WITH THE GIGANTIC BURL

Joshua squats in the shade of a juniper, watches the men for a while. Every now and then one drops his tool, begins digging into the sluice and then pulls something out, spits on it, wipes it with his hands, bites down on it with his teeth, then places it in a leather satchel he wears. By the way the men check the objects' densities with their teeth, Joshua knows they are digging out gold.

He tears a twig from the juniper that shades him, rubs it between his palms to get the stink of his Morgan off. Then he stands, takes nearly the same route he took earlier back to the schooner. Once, in the course of his path, he pauses to view the river, sees the twins wading in the shallows and splashing themselves and each other like children.

Shortly after midday, he finds Renard lying on his back, Renard's body barely graced by a rod of shade. Joshua squats beside him. Renard's eyes are closed, and Joshua thinks at first he's sleeping, but as Joshua stands to leave, Renard speaks.

Did you hear anything worth listening to or see anything worth seeing? Renard asks.

Joshua hesitates. He wants nothing more than the riches he knows Renard and Free Ray's plan can offer him, but something inside him even now wills him to hold on to what he's just witnessed. That something sounds like his father, he thinks, but it's voice so feeble, like an animal that's been starved for days and remains only a fraction of its former self, that it barely manages to make its presence known, is hardly a match for the darker and more powerful self that now consumes him.

Seeming to sense these sensations in Joshua, Renard opens his eyes and sits up.

It is a wonderful day today, he says.

Joshua nods.

In all the places I have traveled, I have never seen so much sun shine in one place, and I have traveled quite many places in the years I have lived.

He removes his gaucho, runs a hand down the length of his ponytail.

Perhaps that sunlight is partly why I have now come back to California, he says. That and the gold, of course.

Renard stands, bends at the waist to stretch his back.

He says, It is no wonder there is so much sun cast on this land. Not even god himself can help but marvel at the opulence of this precious metal.

Joshua is facing Renard, looking at Renard's red hair, when he realizes that he is as tall as Renard is now. It's an odd and disembodied moment when a young man suddenly recognizes his growth, sees it tangible in some way, and it's a moment that doesn't pass by Joshua without affect. Renard has always seemed so much taller than he is, as that eight-fingered man literally looked down on him the first time he met Renard in Mechner's. But now Joshua can squarely meet Renard with his eyes, and possibility seems grander, opportunity more attainable, all in that single look, which is to say that Joshua believes in his new self more than ever.

We should target the ravine, Joshua says.

Renard looks at him quizzically for a moment, then glances around.

Have you seen Free Ray?

Not since this morning, says Joshua.

Renard puts his gaucho back on.

He is an odd man, he says. He has always been odd, but then I am not sure there is a Black man in this land that is not odd, when held to a white man's standards that is.

That's why it makes everything easier if you hold them to their own standards, Joshua says.

These reflexive words hang on Joshua's tongue like ice chips, numb him of himself with their cruelty while Renard smiles. Renard slaps his chest and runs his hands down to his stomach while he takes a deep restorative breath. Then he squints at Joshua.

The ravine? Why would we target the ravine?

For the gold.

I believe that was implied.

I mean, I think there's ample gold there. I saw men tunneling for it and pulling nuggets from a sluice they work.

Which ravine?

Joshua points toward the hill.

Can you be sure of the gold there?

Joshua thinks about that question for a moment. He knows what he saw, and he's certain about how he interpreted it. But the absoluteness in Renard's question gives him pause.

No. I suppose I can't be sure.

Renard doesn't say anything.

It's more isolated though, continues Joshua. Here in camp we're exposed, but behind the hills, near that ravine, it'd be darker there in the evening and easier to escape from.

Renard nods, scratches his hairless cheeks and chin.

And yet, he says, are you willing to kill a man having that uncertainty?

The way Renard scrutinizes his face Joshua can tell Renard's testing him.

I'd imagine there's always uncertainty in murder, Joshua says.

Renard puts a hand on Joshua's shoulder.

Yes, you are right. There is. Why, if there were certainty to any outcome, then how boring and linear the world would be.

CHAPTER EIGHT

The twins are the last to arrive back at the schooner. They find Renard, Free Ray, and Joshua sitting with their backs against the splintered wood and with their arms crossed and their hats dropped over their eyes, as they are now graced with the leisure time of thieves.

Renard tells them about the ravine, and later that afternoon they all take their horses to a copse of stunted oaks where they sit shadowed and with a clean view of it. Three miners tend the sluice in the widest part of the ravine working a triangle of productivity, the other four navigate the tunnel, looking and acting so similarly it's almost as if the tunnel is birthing miners innumerable.

The temperature is steadily dropping, but Joshua can't help his sweating, feeling the drops lingering on his forehead and running down his back. Every now and then his body shivers, and already three times since they stopped in these trees he's reached for his pistol to make sure it's still there. When he catches his hand going for it a fourth time, he mutters to himself to calm down. His stomach tightens. He hasn't eaten since morning, though it's something else entirely he feels wrenching inside him while he stares at the miners he knows are ignorant of this surveillance, miners who mine with the hardy relentlessness of men convinced of a future.

Renard leans forward, props his elbows on the pommel. He picks a finger at his teeth for a moment, scratches his cheek with his pinky nub, then looks at Free Ray with a kind of coy and vicious gesture. Free Ray nods, sets his gaucho in front of him on the saddle. He unlashes the shotgun, working the knots slowly and with diligence, as there's still a half hour or so of too much light.

The shadows of the oaks consume them slowly as the light leaves the ravine and wanders on toward the eastern hills, drawing such a distinct demarcation between fading day and coming night the five of them sit silently and witness the steady mechanisms of the earth. The miners choke their grip on the pickaxes, move their bodies closer to the ravine walls as they work to see better in the lowlight, and the twins squint and throw their heads forward, Clayton poking his over Klayton's shoulder.

Soon, Clayton leans toward Joshua and whispers, We can't see no more. Can you see them? They still there?

The chaotic sounds of the pickaxes breaking the rock become more and more phantomlike as the sun continues setting until it's as if they're hearing the miners almost without seeing them, or seeing only vague shapes of things they know to be people down there. Still, they wait. And the valley darkens. And they wait some more, a great sense of burden settling on Joshua, pressing him into his saddle and making his pistol feel unbearably heavy on his hip. What if there really is no gold? What then? He realizes suddenly that his whole life has been building to this moment, this singular act that has already culminated in his mind and is waiting for his body to catch up to.

Finally, the voices of the miners calling done the day. No more sounds of metal breaking rock or shovels scooping at the sluice, and those vague shapes milling about the way all things do in twilight, seeming to move without cohesion or fluidity or direction, and then Renard straightens up. Free Ray puts his gaucho on and lifts the shotgun, the barrel pointing to the sky. Clayton pulls both his and Klayton's pistol out, holding one in each hand. Renard lightly kicks his horse forward. And it's all Joshua can do to keep from throwing up.

His hand gripping the pistol is clammy, the gun enormous and loose in his grip. He's sure he'll drop it once they get the horses into a run, so he sets the pistol on his saddle, wipes his hand dry on his shirt, and picks it up again, mashing his fingers so tightly around the wooden butt they begin to ache as he follows the others out of the grove.

If the miners can see them coming down the hill, falling it looks like the way the fused shadows of men on horseback tumble over the sandy ground, they give no indication of it, neither stalling nor flinching, nor making any sort of grand gesture toward escape. There's no doubt they can hear the galloping hooves, for the way sound carries between the hills it's like being underwater. Yet, still none of this gives the miners any pause, or any indication of pending danger, as sound belies distance in this valley and for all they know the riding men can be a mile off and still seem as if they are riding from the hill the miners stride toward. But the riders are on that hill, and too soon off of it, charging at the miners on horses starved and emaciated, demonic creatures, horsemen unleashed through the gates of hell.

Clayton fires first, his arms straight in front of him and alongside his brother while he shoots both pistols at once as if he's some kind of professional gunslinger, though with his poor eyesight in the faint light and even poorer aim, he misses the miners wildly. The miners panic at the gunshots. They flock east toward the hills, away from the light, darkness their only savior. In truth, their only option is east, as turning back into the ravine means certain death. They run initially with their pickaxes pumping beside them before sense takes hold and they let go their tools to run faster. Twilight deafened by the gun blasts, the lit powder erupting in vivid, discordant bursts.

Joshua's Morgan comes abreast Renard's horse just as Renard clenches his saddle with his thighs, steadying himself while he fires. A miner falls to his knees, rolls across the dirt before he pushes himself up with one arm and takes off running again behind the others, gripping his shoulder. Before the miner gets very far, Renard fires two more shots, one of which strikes him in the back, and the miner collapses onto his stomach like a static shadow. Renard rides past him, shoots down two more miners with three shots, drops his cylinder to load another, rides upon a fourth miner and empties that cylinder into him.

The remaining three miners split. One turns toward the hill the riders came in from, the other two turn back to the ravine and into the rampage, evidently lost and confused by the panic. Free Ray tacks his horse, heads straight for the miners who flee toward the ravine, almost as if those three are striving to meet each other.

Then Free Ray halts his horse, raises the shotgun, and squeezes both triggers to send one miner off his feet onto the ground several feet back the way he came, a hole nearly blown through his chest. Free Ray jumps from his saddle, takes the pistol in his hand, shoots the second miner in the throat from a distance of thirty yards, a shot he can't possibly have seen well enough to aim for. The miner falls to his knees, scrabbles at the bullet hole with blood-drenched hands like he can plug it, then comes to rest face down in the dirt.

Clayton, who emptied both pistols without consequence, yells to Klayton to stop the horse. He rips the rifle from its scabbard, throws himself down, and scurries after the single, living miner, his steps awkward and jolty as he grips the rifle with both hands. The wind hustles between the hills, and it nearly takes Clayton's hat off as he runs. But Joshua has the jump on him.

He rears the Morgan around and stampedes the miner, feels the miner's body tumbling underneath the horse's hooves for no more than a second until the man lurches out behind the horse.

Goddamn! shouts Klayton still aways off. You done flattened him!

Joshua turns the Morgan, walks the horse up to the miner. His Morgan chuffs wild gray breath into the chilled air. The miner crawls his gnarled and jellied legs forward with one arm. The ligaments in one knee have been obliterated, Joshua notices. On the other leg, his femur quietly works through his skin, inching its way out further and further with each crawling motion like a giant worm. The miner cries and moans an awful pain. When he reaches the Morgan's legs, he stops moving and begins pleading: to God; to Jesus; to the towheaded man who looks so much like a boy sitting that horse and watching him gape-eyed and with an open mouth.

And it's then, while Joshua stares down at the miner, that he realizes he's pissed himself. He's so angry that his vision goes black for a moment.

When Joshua can see again, Renard and Free Ray are beside him. Renard is speaking to him, but Joshua doesn't hear the words. He just watches the man he trampled. Clayton runs toward them with his rifle aimed at the man, but Renard calls Clayton off, and it's like the darkness that settled across Joshua's eyes and in his ears fully clears, the scene suddenly made lucid again.

It is his kill, says Renard. He has earned it.

God…damn, Clayton pants. You rode right over him. Like a…like a…shit I'm tired.

Renard and Free Ray both watch Joshua. They might be smiling at him, Joshua can't be sure now that it's night.

Go on, says Renard. We should be leaving soon.

Joshua shifts in his saddle to feel how wet his trousers are. But knowing won't change what's happened or alleviate his shame, and it's too dark anyway to distinguish wet trousers from dry trousers, so he reaches for his pistol, only to realize he's still holding it, and he dismounts, minding his gimp foot so as not to stumble. He tells himself these wet trousers are simply a reaction, something he has no control over, and that his actions now, deliberate and protracted as they are, these are the actions that define him.

He stands over the wounded miner for what feels like hours though can be no more than several seconds, his own breath plumed in front of him, a soldier poised at the end of an epic battle, except that there's nothing epic about this slaughter. The miner wails into the dirt, as if any mercy can be found in that dusty, indifferent ground, and he rolls around in agony with one hand across his eyes, hiding whatever evil looms over him because he, like all of us, knows too well that seeing is believing.

Joshua bends down. He tugs the gold-filled satchel off the miner's shoulder with no little force, causing a howl of fresh pain from the man that disturbs Joshua initially. But the rich weight of the satchel when he slings it over his own shoulder crushes that disturbance, opens the sinkhole that allows his body to flush with jubilant rage. Holding the satchel back with one arm, Joshua clamps his gimp foot down on the miner's shoulder. Steadies the miner. Bends down again. Touches the pistol's barrel to the miner's chest, thinks better of it, pulls the barrel a few inches away to mitigate the splatter.

The miner cries louder. Joshua lets himself absorb that agony, and when the miner runs out of breath, Joshua is still waiting, as if he expects something darker at the apex of this silence, something more complete that will carry him beyond himself and beyond this moment into a place where action is footless and nimble, unfelt. But the moment passes through the both of them, and they emerge on the other side feeling the same ground, breathing the same air, smelling the same smell, which is tender really, like talcum powder, before the miner starts to howl again.

This time, Joshua doesn't wait. He fires.

CHAPTER NINE

The land is nothing with no moon, like they ride through a dead man's dream, the air so cold as they move through it at a pace they haven't ridden in months. This is what Joshua sees: the miner's hair in his fist; dead-fish eyes rolled skyward; Free Ray handing Joshua his Bowie knife; the knife at the miner's scalp, across it; the hair still in his hand; a head like no head at all; blood dripping on his boots; blood on the knife, blood on his hand; the seven leather satchels, so heavy with gold it's like the bags bear the sins of that raid; three other miners scalped; three other miners scalped.

People will believe the savages raided them.

Renard said that, and he's right, though in truth the Nisenans haven't taken one scalp since an emigrant arrived in California. Regardless, the five of them yipped with a cackling ferocity as they rode away. Like the savages they pretend to be. Like the savages they are. In the distance behind them, they hear the scattered hails of discovery, and what a scene those men will stumble onto, tragic in the dark, horrific come dawn. The five of them ride on into the night with time lost on them, a proud and ceremonial return, trashing the scalps somewhere while crossing bodies of water they crossed before and traveling roads that likely still wear the prints of their earlier journey.

When they arrive at their camp, they skirt it and climb into the hills. Branches invisible in this dark scratch their bodies and faces, and Joshua strains his eyes to see something, anything, to remind him that he's the one who did the scalping, not the other way around. He understands now the helplessness of life, which makes his own that much more nebulous to him. They climb for half a mile, wending a course while the horses sweat and breathe hunger, thirst, exhaustion.

Yesterday, Free Ray hid their schooner in these hills amongst a handcrafted fort of pine, cedar, and oak branches, so they search for the schooner now. He marked the path to the fort with a small rock cairn, or that's what Renard says Free Ray told him. Free Ray leans out of his saddle and scans the landscape. It's so difficult to see. It's so dark. And after all, he hid the wagon during the day, when the land is of a shape and of a quality so different than at night it's unimaginable.

A long while later, Free Ray finds the cairn. They exit the trail, soon are at the schooner. Renard stashes the gold in the wagon bed and burns the empty satchels. The others crowd around the fire for warmth.

It is a shame, Renard says. A leather satchel is a commodity of many uses.

He watches the satchels in the flames.

Then he adds, When not stripped off a murdered man's arm.

The twins retrieve the gold from the wagon and bring it to the fire, where they separate the nuggets into piles by size. They all gaze upon their bounty. That flame-lit gold appears luminous and otherworldly before Joshua's eyes. No amount of imagination could've prepared him for such a sight, and he knows now he'll rob and scalp a hundred more men for such riches. He knows now this is the man life has chosen for him to be, the man he's chosen to be in life.

A little while after that, they sit on the ground beside the fire while the twins rehash the robbery and killings in storytelling voices, using props and cinematic gestures, each one alternating the part of murderer and murdered as the story progresses. The others view this spectacle with much interest and concentration, almost as if what happened did so on some distant day in some distant territory entirely unrelated to them. And then it's early morning. The sun has yet to rise, but none of them have slept.

At dawn, Renard and Free Ray gather up the gold in an empty flour sack and set out into the hills to bury it. They return a few hours later, finding the twins sleeping on their stomachs near the fire's ashes and Joshua chewing a stalk of dried grass. Joshua is still wearing his pistol.

You should eat something, says Renard.

I'm not hungry.

Your body often knows what your mind does not. Here.

Renard hands Joshua a bowl of cooked beans that are two days old and one of the avocados they stole from a migrant's camp. Joshua sets the food on the ground beside him.

You look too thin, says Renard

Joshua glances himself over, nods.

We all look too thin, he says. I'll eat it after a bit.

Free Ray walks over to Joshua with a canteen and hands it to him. The water is cold, and only after he takes a drink does he realize how thirsty he is.

The twins are lying shoulder to shoulder, their faces turned in the same direction with the sunlight on them. Renard steps over the twins with one big stride, toes the fire's ashes to see if there's any trace of the leather satchels. There isn't. How fast that leather burned, the flames shriveling it up to nothing but particles—of ash; of dust; of the sediment of rock to be formed thousands of years from now, and in time that is the fate of all things once living.

Renard reaches a hand toward Free Ray, catches the canteen Free Ray tosses him.

You handled yourself well last night, Renard says.

Joshua looks at him.

Had you ever scalped a man before?

Not before, says Joshua.

Usually it takes some practice, some getting used to. You either cut too deeply and hang the blade on the bone or you cut too shallowly, slip the blade and wind up taking part of your own hand.

Renard wiggles his four-fingers in the air for Joshua to see what the consequence can be.

He says, But to neither of those incidents you fell prey. That is the doctor in you, I suppose.

Joshua clinically examines his own hands. Though he scrubbed them in a bucket of water when they returned to the wagon, there's still some dried blood in his fingernails and along his cuticles, tiny bits of those men carried away from their bodies and repossessed. He spits into his palms and rubs out his fingernails. It does no good.

Renard gracefully steps back over the twins and sits down, and it seems to Joshua there's never any age or grievance to Renard's movements.

It was a thing of beauty to watch, says Renard. Truly a thing of beauty.

Renard pats Joshua's thigh while he smiles.

Now you should eat, he says. Those beans will not last another day, and your body needs the food, lest you make yourself ill before another excursion.

Renard takes another drink from the canteen, then hands it back to Free Ray.

Joshua eats the avocado, then the beans with his fingers, picking each out one at a time and chewing it meticulously, the way he might chew his very last meal on this earth, but there's no savoring to his method of eating, and he feels no abatement of hunger, as he felt no hunger in the first place. The beans are flaky, the taste nearly dried out of them. He eats them while he watches the twins sleep, setting the empty bowl back on the ground beside him when he's finished

Birds call in the trees around him. He can't see them, only hear them, and he doesn't know what kind they are, but he recognizes their sounds, which means he's been in California a good while now, which means how dull and redundant the life of an animal must be when compared to that of a man's.

CHAPTER TEN

Days on horseback follow. Nights of murder, nights of theft. They pay the blacksmith in camp to reshoe their horses, reinforce the schooner's iron tires. They become transients, scattered about the hills surrounding the digger camp with the schooner they move many times over and the buried gold stash they continue to augment. None of them knows how rich they really are. Beyond measure, it's assumed, so of course they must keep stealing, they must keep on their marauding, as there's no measure to wealth that is enough.

That is what they tell themselves, aloud around campfires that burn knapsacks and duffel bags and old rags of shirts and wooden crates and saddle bags and felt hats with the brims bowled by rope and all manner of hides folded up and woven baskets and doctors' bags and trunks and more leather satchels, all items they steal to carry the stolen gold.

Each excursion yields them more and more gold, some excursions more lucrative than others. Afterward, the scalps they've taken long chucked to the dirt to be scavenged by lesser predators, Renard and Free Ray take the gold and bury it where they buried the initial bounty over a month ago.

How many men has Joshua killed now? How many men has he scalped? Not enough. Never enough. That is the insatiable power of greed. Blind to numbers, blind to consequence. Like a virus.

The tenor in the territory has turned. In Monterey on October 13, a little more than a month ago, delegates approved a state constitution, and so a new wind sweeps through the vales and hills to bring with it a new era and usher in a new weather. While there's no such thing as winter here in the manifestation Joshua is used to from Missouri, the temperature is cooler and wetter now, and the body so acclimates to weather that, having lost the heat, he now wraps himself in the coats of dead men while he sleeps. And he sleeps the deep and restful sleep of the contented.

Joshua dreams stories he hears of the Nisenans being attacked, of their camps raided, of cedar-planked teepees razed. The public reaction to their party's plunder has happened in the way Renard said it would. At first, the miners sought retribution for these aberrational killings by capturing and hanging select young Indian men, but as the killings continued, as the miners' consternation grew and the hostility that spilled out of their fear boiled over, they gave up these legalistic killings and turned to slaughtering the Indians not already dying from the cholera or smallpox. And, in it all, in the theft and the murder and the vengeance and the sickness, lies the whole history of expansion in this country, Joshua realizes, for what is history but a confluence of stories recounting death and treasure.

One chilly, gray late-November morning, Joshua wakes long after the others have breakfasted. He doesn't know he slept through their rummaging, but nevertheless he feels refreshed, anew in body and spirit. He walks over to the fire wearing a fancy wool coat he took from a dead Scotsman whose face he can no longer picture, lifts the pot of coffee from the embers and fills his tin cup.

We will target the road to the fort again, Renard says walking up to him.

Renard holds his gaucho in one hand, a crow's feather in the other. Joshua blows on his coffee, sips its bitterness. He looks at the crow's feather, which Renard is twirling between his fingers.

This feather was lying on top of my chest when I woke.

Renard studies the feather some more.

Are you a superstitious man? Renard asks.

Joshua shakes his head.

I would like to think, and have always believed, that I am not either.

Renard smooths the feather with two fingers, then tilts it so that the vane catches the opaque light and turns nearly blue before him.

But you see, he says, there was a steady breeze this morning before you woke, and even though my blanket was ruffled by that breeze, this feather did not move for as long as I lay there and watched it. I am not a superstitious man, but wonders are another thing entirely. For good or for bad.

Renard pokes the hollow shaft snug between a leather band and his gaucho's crown, then puts his gaucho on.

Drink up, he tells Joshua. We are leaving soon.

Out of the hills they ride with a contemptuous virtuosity. Late afternoon finds them past Mormon Island at the junction of the American River forks and into the pitted dirt gulley alongside Sutter's Fort Road, where they make no efforts to conceal themselves, lingering in plain sight due to sheer vanity and for the genius of it, as the miners are watching cautiously for ambushing men they think they wouldn't be able to see so clearly. They stake the horses so that they will be visible for a half mile in either direction on the road. They keep their gold pans and pickaxes lashed to their saddles, tuck the pistols inside blankets they now sit on with the yawning afternoon set to frame their tale of deception: men seeking a respite from the hardship of mining on their way to the fort.

Companies pass them in turn. The five of them pretend to be absorbed in a game of cards, or they pass around a whiskey bottle they acquired on an excursion three days prior. They know these companies carry gold, but the companies themselves are too big to target with too many variables, and they're waiting until late evening anyway, when lesser light will aid their attack.

The sky never clears. Come sunset the clouds glow with an ethereal, rosy hue.

What a beautiful sky, says Klayton.

His voice is thin and raspy like a dog's moaning. The others lean back to regard the sky.

Almost makes you feel poorly, don't it, says Klayton.

What do you mean? asks Joshua.

I mean that sky is as beautiful a sky that I ever seen, which likely means these men coming down this road are looking up and thinking the same thing. And a few of them ain't never going to see a sky like that again. It kinda puts the guilt in you, that's what I mean.

They might could see it when they get to Heaven, says Clayton. Or they might could see something even more beautiful up there.

Shit, says Klayton dismissively. Ain't no man who ever set foot in this valley is going to Heaven. Heaven's gates have been locked shut to our hearts.

That don't make any sense, says Clayton.

About the hearts?

About the gates.

Joshua used to live with a preacher, Renard says. Perhaps he could tell you whether there are gates or not.

Klayton narrows his eyes and snorts bull-like.

That true? he asks.

I don't know anything about any gates, says Joshua.

No, says Klayton. That true about the preacher? That you used to live with one?

Joshua glances at Renard, then looks back at Klayton.

I wouldn't say I lived with him. I stayed with a preacher for a bit, yeah, but only to share a room. For the economics of it. There wasn't anything more to it than that.

Sounds like living to me, says Clayton. Seems like you a man of two minds then. A preacher and a doctor.

Like I said, I wouldn't know anything about any gates, says Joshua.

He stands and walks over to his Morgan. He strokes the horse's mane and ignores the others, whose eyes he can feel fixed on his back.

I had a mind to become a preacher once, Klayton says. Thought I heard the voice in my heart. But I can't read. Ain't no kinda preacher can preach a scripture he hisself can't read.

No one else speaks for a moment, perhaps as taken aback by Klayton's revelation as he is. The silence discomforts Klayton.

That was a long time ago, he says. How much longer you figure we going to be waiting?

Why? asks Renard.

I got to piss is why. And I don't want to be pissing when the shooting starts.

I am not going to direct you when and when not to piss.

I'm pissing then, says Klayton.

He trudges behind a bush. Clayton waits a minute, giggling to himself, before he yells: Klayton! A target's coming!

There's a lot of rustling in the bush before Klayton throws himself out of it like a man who's been lost for days, hopping over to the others while hitching his trousers up, one leg wet with piss.

Where?

He scans the road, but Clayton is already rolling on his back in laughter.

✳

AFTER ANOTHER HOUR of waiting, a single schooner driven
by two men comes into view. Free Ray stands and walks over to his
horse where he's hidden the shotgun, and the others understand
what's coming.

They mount their horses, pistols in hand, and bring them onto
the road. If the men driving the schooner even had a mind to turn
around and flee, it's impossible now. The horses are brought to a
gallop and a wall of dust mounts behind those five thick with the
impregnability of chance as the approaching schooner lurches to a
halt, the drivers frantically throwing their bodies around and yelling
words incoherent to the charging band and reaching for something,
guns most likely. The five of them are already firing, the shots blowing splinters from the schooner and sucking the legs up from one of
the oxen. The animal collapses, and the schooner lilts to that side.

The drivers aren't yet harmed. They have their backs to the band,
flail their arms as the band nears and as the obscure figures gain clarity in the closing distance until, suddenly, the drivers turn around.
They hold shotguns in their hands, and behind them the bodies of
four more men rise through holes in the bonnet like reptiles hatch-
ing through rubbery eggs.

Shit! Joshua yells.

He whips the neck of his Morgan so far to the left he thinks he
might break it.

A barrage of shot whistles past him. Renard's horse stumbles but
rights itself, and Klayton tacks the twins' horse toward the gulley
just as Clayton yelps in pain and slumps limply against his brother's
back.

Clayton! Klayton yells. Clayton!

But he can barely hear himself amidst the noise.

The five of them are split. The twins and Joshua on one side of the road, Free Ray and Renard on the other. The men in the schooner fire without pause, fire like they plan to gun down those riders and then gun down the souls that might escape from those riders' dying bodies. The horsemen charge past the schooner through rancid gunsmoke, their ears deafened by the blasts, and the firing stalls for a moment, then commences again at their backs, though the sound is lighter, like there are fewer guns now. None of the riders look back, the night so heavy on them like a curse.

Back at camp Free Ray builds a fire. Klayton sobs and mumbles incoherent prayers while his brother lies unconscious. Using a torch for light that Klayton holds, Joshua strips off Clayton's sticky shirt to examine the wound, though his movements, as determined and hurried as they were initially, slow now as he takes in Clayton's half-nakedness.

While Clayton's face and arms are browned by weeks in the sun and grimy with dirt, his chest and belly are remarkably clean, the skin smooth and grotesquely pale now that his body is purging blood, a thick clump of dark chest hair reaching from shoulder to shoulder and crunchy when Joshua digs through it to find the bullet hole. Joshua can see the last two ribs reveal themselves each time Clayton exhales.

What do you see? Klayton asks.

He's shot beneath the collarbone, Joshua says.

What's a collarbone?

Without answering, Joshua prods at the bullet hole again, the blood warming his cold hand. He removes bits of cloth and silk from the wound while he searches for the shot, pokes at Clayton's collarbone and shoulder blade to see if anything's broken, then lifts Clayton's arm and rotates it in small circles as gently as he can. His shoulder still works.

He digs a scalpel out from his medical bag, splashes it with whiskey, then cuts open the wound, using hemostat pliers to extract the debris his fingers can't reach or adequately grip. Then he rolls Clayton toward himself, holds Clayton up on his unwounded side with one hand while he instructs Klayton to hold the torch as close to Clayton's back as he can without burning Clayton or himself. He inspects the wound from the back.

He's got a hole here, Joshua says finally. I don't see any lead, so the shot must've passed through.

He lowers Clayton back onto the ground.

By chance alone, Joshua adds.

Klayton hovers over Joshua with his one empty hand frantic and twitchy and miming every deliberation Joshua makes, his face contorted from so much sadness. Joshua doesn't want to listen to Klayton crying anymore, so he removes Clayton's blood-covered trousers and shoves the man's clothes at his brother.

Give me some room to work, he tells him.

Klayton hands Free Ray the torch, walks over, and throws the clothes into the fire. Then he strips off his own blood-stained shirt and trousers, burns them too, as if wearing your own blood and that of your brother's portends some inevitable and painful culmination. He stands beside the fire in only his union suit, hugging himself and watching Joshua, wiping his eyes and nose with his dirty sleeve every now and then.

He gonna be all right? Klayton calls out after a while.

Joshua doesn't look up and doesn't respond. He's pouring a thin stream of whiskey into Clayton's wound, watching to be sure it runs all the way through it and out his back.

He gonna be all right, ain't he? It ain't that bad?

He's been shot, says Joshua washing his hands with the whiskey. That's always bad.

This truth seems to momentarily break Klayton. He gags as if he's about to vomit and turns toward the fire, the flames angry and exposing the dirt that layers his face.

Renard removes his gaucho and stares at the crow's feather. Joshua can't fathom how that feather didn't blow off Renard's hat as they fled. And judging by Renard's expression, neither can he. Renard pulls the feather out of his hat slowly, as if he expects it to be a much more difficult task than it is, then wonders at the feather a few seconds more, wonders at the unearthly power it contains that no one can decipher though that which he despises any want of knowing, before he breaks it in half and drops the pieces fluttering to the ground.

That had nothing to do with this, says Joshua.

He's balled one of his own shirts and now pressures Clayton's wound with it to try and slow the bleeding.

Maybe, says Renard. Maybe not.

Renard tucks in the tails of his shirt that have come out, hikes up his trousers, and readjusts his coat. He smooths his ponytail, dusts off his ever-smooth face.

If you want to do something that matters, says Joshua, you can hold this shirt for a bit.

Renard looks at the wound. It's pitted and horrible in the torchlight. He leans to inspect Clayton's face as if gauging what amount of good his help will or won't do. He shakes his head.

By chance alone, he says. Was that not how you described it?

Joshua scoffs. He removes the shirt from the wound, wrings the blood out of it onto the dirt, puts the shirt back into place.

We may choose what lives we lead, says Renard. But those lives are merely composites of the many moments we spend running from chance.

So none of this does any good, says Joshua. My medical knowledge. My training. All of it for naught in the end. That's what you're saying.

It has nothing to do with good or not good. Death is simply a matter of when. And all of this, all of what you are doing, only delays that.

CHAPTER ELEVEN

Clayton remains unconscious for two days, but he refuses to die. He has more life in him than Joshua initially thought. Even Renard remarked about the strength of this short man.

There was a time that I would have thought him susceptible to a bad look, Renard said.

Each day Joshua cleans the gunshot with water and treats it with camphor he found in the medical bag of a doctor they murdered, then he patches it with rags of shirts. Klayton sits beside his brother as long as the sun is up, holding Clayton's hand and speaking to him quietly about nothing in particular. He says that he wants to keep his voice in his brother's ears, though Joshua notices that Klayton refuses to look at Clayton's face while he talks. He'll look at his brother's hand, or chest, or legs, or at the familiar land around them, but not his face, as if Clayton's so-pale face frightens him, as if looking at it will in some way give that edging death credence and thus offer Clayton to the afterworld in an act relinquishment.

Rain falls hard and fast the day Clayton finally sees fit to open his eyes. Klayton and Joshua had gathered the remaining sacks of rice and flour, piled them at the head of the schooner, and carried Clayton into the bed, so that when Clayton does open his eyes mid-morning, all he can see is the sterile canvas, and perhaps he thinks for a moment, with that blankness above him and the rain hammering the bonnet in an unsoothing manner, that he's dead. Clayton tries to sit up, but his body won't have it, like it isn't his body at all. He moans, but the rain talks over him as the earth doesn't care one bit about his pain. His arm is slinged by an old blood-stained shirt. He twists his head to the side, which is all the movement he can summon, and he examines the sling peripherally. Then he straightens his head and lies there, the day and the time unknown to him, and likely he's trying to recall the events preceding this injury when someone climbs into the bed and Klayton appears over him drenched by the rain with a look that is at once shock and euphoria.

Klayton doesn't say anything. For a moment, he doesn't even flinch. Then he sits down, takes his brother's hand, and begins crying. The two of them don't speak, as what passes between them is stronger than words.

Joshua, Renard, and Free Ray are huddled underneath a massive pine, their coat collars turned up to the rain, shoulders slumped forward, their heads bowed to keep the water from their faces, the way they might appear at a funeral. They all hold steaming cups of coffee inside their coats, and they wait for word from Klayton about the status of his brother. After a while and Klayton not returning, Renard taps Joshua in the leg with his boot and tells him to check on the twins.

Joshua hands Renard his cup, pulls the ends of his coat together with one hand, and hobbles over to the wagon. The ground, desiccated and dusty for weeks, has transformed to mud entirely, thick and soupy, and his gimp foot proves close to useless for balance.

I'll be goddamned, Joshua says once he reaches the schooner and sees Clayton awake and the twins holding hands.

He doesn't bother climbing inside. There's no room for him anyway.

TWO WEEKS LATER, while they remain in camp to let Clayton rest and heal, they run short on food. On a day the sun rises vibrant and crisp having shed the weight of summer, Renard wanders off and comes back a little while later with some of their gold, and Joshua heads to Sutter's Fort.

Was there any trouble? asks Renard when Joshua returns the next evening carting a wooden sled piled with bags of rice and flour, a greasy pack of beef steaks, five sticks of hard candy (one for each of them), some apples, and a few medicinal powders.

No, says Joshua taking his seat around the fire with the others.

And the road? Any posted sentries or defense measures of the like?

Nothing that matters.

You see? says Renard to the others. Memory here is fleeting. Every man is too focused on getting rich.

I don't believe that, says Joshua.

What is that you do not believe?

That every man here only wants to get rich. That isn't true.

Renard laughs.

Of course it is, he says mockingly. When a man opens his eyes, he searches for gold. When he closes them, he sees gold.

They ratified a state constitution, says Joshua.

They did what? asks Klayton.

I heard it at the fort.

When's it gonna happen?

I don't know, says Joshua. Soon I guess, now that there's going to be a governor and all. I don't imagine they would write a constitution and then sit on it.

Statehood don't matter as far as I'm concerned, says Klayton. There's still gonna be gold and men to take it from.

Joshua shakes his head.

There's too much law in a state, he says.

Here is a man who truly understands law, Renard says pointing at Free Ray. Ask him or any other of his kind, and they will tell you what capacity law generates.

His law ain't white law, says Klayton.

That may be, says Renard. But there is always law, even for white men.

I'm talking about divine law, says Klayton. It's the divine law they are violating.

Divine or otherwise, there is never such a thing as escaping law, Renard says. No matter how white your skin or how far west you travel. That is why you must live beyond it. Those men who are always fleeing law are the men who die burdened by unsatisfied lives.

Are we living beyond it? asks Klayton.

I believe we are, says Renard.

I figured we was. I like living beyond it. There ain't enough freedom otherwise.

Freedom to do what? asks Joshua.

Whatever it is you want, says Klayton. That's what freedom is.

That's reductive.

I ain't sure what that means.

Free Ray laughs.

Something funny about that? Klayton hisses.

Easy, Joshua says. Reductive means that you're oversimplifying things. Not every action or intent carries the same weight.

That's what I figured, says Klayton.

Every man here has as fair a chance at living as every other, says Renard. And nothing has to change.

Renard turns to Free Ray.

He says, Even you, my friend, must know that one day there will be no more territory for you and your race to escape to.

Free Ray leans back, retrieves a log, tosses it into the fire.

It already has changed, says Joshua.

Renard's face tightens.

I think last night's stay in the fort's hotel weakened you, Renard says. Remember that there is always a bed somewhere that you can take if you so choose.

The next morning, Joshua is out of their camp by first light. There's nothing else to do while they wait for Clayton to get his strength back, and digging gold, regardless of how much he does or doesn't find, is at least an action that has the potential to compound his wealth.

He creeps through the trees and brush surrounding their camp so as not to wake the others before he comes out to the trail, winds down the hill with long and heavy footfalls, everything around him stilled by dawn and the singing of birds sourceless and chaotic. The closer he comes to the bottom of the hill, the greater the sound of the miners encamped near the river. They move about with the new light casting a freshness on their faces and bodies that belie the true nature of their toil. The light hazes the camp, makes all either plumb or flat, oversimplified, and Joshua passes through it a déjà vu being and wades out into the river with the water calm and dark and he commences digging.

There is less haste in his efforts, less effort in his efforts, truth be told. He works more for the sake of working, with little concern for the outcome or the product of his own labor, and he finds catharsis in this sort of digging.

He does find gold. It doesn't amount to much, not even an ounce, but when he looks up and sees the other diggers with their faces inches from their pans and their arms working frantically in a pleading manner to wash the gravel down to pay dirt, he believes he understands more than these men. A thing greater than these men, and greater than himself. And so he stands there, like the kings of old, though by the sheer look of him he's nothing special, stands there knee-deep in the American River, the sun rising steadily to his left, an empty gold pan in his hand, a thimbleful of wet gold in his leather pouch, just barely a man but already beset by that arrogant belief that besets all men. That founded America, that opened the California Trail, that coined Manifest Destiny.

CHAPTER TWELVE

The next few days are wet ones, the mud climbing to their ankles and submerging the animals' hooves; the pines whispering while it rains, a soothing sound Joshua never gets tired of no matter how many times he hears it; the American River swelling tremendously, rushing through the valley with a ferocity previously unseen, which makes it far more difficult and dangerous to pan. The five of them do what they can to keep their powder and guns dry, though the rain falls with such consistency that by the time it stops, they have to postpone their excursion another day, have to lay their arms out on blankets to dry in the sun.

Midmorning they leave their camp, Clayton well enough to ride though not yet well enough to make use of his right arm, which he keeps in its sling while his gunshot fully heals. They head back downriver the way they went during their very first excursion. They will no longer target the fort road, an unspoken agreement.

The day is warm with the sun finally on them, like the weather itself has been waiting for their reemergence and now glorifies their vicious intentions, and they ford the American River by early after- noon, gallop until they ford the river again a little later. The miners populating the valley give their band little thought as they ride on through, offer not much more than a cursory glance in the band's direction, the cycling of new faces in and out an all-too-common occurrence.

They finally stop riding late in the day well north of Old Dry Diggings, a solid twenty-five miles from their camp. The horses are tied to a sycamore sapling, after which they sit cross-legged along the riverbank with their feet in the water to ease their blisters, sup- pering on dried meat and tortillas they packed, almost as if they are school children on a picnic.

Upriver a miner perches on a large rock near the bank and rocks a cradle, his floppy-brimmed hat tattered and sunbleached, his trou- ser legs bunched at the knees where the wool disappears into the leather of his boots as he scoops and pours the half-gallon tin dip- per. He wears a beard that drops to his clavicle and is as dense as a thicket of thorns, so dense his chin probably hasn't seen the sun in months. Beyond him a group of seven men work a sluice, all of them hatted and bearded and parading up and down the length of the device that extends for more than ten feet perpendicular the bank, some scooping auriferous gravel with half-gallon dippers and pour- ing it in at the top, others wielding pickaxes or pitchforks, walking along the length of the sluice and loosening the larger rocks and clumps of dirt to aid the flow. Beyond that group still more miners scattered and panning throughout the river, and the land heavily timbered, and skylong roll low white clouds that seem to puff from within the earth just past the horizon like those clouds are blown from magnificent internal smokestacks.

After a while, the five of them pull their feet out of the water and put their boots back on, though at no point does Joshua take his eyes off of the miners. There's something admirable in the miners' determination. Joshua thinks back about the trail these miners traveled to get to this point, where circumstance has conjured all of them to this river at this moment, and he acknowledges that determination, even values it in a weird, almost principled way. Low light cascades the river as the sun sets. The sky goes gold, then silver, and it's a wonder when you look for it: the world brimmed with the hue of those precious metals.

Free Ray leans back onto the smooth rocks, put his hands behind his head, covers his face with his gaucho even though evening is now administered.

You plan on only lying there? Clayton asks.

Free Ray doesn't move or respond.

You fucking mute, says Clayton.

Free Ray tips up his gaucho and looks at Clayton blankly for a few seconds.

I know one thing you thinking that you ain't ever got to put words to, Clayton says. You lucky there ain't no slavery here.

Klayton chuckles. Clayton adjusts his sling, then turns to Renard.

What're we waiting for?

The scattered panners have left the river, but the man rocking the cradle still digs, every now and then sifting through the finer sand along the riffle-bars. The sluice is likewise still being run, illuminated by lanterns set on the rocks alongside it. Renard glances at Free Ray, and with that unceasing stoicism the others have come to expect from him, Free Ray dons his gaucho and stands.

Let us go then, says Renard.

The five of them tie bandanas over their faces and approach the men on foot. The ground is squishy above the bank, and they line up nearly side by side until the twins skirt off to target the single man working the cradle and Renard, Free Ray, and Joshua continue toward the sluice, each holding his pistol in hand behind his back in a wanted sneak attack.

A pistol shot sings out unexpectedly.

Joshua, Renard, and Free Ray are still a good distance from the sluice, but they freeze. The miners at the sluice freeze, too, puzzled and staring at those three while the sluice still works its gravitational logic, then looking behind those three with astonishment as a flare of sparks that seems so intrusive to the coming dark accompanies the second pistol shot, which quickly follows the first one.

Joshua glances back. He sees the man at the cradle stumble into the river toward the opposite bank with one hand holding his leg, falling and righting himself frantically to stumble on. Klayton and Clayton stand on the bank, pistols aimed at the man's back like they are target shooting. They fire simultaneously, spouts of water a perimeter to the injured miner's path.

When Joshua turns back, the men at the sluice have already abandoned their own digging. Those on dry ground flee toward the hills, those in the river flee up the bank, and a volley of gunfire chases them all. The gunfire a hollowing sound that hammers their chests and all but one of the lanterns kicked over, the chimneys shattering as the flames pop to blackness, and in the end the air smokes with gunpowder and twilight bares spots of white that float across the shooters' vision. Three men lie lead-ridden in bloody piles of earth near the sluice, one stares skyward with tears in his eyes while Joshua caves his forehead with the butt of his pistol, and the single miner working the cradle, who the twins finally managed to shoot dead in the water, aimlessly drifts downriver like a log.

Where's the gold? Clayton shouts.

He's upended the cradle and sludged through the quicksilver with his one working arm. Now he stands, a silver-caked hand held above his head in consternation.

You see any, Klayton? No? We ain't finding any!

Look harder! yells Joshua.

I can't hardly see no more, but I know there ain't none here! Clayton shouts.

Joshua ignores him. At the sluice, he and the other two are having as much trouble as the twins are in locating any gold. Joshua thinks it impossible for the men they just killed to have found no gold in the course of their diggings. There has to be some gold, even if what that "some" is proves incremental.

They comb the sluice from top to bottom, first with their hands while it continues to wash the gravel until, without much fore-thought, Joshua kicks the device to topple it, then sifts through the contents that have spilled and spread across the ground in a wide and still widening swath of dirt and rock. That searching also proves useless.

As dark as it is now, Renard walks over and retrieves the one lantern still aflame. Free Ray and Joshua gather around him, their faces ducking in and out of the orb of light like curious fish in a black lake, and they scan the ground for that fortuitous glint, hunched and hobbling like three old men as they walk so slowly and with nothing of the fury that preceded this act, almost as if that fury and that murder manifested itself in beings entirely distinct from these three. They keep on in this manner well into the night, because there's nothing so disheartening as wealthless slaughter, but, like the twins, they find nothing.

Renard chucks the lantern into the dirt. The ground instanta-neously absorbs the flame. They return to their horses bearing the scalps of the men they could scalp. Cold tails in on the dark, and by the time they reenter their camp, their fingers hardly work and their lips feel thick and heavy forming words.

I can't stop shaking, says Joshua.

He sits so close to the large fire he can smell the toes of his leather boots cooking.

Perhaps there is a positive to be had in tonight's failed excursion, says Renard.

His arms are crossed at his chest and his knees brought as close to his arms as possible.

And what's that? asks Clayton.

Free Ray and I are not subjected to this cold in the woods, as there is no gold to bury.

I ain't in no mood for funny, Clayton mutters.

He spits into the fire.

It's hard to believe it's this cold after a warm day like today.

Joshua's words squeeze out of him like each one represents one less modicum of heat his body now contains.

It ain't that cold out here, says Clayton.

Yes it is, says Klayton. You ain't got to be so sore about everything simply because we didn't find any gold. It's one night is all. One excursion. There's plenty more to be had, and plenty more gold to be buried on nights as cold if not colder than this one we're suffering through.

But Klayton will be wrong about this assumption. In the weeks following, they kill more men. With their guns. With their knives. With their hands. Running men down with their horses until the men are crushed between hoof and dirt. When it rains, Joshua suffocates men in the mud or drowns them in the shallows along the banks, legs kicking for life while he smashes faces against rocks, noses and eye sockets shattering well before the men suck in enough water to flood their lungs, the men shitting themselves, their bodies singing with expelled gases and that sound triggering sensations from his childhood when he explored cadavers alongside his father and listened to the symphonies of decomposition. He sees parts of the body he's never seen outside of the stenciled illustrations in his father's medical books, runs ligament and tendon and bone through his fingertips to search for the blackness and greed that sticks to his own skeleton like resin so that he can dissect the primal capacities of this world, his own laboratory. He hears cheek bones rattle like dice in a cup and pictures the men's newly misshapen faces, their now-obstructed airways, how the brain can only handle so much impact before it too bends and warps and that which makes men men begins to disappear. He takes so many scalps even the scavengers stop feeding on them, stomachs saturated by human blood. And he and the others accrue not one more ounce of gold.

CHAPTER THIRTEEN

On a December day spitting rain and paled by a hedge of clouds, Clayton walks over to the schooner that leans now with a busted rear wheel, climbs inside the rickety bed, and emerges again with a shovel held at arm's length, the blade of it aimed skyward the way a military flag bearer carries a ceremonial flag. He's taken off his sling, and he carries the shovel with his right and previously unused arm, as if to prove some strength of character, or some ultimate conclusion he intends to convey through the strain of this effort. The ground is pure mud, and he walks slowly, rolling each foot from heel to toe to steady himself, his back straight, his head never averted from the direction he travels, neither watching the ground nor the shovel, his eyes fixed angrily on Renard, who proves to be his destination.

There burns no fire on account of the saturated wood. The others watch Clayton, sitting on wooden crates or upturned cooking pots they carted all the way from Missouri and now have no other use for. No one seems to know Clayton's intentions, least of whom his own brother, who shifts anxiously on his crate, his hands clamped underneath his butt to keep them warm and dry.

Dig it up, insists Clayton when he reaches Renard.

He drops the shovel at Renard's feet. Then he stares at the red-haired man, who watches him curiously and with an evident degree of comicality. The splattered mud ends up on Free Ray's trousers, and after it does, Klayton rips his hands out, holds them shaking in front of him like he might have to do something with them that he doesn't want to, something cataclysmic and ever-changing. When Free Ray doesn't react, when he simply wipes the mud away, Klayton shoves his hands underneath his butt again and eases slightly.

All of it, says Clayton.

And what would you have me do with it once I dig it up?

Clayton bends down and retrieves the shovel, shoving it into Renard's chest and muddying the coat Renard has buttoned up to his neck for warmth.

I ain't going on no more excursions with the chance of dying poor, says Clayton. And right now, with that gold in the ground, I ain't no richer than I was while crossing this country. Dig it up. Then we can divide shares.

Renard takes the shovel. He examines the mud stain on his coat but doesn't wipe it away. The rain will take care of it, so instead he looks at the stain more with the intent to study it, to find the answer in it, if there is such an answer, or at least to consider the consequences of this evolving dissention.

When Renard looks back up at Clayton, he smiles. There's something horrible in that smile, an inexplicable and ill-meaning something that makes Clayton wince and take a quick step back.

When the rain ceases, says Renard. Then you can take hold your share.

Over the next two days the rain continues, and it's like time stands still.

The third day, having woken to the same meteorological scene, Clayton and Klayton take their gold pans and slog down to the river. They skate the mud downhill on worn soles that do little in keeping their feet dry until they reach a bend in the trail, view a mining camp below that has so grown in population it's nearly unrecognizable to them. From where they stand, they can hardly see the ground given the number of tents sprung up. Joshua, with nothing else to do, has followed the twins without their knowing. He comes around the bend not realizing the twins have stopped, and the twins fling around with their pans held out like weapons.

You tracking us? Clayton says.

As if I've got nothing better to do than track you two, says Joshua.

Then why you following us?

I'm not following you, Joshua lies. I'm headed to the camp, and there's only one way up and down this hill.

Clayton wipes the rain from his eyes, studies Joshua.

You ain't carrying no pan, he says. So what is you planning on doing in camp?

Joshua shrugs.

All right, says Clayton. You ain't got to tell us your business. I suppose it don't matter anyhow.

When they reach the camp, they navigate the tents and head to the road near the river, where they stop in a line and survey what lies before them: men waist deep in the rushing water, ropes strung around their waists that are lashed to wooden stakes driven into the bank as they fight the racing current with their pans. The twins glance at each other, shrug, cross the road to the river, and drop their coats in a pile on the bank. They hold hands while they step into the turbulent water, dropping so suddenly to their thighs that the river nearly takes them down before they right themselves. Just a few feet from the bank, they take turns digging gravel, each using the other for leverage.

Joshua watches the twins struggle to pan, his shoulders tucked against the rain, when he feels something tug on the back of his shirt. He turns around.

Surely it has been a good many days since I've last seen you down here at the old American, an old man says.

The man, who goes by the name Surely, has a beard blackened by shoe polish that hangs to his stomach, wears a bicorn hat with a musket-ball hole in the front (a relic from the days the Spanish still laid claim to this valley), and he is smiling all gums.

Joshua glances back at the twins. They're still panning, still sharing their fate.

I haven't been around this camp lately, he says.

The old man nods.

Your compañeros, the old man says pointing to the twins.

Joshua nods.

The old man peels his lips back with his dirty fingers, prods one of the sores in his mouth, examines the blood before he wipes his finger on his sleeve.

It'll be quite soon, Surely says. The Lady tells me so, though surely I would welcome death much sooner. A true wonder of God's creation, The Lady is. An even mightier wonder amongst this man-racked landscape. We should all be so fortunate as to be graced with such prescience as The Lady.

The old man looks into Joshua's eyes like in that vibrant blue is printed the future, which, if the old man can make sense of it, will give new and transcendent meaning to the so-ephemeral life upon which he himself can only speculate.

Joshua doesn't respond.

The old man smiles again, turns on his heel with the kind of grace and fluidity he could've only learned in some long past and now archaic military service, and leaves Joshua, wobbling a few paces down the road before he stops another man, begins again his lip-service to The Lady.

Small and rustic, The Lady's cabin is beshackled by charred

pine-plank walls. The mystic flag cut from bonnet canvas that marks her establishment and bears that all-seeing eye hangs damp and wrapped around its knobby-branch mast even though the rain has finally stopped. In front of her white-painted door, a line of grimy and fidgeting men wait with a patience so uncommon in the valley, all yearning for a window into their own futures.

Joshua told himself he'd visit The Lady purely out of curiosity, but standing in line it begins to occur to him how silly this is. He starts to walk away, but when another man steps into the line to take his vacated place, and Joshua sees yet another man coming not far off, he finds himself jumping back into line to assure his place before that second man can move in front of him.

Nearly an hour of waiting in that line. No one speaks to the others around him, out of some foregone conclusion perhaps, like they believe the accuracy of The Lady's reading will be jinxed by speech, or perhaps their reticence is due to a shared sense of hostility. If everyone in this line seeks fortune and seeks The Lady to confirm a tangible path to that fortune, then certainly some of them are bound to walk away with bad news, and so each silently wishes that misfortune upon his neighbor. So many neighbors. They all smell churned, a mix of sweat and the river, and they wear desperation on their faces the way other men wear glasses, which sickens Joshua. These men are weak. These men are not him.

Just outside the door now, Joshua hesitates again. How much that doctor-father of his would scoff at the idea of a fortuneteller, a thought that makes him chuckle, because of all that his life has become, this is the thought that gives his conscience pause. So, he thinks while he enters The Lady's shack, this is my morality.

Inside it is so dark that Joshua stands for a few seconds in the single room to let his eyes adjust. His nose stings from the sharp smell of burning pine, the air stale and thick with too much vacated human breath. A gruff, over-smoked voice beckons from nearby.

Come closer, come closer.

Joshua sticks his hand out and shuffles his feet forward like a newly blinded man, trying to feel his way to wherever The Lady (he presumes it's The Lady who's spoken to him) is. But nothing guides him. Not the voice. Not his own eyesight.

He stops again, waits. Slowly the room gathers shape, the darkness settling in shadows along the corners and a low wooden table holding a stack of large cards revealed just a few feet away. He sits down in the wooden chair across from The Lady, realizes only then how short she is, for sitting he is still a whole head and shoulders taller. She can't be much more than four feet tall. Her scarecrow hair swallows her thin face, which is pale and younger looking than her voice suggests, and she purses her lips while she deftly shuffles the cards without looking at him. Joshua can feel the thin wind sleeking across his arms while she shuffles.

You not like me, she says.

She has a heavy accent Joshua hasn't heard before, the words themselves rough and dense when she forms them, as if each one takes her a lot of effort. He's unsure what her statement might mean and how he should answer it, so he says the only thing he can think of.

No.

When he realizes how ambiguous his response is, he clarifies: I mean, I don't know you.

The Lady nods, her hair bouncing.

You not trust me, she says.

I don't know you, Joshua repeats.

His voice sounds like he can't even convince himself of his answer. He clears his throat, looks away from her.

In each corner of the cabin, a dead rooster hangs by its feet from the rafters, blood having stained the bird's ruddy and matted hackles, the wattles and beaks cut off, and a string of red beads shaped around the necks and up to the combs of the birds and then catenaried across the walls. There's no light save for what sneaks through the structure's loosely fitted planks, and even that light is a deep gray, the cabin itself a kaleidoscope that seems to absorb all brightness and reflect only darkness, as if darkness is the one true color, the world at its lifeless origins.

Here, The Lady says. Touch one.

She points at three stacks of cards with her head still down, the backs of the cards showing. Joshua places his hand on the middle deck. She pushes the other two decks to the side, picks up the deck he pointed at, and flips the top five cards face up in a row. The rest of the deck she sets with the other discarded cards.

She studies the row, first with her face so close to the table her broad boxer's nose brushes the wood, and then with her hands, though the cards, as far as Joshua can tell, are all the same. She makes short, grunting noises in the manner of a pig while she examines them with such deliberateness and calculation Joshua begins to think this reaction is intended to assure him that his fortune will be told with clarity and understanding.

He waits. He waits some more. He grows ever more uncomfortable with her silence and the dense air that's beginning to make him sweat.

Finally, The Lady lifts her head from the table and looks him directly in the eyes. Her own eyes are so wide and empty they shimmer in the lightless cabin, and Joshua wonders if those eyes can truly see innumerable signs, like they've been crafted out of some precious stone for her and her alone in all creation. And here, in this valley, on this day, their destinies converging with the clarity and certainty that fate had always dictated, The Lady can unearth tomorrow for Joshua, riddle his future with hope and fortune to finally and always strip him of his beleaguered past.

I see but only little, The Lady croaks.

And whatever believability engendered itself in Joshua vanishes.

The sun rising on the world so that everything mystical and mysterious is suddenly made real again, made mundane by the force of logic and enumeration.

Joshua leans back in his chair, finds himself stifling hostile laughter. I see...

The Lady pauses. She throws her head to the table again for a few seconds before she lifts it and continues.

My sight. It cloudy. Cloudy like the morning. But I see waves of water, something, a bright shiny beneath.

Joshua stands. He can't bring himself to listen any longer. But when he turns and starts for the door, The Lady shouts, You! Pay!

Joshua glares back at her for a moment. She holds her hand outstretched with her palm up, those hugely empty eyes discovering their own tangibility and hawking him. How easily he could break her neck, or smash her head with the chair, violence so often the path to reprisal now these thoughts are effortlessly conjured. Instead, he reaches into the pocket of his trousers and pulls out a one-dollar gold coin he acquired at Sutter's Fort. Too much exertion would be spent enacting her death anyway, he thinks.

The Lady takes the coin brusquely, puts it between her bulbous and wrinkly breasts, then begins scooping up the cards with one hand while waving Joshua out of her shack with the other.

Into the self-same world he goes again. Past that line of men who seek knowing where knowing isn't to be found, for this is a false world governed by a false commodity. Afternoon will come as dull and colorless as dawn, but before it does Joshua stands on the road half-watching the twins pan while his mind inadvertently wanders over thoughts of his past he forces himself not to acknowledge.

Not long standing there, he sees the twins surrender their efforts and head for the bank, still holding hands for balance as they move with the same gait, the same uncertainties, the same everything. They come nearer the bank each the other's reflection until Klayton stops, lets go of Clayton's hand, plunges his head and shoulders into the cold water. His hat dislodges from his submerged head and floats downriver. Klayton stays under for time enough that Clayton begins to yank on his brother's arm, then Klayton stays under a bit more so that Joshua approaches the river, wondering if he will actually come back up.

He does finally, whipping back his drenched head, huffing breath and shivering and holding in his fist a gold nugget that consumes his hand.

Goddamn! exclaims Clayton almost falling chest first into the water as he lunges toward Klayton's hand for the gold.

Klayton rips the nugget away. He turns his back to his brother and stares at the nugget in disbelief.

Let me see! Let me see it! pleads Clayton.

He tugs at his brother's arm, but Klayton resists him. Clayton slaps his brother on the back of the head. Klayton whirls his head around.

I found it, he hisses wiping the wet hair off his face. I'll show it to you when I see fit to show it to you.

Klayton pushes his brother hard with his other hand, which sends Clayton sinking into the water up to his chest. Clayton scrambles around like a drowning man until he gets his legs underneath him and stands stiff-bodied against the current and panting. A jagged rock bigger than Clayton's hand drips opaque water between his fingers. Klayton doesn't see this rock. He's still staring at the gold he miraculously stumbled upon, is pondering everything but the one thing he should be: the tragic designs that riches weave.

Clayton sets one foot behind himself for balance. He rears the rock as high as he can. He smashes it down into the back of his brother's head.

The sound of Klayton's skull shattering horrifies Joshua, shakes the other men who stopped and congregated when the commotion between the twins began. It's a dull, unechoing sound, one that momentarily curbs all aftermath in its signifying finality. Klayton's entire body goes limp. The nugget drops and tumbles in that river to be found again on another day while Klayton sinks straight down at the waist like he's being tugged under. He bobs up several feet away on his stomach, his head hemorrhaging, the blood shaping his hair to the unshapened bone, his body twirling in the current like a discarded sack of clothes.

Someone goes after Klayton's body. A man who tears off his boots and clothes, who fights the current with a leviathan's strength to drag Klayton to the bank. He lies Klayton on his back, the California tan already stripping from Klayton's flesh. Couple that with the way Klayton's limbs and head flop like there's no bone, and Joshua knows it means there's no possibility of life in him. He can only watch. As can Clayton, who seems stuck in place and in time by what he's done, so much emotion evidently coursing through him while he watched his brother float downstream that each feeling canceled the others out so that he appears utterly emotionless now, and his mind has simply stopped working.

Once the swimmer steps away from Klayton's body, Clayton shifts his unthinking gaze to the rock, which he still holds in his hand. He gazes at it like it has its own agency, remaining in that pose for nearly a minute before three lanky men remove their coats and wade into the river and snatch Clayton by the neck and arms.

Clayton drops the rock when the men grab him. The moment he does his mind reinitiates. He howls with so much anguish Joshua knows he will never again hear such a sound in his lifetime.

The tears consume Clayton's face like the breaking of a magnificent dam, and he flails his arms and legs all the way to the bank, trying to free himself from those men. Not because he fears the consequence of others, but because the only adequate reparation of this act would be death by his own hand.

The men drag him over the rocks and onto the bank, pin him on his back in the dirt. Clayton goes still, his sorrow overwhelming him so completely he too falls limp, just drains his eyes while he chokes on his own spit. Other than the sounds of Clayton's crying and choking, and given how ominously Clayton's own horizontal posture mirrors his brother's, it's nearly impossible for Joshua to distinguish the dead Klayton from the living Clayton, and perhaps that's what Clayton wishes for more than anything in the world right now.

A circle of onlookers has formed around Klayton. There's murmuring, confusion. The men shift their eyes from Klayton to Clayton with bemused expressions, scratching their beards like they're seeing the then and now in a single, time-smashed instant. Someone bends down and puts his ear to Klayton's mouth, moving it closer and closer until his lobe nearly wicks bluing lips. The man jumps up, shivers like a cold brushes him, and another man bends down, also puts his ear just above Klayton's mouth only to affirm what the first man believed, what all of them knew to be true from the moment the swimmer retrieved his body from the river.

Joshua slowly approaches the circle, pushes his way through so he can see. The urge to save Klayton, to fulfill some sort of doctorly-duty hasn't occurred to him, and he ponders that now, standing over Klayton for a minute and looking down at him with such detachment and stoicism it's like he doesn't know this man, and, in truth, he feels at this moment like he doesn't, since the dead man lying on the ground resembles nothing of the man he did know.

When Joshua turns back, Clayton is already bound at the wrists and ankles with rope and brought to his feet. Men are shouting in unison, Take him to Old Dry Diggings! Many wave their gold pans in the air like this is a valley full of judges all set to bring down the ordered and democratized gavel of justice. January of this year it was that California recorded its first execution for murder, so the territory must have a taste for it now, and what better way to satisfy the palate for blood than a man who would bludgeon his own brother to death over a fist-sized gold nugget.

Joshua starts toward Clayton. He feels like he should say something to him. So many goodbyes he's already experienced in these seventeen years without Goodbye, and what drives his desire now is more a lingering and long-sought-after sense of closure than any indebtedness to Clayton. He knows he wants to say something, but he doesn't know what to say. He sees that Clayton hasn't stopped sobbing, and how easily the men move him around, he a puppet to these proceedings and what preceded them, already having relinquished the rest of his life to whims and chance it seems. Joshua walks slowly, trying to compose some thought, some remark that seems justified or appropriate. He holds his coat tighter around him, feeling the chill in that valley and the coldness of Clayton's act in his own blood, when he notices a hand pointing at him.

It's Surely's hand. The old man speaks hurriedly to a group of men who eye Joshua with the same disdain they eyed Clayton. Joshua looks at Surely full on. The horror in the old man's eyes is unmistakable.

Joshua lets go of his coat. He tears through the camp and heads back for the hills, not even bothering to look back at the men chasing him, or to see Clayton's feet tied to a horse and the one still-living twin from Georgia dragged down the road toward Old Dry Diggings where he will certainly be hanged, if that mode of travel doesn't kill Clayton first.

CHAPTER FOURTEEN

No time wasted in abandoning camp. They gather their duffel bags and guns, the twins' more valuable possessions, some food and cookware, then leave everything else, including the schooner, and scatter the mules. Joshua even leaves his medical bag, remaking his life once more. They ride deeper into the hills and dig up their gold just before night sets in. They split the gold evenly between the three of them, bag it and lash the bags to their saddles, hoping the horses' knees don't buckle under the weight. The three of them aimless after that. They wander the valley on horseback, dawn breaking a future for them that's as fresh and clean as a newborn's skin.

They travel northwest, further into the hills where the craggy rock and dense pine welcome all sorts of vagabonds in its various hideaways. No one speaks about the twins, and perhaps Renard sums it up best when, during their first night as veritable fugitives, he shovels a handful of rice and brown-spotted avocado into his mouth and says while chewing: So we become richer still.

Joshua nods, but in truth he feels himself apart from everything, as if he's been stitched to a portion of the ground that doesn't turn as the earth does and the world keeps moving on without him. Every time he closes his eyes the image of Clayton smashing Klayton's skull is the only thing he sees. He feels nothing while watching this image. He sleeps. He eats. He drinks. He dries his pistol each morning and spit shines the barrel in the evenings in the rote and primitive manner that he feels himself returned to, time unwinding itself so that each day is one step backward and soon he will be alone on a deserted and inhospitable world spouting nascent bouts of lava where even the vaguest notion of a god can't exist.

They camp for four nights in sight of no one. They stay alert for mountain lions and scavenge late-season berries to feed their horses, which seem each evening so close to death the three of them expect dead horses come morning and their fates inevitably sealed as a result.

On the fifth day, Joshua wakes with his head heavy and clattering like it's been filled with sharp gravel. His stomach is so queasy he soon shits out the last bits of food the three of them rationed, then succumbs to episodes of diarrhea that eventually go colorless. By midday, there's no food left.

Blow dry your cylinders, says Renard. The moisture can flood the cap spark.

They pack everything with them as they ride once more, true nomads heading south out of the hills back toward the American River while they carry death in their hearts and seek easy food and shelter. The trees are mostly bare and hazed by mist and nothing, no lingering brittle five-fingered oak leaf nor the sloppy wet dirt cleanly parted by horse hooves, will focus for Joshua, his mind detached from their angst and their intent though he rides his Morgan with such acuteness seeing him you would never know that to be the case. Soon, they come to a crest, and in a narrow and rocky valley they catch sight of eight Chileans winnowing in front of a dynamited tunnel, a slaughter so convenient that Joshua convinces the others it isn't worth the sweat they would break to execute it. Instead, they trade the twins' knives for one of the Chilean's vivid wool blankets and some food, and that night they crouch silently around a large fire not far off, wrapping themselves in that single blanket and eating a robust meal of salted beef, tortillas, and beans.

In the gray and foggy morning of the eighth of December, they pack the blanket and pack themselves. Joshua coughs up a thick wad of phlegm, spits it out. His throat is sore, his head aching, so he gazes at the Chileans while they work to take his mind off of his own ills, admiring their squat stature and quick movements, their black hair so different from his own.

There's no wind while they mount their horses and continue on through the valley, ascending the western slope by high-stepping a mound of scree, but when they reach the peak, they turn their heads away and draw low their hats, so sharp and cold is the sudden wind. Joshua begins to cough a cough that will last the rest of the day. The gray never burns off as they follow their own path. They wind through pine and sidestep rock and climb and descend and climb some more. The American River runs somewhere to their left, or at their backs, they aren't exactly sure, but they aren't seeking it anymore. They aren't seeking gold anymore. Long after they began riding they finally stop. Free Ray dismounts, reaches into his duffel bag, pulls out one bandana filled with tortillas and another filled with salted beef, the very meal they ate the night before, such that life for Joshua has begun to repeat itself, a series of redundancies only differentiated by his aging, the wrinkling of his skin, the experiences that burrow inside his heart and mind, fewer teeth. They eat on the ground, each of them delicately leaning against tree trunks to ease their backs. Their bodies aren't yet situated for such riding again, so these last several days were difficult and painful ones, and they use this sedentary moment to revive. Soon though, they find themselves overtaken by shivering, and the cold on their hands makes their knuckles sore and stiff. If there was a sun, they would've sat in it, but as it is the entirety of their world is one big shadow. Even after Joshua finishes eating, he is still hungry. The diarrhea has finally passed, and the intermittent fasting that accommodated that illness now renders him hungrier than he's felt in all his life. The depth of this hunger fatigues Joshua. He can barely keep his eyes open, the landscape beckoning him to sleep, the world winking in and out of view for what seems a long while until he feels something hitting his boot.

We are departing, says Renard.

Joshua didn't know he'd fallen asleep, nor can he tell how long he slept (if it's afternoon or evening now), as the sky is nearly the same color it was the last morning he remembers. He rubs his crusted eyes and stands awkwardly with his gimp foot not wanting to work. He wipes the dampness from his face first with damp hands, then a damp sleeve, before he stretches his back out. This futile routine of refreshment completed he climbs up on his Morgan, and they leave those trees, pushing further into the hills and stopping again only when they hear singing.

The sweet voices creep out of a glade below them, carry on the wind that blows at their faces, which means they can hear those voices as clearly as they can see their hands on their reins. The voices are both men's and women's, some so high-pitched they can only belong to the elastic chords of children, and they sing for the heavens in English. Joshua wonders at first if he's imagining this song. He leans forward to capture more of the sound, to understand why he suddenly feels the holes he hadn't realized existed in his world are being patched, that the fractured scope of humanity is being fused back together. He thinks at first the delicate sounds coming from the children are dying animals, until he realizes they are a kind of human he'd forgotten existed. He feels the women more than hears them, a slow-burning shock to his system the way he experienced sugar for the first time, activating cells that have been dormant for far too long and that spark a remembrance much deeper and much more profound than anything the brain can muster.

He looks at Renard and Free Ray, sees from the looks on their faces that they hear what he hears. So this song doesn't only exist in his imagination. As the three of them kick their horses down the hill, Joshua feels something else building inside of him, a sensation that mirrors the one he felt on that very first evening while he and the others waited on the hillside above the ravine and watched the first miners they would steal from and kill. What will he find when they cross this threshold back into a re-peopled place? Who will he be now if not simply a man in a man's world?

They soon come upon the glade. Roughly fifty people huddle under a sort of porch that's framed by twenty-foot-high posts and canopied with fragrant pine branches. A narrow stream ribbons at the edge of the forest just beyond the glade, not the kind of water that will harbor any gold so the kind that goes largely ignored by the seekers. Scattered about the glade are the skeletons of partially built cabins, and piled inside the incomplete cabins are pallets of blankets, trunks of clothes, loose saddles, tents, lanterns, wooden crates, a few muskets, a chalkboard leaned against one cabin wall with the alphabet written on it, still-smoking fires, and all manner of cookware and cutlery Joshua can imagine. This place is no camp. This place is the start of a village.

A man dressed in all black stands in the center of the congregation. He is no wider than the posts supporting the structure, and the slack linen sleeve of his right arm is pinned to his shoulder. He sings with a voice three times his size, and with the singing finished just as the three of them sidle up to the group, the man begins preaching in the same volume.

Strike upon this world the riches of man!

The man holds his closed bible with his only arm, moves the book slowly across the congregation like he's performing a group exorcism.

Strike upon this world man's vices, man's desires! So lewd and putrid they become when let loose in this unhallowed land. Strike yesterday! Strike tomorrow! Strike now! For you who so art hearing this plea may prevail, may gift unto here a new day that dawns with His riches. With His Grace. For what does it profit to gain the world while losing your soul? People of Christ.

The preacher goes silent. He's caught sight of the horsebacked men and stands now as if statued in this singular moment. It takes a minute for the congregation to turn their gaze toward Joshua and the other two, some so caught up in histrionic prayer they don't realize the preacher's silence is anything extraordinary, others simply unaware of the circumstance, as they are standing with their eyes closed or while so fixedly watching the preacher the world apart from him is nothingness. When finally the presence of the three strange men is made evident to everyone, no one utters a sound. They shift their gaze from the horsemen to the preacher, waiting for the preacher to make sense of this curious, unexpected incident.

The preacher clears his multifaceted throat. He tucks his bible under the nub of his right arm, wipes his brow with the palm of his hand, runs his hand down each half of his parted hair. When he speaks again, he does so with a tone deeper than a man that thin should ever be able to muster.

Welcome, gentlemen, he says. You are most welcome. All men are welcome in the eyes of our Lord Jesus Christ.

The preacher looks warily at Free Ray.

He says, Most especially those requiring His Salvation. My name is Paul, as in the apostle. Welcome to our humble sanctuary.

Paul removes the Bible from his nub and presses it against his heart, scans the congregation while he smiles and nods. The congregation smiles, nods in uniform along with him.

God blesseth the strong of mind and the devoted of heart, Paul says.

Amen! roars the congregation, which startles Joshua.

Paul motions to a tree near one of the partially built cabins.

He says, Hitch your horses, gentlemen. The day is late, and by His Grace an ample supper is soon to be upon us, to which you are certainly welcome. But first please join us in a final Worship on this most glorious day Heaven doth provide us.

Joshua glances at the sky. Still the same lifeless gray, a dull and sullied place for such a god to live. The preacher smiles directly at Joshua when Joshua looks back at the congregation, and Joshua frowns. He knocks the Morgan's ribs with his heels, follows after Renard and Free Ray, who are already dismounting near the tree and hitching the horses to the trunk.

The preacher has struck up his sermonizing again, and the congregation, now largely ignoring the three aside from some cursory glances, have resumed their contrition of sighs and murmurs, punctuating the preacher's firebrand style with loud and boisterous, Amens!, when necessary—and even when not.

Good unto you, children of the Lord. Good unto you for believing there is THE way. Not A way, nor ANOTHER way. But THE way. Hear me when I say again. THE way. So much of this meandering world twists and turns like that creek that doth babble to my rear.

Paul shoots his Bibled hand behind him and points at the creek that's invisible through the tree line.

He says, We are apt to get lost in those bends, sucked down by the eddies life's turbulence creates where, on that blind and murky bottom, there reigns doubt, unbelief, temptation ripe for Satan's foul plan. Trust in me all you listeners, all you heedful minds among us. Satan has his plan, and his plan he will enact, if even, like the canine who preys on your fear, he smells a hint of weakness. But!

Paul shoots his one arm into the air with his Bible outheld, pauses while all in the congregation hush. He turns his eyes from one congregation member to another, as if to make certain that all eyes are on him and him alone.

But! he shouts again.

Then, with Paul's cadence rising with each word as the congregation stirs in anticipation of his climax, he says, Do not mistake yourselves. You cannot crosseth the creek alone. Can the blind man lead himself home? Can the deaf man hear the thief stalking him? Can the speechless cry out in protest of Sin? No! We are but simple beings, crafted in His image and yet broken by our own strangeness, afflicted by this earth.

Paul flaps his loose sleeve.

He continues, As a community, we can be made whole again. So a community we shall be. For to bask in the warmth of His Grace together is to be far richer than any mountains of gold ripped from the river's mouth in the individuation of greed and gain.

Amen! the congregation cries out.

Some drop to their knees in prayer. The preacher bows his head, holds the bible to his heart, begins praying. His dirty face is streaked by tears when he finishes. The sermon ended, everyone in the congregation goes up to Paul and shakes his hand. They nod silent greetings to Joshua, Renard, and Free Ray as they pass.

Renard and Free Ray watch these men and women indifferently, almost abjectly. Joshua tries to follow their lead, but every man with a clean and shaven face, every woman, and every child push him backward to the world he long ago left. When a girl who can't be

older than fifteen and who leads an older balding man by the elbow
approaches, she glances at Joshua. She looks so much like a boy with
her short hair, her chest straight enough to balance a pail were she
lying on her back, and a square face that looks innocent and baby-
like, not yet ground out by the world's hardness. In fact, he wouldn't
know otherwise if not for the dress she's wearing, and his heart skips
at the fleeting misdirection. He feels something grip him like he
hasn't felt in a long while. A kind of longing, a kind of warmth. He
follows her with his head, keeps his eyes on her still as she makes her
way to one of the farthest cabins, where she sits the older man on a
stump before she pushes up her dress sleeves, crouches over a pit of
coals, and begins stirring the contents of a large pot.

Renard leans in while Joshua watches her.

Now that is a dress that hides a true joy, he whispers.

Joshua's skin goes cold. He whips around to face Renard, but as he
does, the preacher walks up with his Bible tucked under his nub and
extends his hand, first shaking Renard's, then Joshua's, and lastly, if
not slightly begrudgingly, Free Ray's.

I see you've met Mr. Wurley, the preacher says. And his daughter
Elizabeth.

Joshua looks away from him.

My name is Paul, says the preacher.

You said that already, Renard says.

Paul smiles.

And evidently you listened, says the preacher.

CHAPTER FIFTEEN

The congregation sings up the sun with psalms followed by a chanting prayer Paul leads with great ferocity. He calls this encampment Antioch, and once he sets to his sermonizing, he rages about with his limp sleeve and waves his bible in the air like a maniac. The congregation is nearly in tears, some so overwhelmed they prostrate themselves on the wet ground with little regard to the mud that sticks to their faces and soils their clothes. The sky is a piercing blue, bluer than Joshua has seen in weeks. Paul must be taking this clarity as something of sign. He calls on his congregation to perceive it, and in perceiving it, understand the Grace of God made tangible through all manner of symbols. Those on the ground roll onto their backs to turn their faces skyward. Those standing fling their arms behind them, arch their banks and close their eyes, feeling the sky without seeing it.

Joshua watches this preaching spectacle from their camp. He and the other two are eating their last pieces of salted beef. Paul offers them a knowing look every now and then. At one point, while going on about the miracles of Jesus, Paul looks over and Renard tips his hat, a gesture which, aside from disconcerting the preacher or catching him off guard as was perhaps Renard's intention, is greeted by Paul's cursory nod so synchronized with his sermon it's as if the preacher built in that nod long before the actual incident. Some sort of prescient inclination offered by a dream, or a life preceding this one. Stirred by his failure, Renard bends down and chucks a log into the still burning fire. Sparks flare. The wood pops. And for a moment almost too fleeting to recognize, but a moment enough, Paul's words get interrupted.

That evening, once Paul finishes his evening sermon and the rest of the congregation rest before supper, Paul joins the three of them.

Such a beautiful day it is, he says. A day especially fit for His Praises. God has, in all his magnanimity, blesseth'd us with this sunshine.

The preacher's ghost of an arm seems possessed of its own agency the way the sleeve constantly flaps. Joshua wonders who (or what) performed the amputation.

Paul clears his throat. He folds his arm across his chest, gathers his loose sleeve in his hand to give him the appearance of having crossed his arms. When he speaks again, his tone takes on the rounded register of his preaching voice.

He says, Now that the Lord has brought you to our hamlet, what is it that you gentlemen seek in Antioch?

No one replies. Paul waits, patient and composed as a preacher is want to be, as Joshua remembers that preacher in Independence always was. The dull chatter from the congregation drifts through and among the four of them while they remain silent. Joshua hears a child call out Mommy. He's never once spoken this word, never formed it on his lips. When he thinks about this word now, it hangs empty in his heart.

There's nothing we seek, Joshua says finally.

Nothing? presses Paul.

Nothing here.

Paul glances at the horses, then surveys the contents piled around the fire.

Ah, says Paul. You are all gold seekers. Tell me then, have you found yourselves lucky in your excursion?

Renard and Free Ray laugh so fully they momentarily catch the preacher off guard.

Yes, says Renard.

There's so much irony in Renard's voice that even Paul, ignorant of their past, might guess at what he's implying.

We have found ourselves quite lucky, Renard says.

I see. And what exactly do you plan to do with your newfound wealth, fleeting as it is of course.

Fleeting? says Joshua.

Any wealth wedded to mortality is fleeting.

We will do what all men of great wealth do, says Renard.

There is another long silence. Finally, perhaps feeling a little baited into his question, Paul asks flatly: And what is it exactly that all wealthy men do?

Renard smiles.

Nothing, he says.

Paul scoffs. He lets go his sleeve, puts his hand on his knee while he sits up taller. He leans toward the fire, his face slick in the firelight, his oily black hair waxlike.

Idle hands, says Paul shaking his head. We must all, Believers and nonbelievers alike, beware idle hands.

Renard glances at Free Ray, the two of them sharing some unspoken secret that's lost on Joshua.

Why are you here? Paul presses Renard.

The same as you and your party I suppose, says Renard.

Paul smiles coyly, smooths each side of his hair.

We are not a party. We are a congregation, a family. And what is it that you suppose my family and I are here for? he asks.

Freedom, says Renard. And opportunity.

Yes. The many histories of persecution. But we are not Mormons, as you may suppose. Our persecution assumed a different face than that staring down the bedeviled Mormons.

So you fled, Renard says mockingly.

Paul nods.

Who in this territory has not fled whence he came? I imagine, sir, that you and that most notable odor you bear have fled at times too.

It is ironic, is it not? says Renard. The law you escaped seems to be chasing you and your congregation once more.

We fear no reckoning, be it Divinely wrought or manifested by man.

Renard laughs. He stands, unholsters his pistol, holds the gun out toward Paul.

Here, he says. Take this then. It sounds like you may have to reliven the stories of the old testament on your way to the golden gates.

Renard keeps laughing. Paul doesn't seem used to such combatance, and he stands as well, hardens his tone.

Paul says, You gentlemen are welcome here in Antioch. But take note that the hospitality afforded you here, which is likewise afforded all those you see before you, is done so according to the graciousness and resolve of each his own heart and each his own mind. We do not offer charity. We do not offer respite. We offer Spiritual growth, diligence in labor, and community. In sum, a greater richness than this material world can ever offer, though offered only to those so willing to accept the Faith to which we adhere. For that you are most welcome to stay and join us. Otherwise, gentlemen, I should bid you goodbye now, and come sunrise watch you and your carted souls depart over those hills.

Paul places his hand over his heart, dips his head to each one of them in turn. He turns on his heels, starts off toward the chapel.

Who are all these people? Joshua calls after the preacher.

Paul stops and turns around. He studies Joshua for a long moment, as if trying to figure out exactly how he will answer a question that offers so many possibilities. He glances over his shoulder at the rest of the congregation, then looks back at Joshua.

They are followers of Christ, he says. Believers in the Word and Faithful servants to His purpose.

I mean...

Joshua pauses. He steals a look across the glade at Elizabeth.

I mean, he repeats. Where are they all from?

Where are you from?

Missouri.

Yes, says Paul. We have several members from Missouri.

Joshua waits for Paul to continue, but the preacher only dips his head again, this time slighter than the first, then walks on to the unfinished chapel. There, two stout men argue about the planing of a log, their combative voices softened and angry gestures quelled when Paul approaches, and very soon after the two men are shaking hands, one returning to the log, the other retrieving a hammer and setting to work with a different man while they struggle to mount a stained glass window that rainbows in the sunlight.

That preacher-man likes you, Renard says to Joshua. You must have a knack for charming men of god.

He doesn't know a thing about me, says Joshua.

Yes he does, says Renard. You told him everything he needs to know.

How do you figure?

Inquiry is the gateway to belief.

I didn't ask him a thing about anything like that.

But you asked him a question.

It had nothing to do with belief.

Everything has to do with belief when you are talking to a preacher.

Joshua shakes his head.

It doesn't matter anyway, he says.

You are right, says Renard. It does not matter.

Joshua rubs his arms together as a shiver overtakes him. He sticks his hands in his armpits to warm them further, looks out across the glade to find Elizabeth. She is kneeling near a fire and wiping her father's face with a rag. When she finishes that, she slings the rag over her shoulder, picks up a steaming cup from the ground, and tips the cup to her father's lips. Even though it's cold, her dress sleeves are rolled up, a spartanness that shames Joshua. He pulls his hands from his armpits and straightens his body to stem his shivering, but he keeps watching her. She tends to her father until her father has his fill to drink and then they both kneel in the mud, he being helped to the ground by her before she takes to her knees. With her father's hands in hers, they bow their heads in prayer. While she prays Joshua wills her to look at him, watching her so intently that soon he begins to feel his gaze a kind of violation. But he doesn't turn away. Her face looks even softer, more beautiful in the firelight, like an illusion, a mask she wears to cover the true and gritty life she is hardly ignorant of. He waits for her to glance his way, and after she doesn't, after she and her father finish their prayer and they hug and she helps him back to his feet before leading him back to his stump, she starts sawing at a felled pine trunk. Joshua has never seen a woman work like a man before. He finds himself willing her back to that manifestation she assumed in that moment he mistook her for a boy, but she will never resume that form, bound by a reality that neither she nor he can ever avail themselves of. The despondency in this realization overwhelms him with a longing he hasn't felt since he left Missouri, and, feeling it now, this longing seems hardly capable of being contained in that single word: compassion.

You are cold, says Renard.

It's not that cold, says Joshua turning back to look at the fire. Besides, we have the fire.

True. Fire is a veritable wonder of nature.

Free Ray spreads some of the coals out along the perimeter of the fire with a stick, then places the coffee pot on top of the coals.

She is a beautiful creature, says Renard.

Who is?

That one.

Renard points to Elizabeth.

Joshua doesn't want to talk about her, but he knows Renard will only continue to push the matter.

I suppose she is beautiful, he says. But there are a lot of beautiful people, in a lot of places.

Not like her, insists Renard. Not here. And besides, your proclivities prevent you from an objective assessment of women. Does that not disrupt the value of your scientific mind?

I could say the same for you, says Joshua.

Renard smiles while he looks out across the glade. Joshua can see the flames tinyed and mirrored in Renard's black eyes and the lust those flames lay bare, or the lust those flames magnify, and, almost without thinking about it, Joshua stands and walks over and steps in Renard's sightline to block out Elizabeth. He picks up a log, tosses it into the fire.

Good, says Renard looking up at Joshua. There can never be too much fire on a day as cold as today.

Renard keeps his eyes on Joshua as Joshua sits back down, then turns them to Free Ray.

Well, he says. It seems we have been given an ultimatum. I see no need for this village and its fervent inhabitants. Agreed?

Free Ray pulls out his Bowie knife, runs the blade over his

cheekbones in a dry and hasty shave. He stares at Renard while he does so, his face flat, as if it's painted on canvas. Something about this dissention strikes Joshua as new and unexpected, yet deep down he realizes that such angst always welled within all of them, and, like that gold that takes centuries to push its way high enough through the superficial rock and dirt so it can be discovered, the preciousness inside of them, that which they alone harbor and control, is beginning to reveal itself.

It would be silly to stay, Renard insists.

He stares at Free Ray as Free Ray continues to ignore him, Renard's eyes hardening, his cheeks pulsed when he clenches his teeth.

He repeats, It is silly to stay.

Free Ray holsters his Bowie knife, brings up his knees, and shakes his head.

Renard huffs and lets go his stare. He turns to Joshua.

And what do you say? Staying seems a far-fetched option.

I don't think we have a choice, says Joshua.

Of course we have a choice. You and I, we will always have a choice in this world.

Free Ray crosses his arms. He glances at Renard, then fixes on Joshua. Joshua shifts his eyes between him and Renard, both of them watching him, waiting to see where he will situate himself. He scoots closer to the fire, eyes the flames.

Joshua says, Staying seems to be a small sacrifice for good meals.

He shrugs.

Besides, he continues, what's one more falsehood amongst thousands?

SHORTLY AFTER DARKNESS settles, Free Ray unties the gold secured to his saddle and grabs the shovel. He starts toward the woods beyond the creek.

Wait, says Renard as he stands. I will come with you.

Free Ray waves Renard off without looking back, goes on alone to hide that portion of the gold. He returns an hour later, carries off the gold from Renard's horse, then a half hour after that the gold from Joshua's Morgan. When he returns for good, he sits beside Joshua. Renard rises silently, removes his blanket from his saddle, and wraps himself in it. Then he lies facing away from the other two until he falls asleep.

CHAPTER SIXTEEN

The eleventh of December, the rain pours like the shedding of giant tears for some yet known though impregnable grief. Nothing is spared the wetness. The congregation crams inside the half-built chapel, the only structure with some semblance of a roof. The members who don't fit beneath the roof stand just outside of it, and there must be some unspoken hierarchy in the congregation, as those trapped in the rain never jockey for a position beneath nor complain of their state, all eyes and ears turned to Paul, who's completely dry and tucked against the wall between two stained-glass windows where no wetness can find its way.

Standing at the very back of the congregation, with the rain battering the wood and battering his head, Joshua can hear the preacher's deep and solemn voice but can't understand the words Paul speaks. Soon, the mud inside the chapel grows so thick it begins to rise. It seals over the toes of their boots, crawls up their heels, and laps their ankles the way waves might, all the while growing soupier, more water than mud eventually, all of them mired in a swamp and sinking.

Still, the worship continues. Eventually, a stale loaf of bread is passed around for communion, though it too suffers that saturation, so soggy once it leaves the roofed part of the chapel that members are forced to take what remaining pieces of it slop into their hands. A goblet of wine goes around next, each taking his or her turn to drink while the rain refills it and the wine, just as it did on that miraculous day centuries ago, never loses its mark in the cup.

Paul doesn't seem to notice that Joshua, Renard, and Free Ray refuse the bread and refuse the wine. Either that or he doesn't make a show of noticing it.

After communion, the congregation joins hands in final prayer. Elizabeth isn't far off to Joshua's side, and Joshua reaches his hand out toward hers. To his great astonishment, she takes it. Her hand is rough, much rougher than he imagines a woman's hand would ever be. He holds it for what seems only a few seconds, or time less than that, even though Paul draws that prayer out as if it's the last prayer that might well be uttered from his lips. And perhaps it is. If this rain keeps up, Antioch will quite soon be less a burgeoning village and more the wasted planks of an unfit ark.

By late afternoon, though, the rain does stop. Joshua is put to work felling trees. The work is grueling and painful. With each blow of the ax, his body reminds him how easy it was to slaughter, how the energy his muscles and bones must absorb with this labor is nothing like the release of taking a man's life. The man he works alongside, whose body is all massive arms and shoulders, appears tireless. Exhausted and embarrassed by his evident weakness in front of this man, Joshua soon wanders off to take a break. He spots Elizabeth.

I'm Joshua, he says when he approaches.

Elizabeth doesn't look up. She's fiddling with a small contraption of springs, chains, and sharp metal teeth.

She says, Paul told us.

What are you doing?

Setting a trap.

Joshua waits for her to clarify. She doesn't. He bends down to get a closer look at the contraption, at her work.

A trap for what? he asks.

Hares, squirrels. Smaller animals mostly.

Elizabeth's responses are blunt and matter-of-fact like the truth should be so simple and straightforward. Joshua stands again, looks back at the massive arms he was working alongside, which have already felled three more trees.

I've never seen a woman setting a trap before, Joshua says turning back.

Elizabeth looks at him. She smiles banally, all of her imperfections somehow making her more real now—the mole above her left eye, the scar that cuts from the top of her lip diagonally up her cheek, a narrow and black hole where a front tooth should be.

We do, she says.

She finishes setting the trap, then stands up and dusts off her hands.

She says, I caught a fox here not long ago. My father and I made a shawl of its pelt. We sold the shawl of course, to a gold digger who said he would trade it in San Francisco for more equipment. Beyond our essentials, we don't have much need for material objects here in Antioch.

That trap can hold a fox?

It can hold a fox.

It looks quite small, says Joshua. I would think a fox is too big for that. It could just get away.

It didn't though.

Elizabeth steps toward him, as if she's going to engage him further. Her dress is still wet from the rain and clings to every slight curve of her body. Joshua can smell her in all her ripeness, can see the sweat that clings to her neck glistening in the nascent sunlight. Small, physical properties that engrain his compassion for her even more. She looks at him, waits for a moment, waits for him to understand what her look means.

If you catch another fox, will you make another shawl? Joshua asks.

Elizabeth sighs, as if these questions annoy her.

I won't catch one, she says. The others are smart enough not to return here. Which is why I'm not relocating the trap. I don't need another shawl.

She pauses, waits again for Joshua to read the meaning in her silence. But he can't read it. Even trying as much as he is he can't read it.

She says, You should be getting back to your work. You've abandoned David, and you might have finished by now if you'd kept at it.

By the time the day's work is finished, Joshua is famished. The smell of stew that lingers in the air is his only thought. There will be no worship this evening, Paul declares, so successful was the one this morning that tonight is a celebration of sorts. They have withstood the rain, as if that rain symbolizes some test of faith, and shown themselves committed to their faith even in a chapel half-constructed. And so, a feast will be had.

The stew is served up in shallow wooden bowls along with more bread, and halfway through supper Paul jogs off toward the chapel and returns with a fiddle, sits next to a woman who likewise has a fiddle. The two begin to play, the congregation gathering around the two fiddlers and clapping their hands and slapping their knees.

Even the most faithful have a life beyond god at times, Renard says to Joshua.

The three of them mingle alone and apart from the others.

I can't figure why they're so happy, Joshua says.

Because they are still living, I suppose. Sometimes that is reason enough.

I guess so. For them at least.

For many, says Renard.

Joshua turns away. Renard says something else to Joshua, but Joshua isn't listening, then Renard turns and whispers to Free Ray, and Free Ray smiles when he looks out at the congregation, nods.

Renard taps Joshua on the shoulder.

You should not watch her so intently, he says.

Watch who?

Women can feel your eyes.

What's that supposed to mean.

Exactly what it does. They can feel men watching them. A kind of instinct, or a sense if you want to call it that.

I wasn't watching anyone.

It is like the doe who can sense the wolf, or the mouse who can sense the hawk. That instinct balances things.

A doe? A mouse? I don't know what you're talking about.

Yes you do, says Renard. So does she.

Joshua spoons the rest of his stew into his mouth, sets the bowl on the ground. He wipes his hands on his shirt, puts on his hat, and walks over to Elizabeth, stopping just behind her. She turns and looks at him when he arrives.

Did you finish your work? she asks.

Joshua nods.

He asks, Did you trap any animals?

I'll see in the morning, she says.

Joshua smiles and Elizabeth smiles back with that same banal smile she gave him this afternoon. While there's nothing else in that expression that suggests anything, her simplicity, her complacency soothes Joshua, and he finds himself regarding her with the warmth and affection he believes one would have for a sibling, a thought that, inasmuch as it brings him solace, tails with pain, for he is entirely alone in this world, and when he dies there will not be a single trace left of him on this earth. There's hardly any companionship in these valleys, and there's an even greater lack of love, both of which Joshua, at an age too far beyond his years, suddenly and viscerally feels the absence of, and at seventeen, has no idea how to rectify. Because a young man isn't meant to become a man without knowing this.

Elizabeth taps her knee with one hand now as Paul and the other fiddler have switched tunes, and Joshua steps closer, lets the back of his hand brush against her untapping hand. She glances at him when he does, stops swaying, and leans so slightly away that the back of his hand can still barely grace hers when the wind blows just right.

The both of them stand there, and the lust Joshua felt initially when he mistook Elizabeth for a boy returns to him. It exists outside of Elizabeth now, which allows him to long for her and long for the idea of him simultaneously—one the holistic love of family, the other a singular and passionate need. It never occurred to him until now how lonely his father must've been without the latter. A loneliness entirely apart from Joshua, but something he would've never understood then (would've been hurt by) and hardly understands now. If he doesn't quite get it, though, his bones sense it, ached by growth and by yearning. He feels sorry for his father and his father's life of sacrifice (as he feels it surely must've been), but along with that sorry he resents his father for the governed life his father chose. Because there comes such a time we all outgrow our parents' weaknesses, and the best of us try to track that wondrous, uncharted path into the blind and tenebrous beyond that lies outside that influence we can never truly shed.

*

LATER, THE CELEBRATION long ceased and his blanket still too wet for use, Joshua lies bundled beside the dwindling fire in his coat and mittens, Free Ray and Renard sleeping around him in the same mummified manner so that, like a Pagan symbol, they form a sort of triangle with the fire the epicenter. He's thinking about Elizabeth and pseudo-Elizabeth, then even later dreaming about them, but when he's shaken awake with the night still so dark and so cold, it's Renard who stands over him, that man's pale face bright like a moon.

Get up and follow me, whispers Renard.

Joshua acquiesces. He's too cold to continue lying here now that he's awake, and the urgency in Renard's voice intrigues him. With a shovel hoisted over his shoulder and no moon to guide them, Renard forges their path through the woods.

Where are we going? asks Joshua.

To dig up the gold.

Why?

Renard doesn't answer him. He seems to know where he's going even though he didn't bury the gold, navigating the woods nimbly the way a deer does, or a fox, and Joshua follows close on his heels, often slipping in the dark in the mud with his gimp foot.

Did Free Ray tell you where he buried it?

No.

Then how do you know where it is?

Renard stops, turns around.

That man has always thought himself cleverer and more capable than he is, Renard says. Besides, anything can be tracked if you know what to look for and how to look for it.

Renard starts off again. After an hour, they stop a second time, Joshua sweating against the cold. Renard jams the blade of the shovel into the mud at various locations until he finds what he's looking for and begins digging. When the hole is deep enough, he leaves the shovel upright in the ground, lowers himself into the hole, digs a bit longer with his hands. From where Joshua stands, shivering now in his stillness and his jaw aching from chatter, he watches Renard disappear into that hole and emerge again a minute later with a sack of gold that he labors to lift.

It is time for us to leave now, says Renard still standing in the hole.

Leave Antioch?

None of them have ever referred to the village as Antioch before, and Renard looks up at Joshua now as if doing so validates Paul and the community in some way.

You like it here, says Renard.

No I don't. I'm not sure we have enough food yet, is all.

We have what we need, and there is plenty to be got apart from this place. You should know that well enough by now.

Joshua turns away. He can see hardly anything in these woods, save for the vague and obscure outlines of objects he knows to be trees.

What about the weather? he says turning back. You think striking targets with only three of us and rain like we've had is going to be easy?

I do not think of it as either easy or hard. I think of it as necessary.

It doesn't make much sense.

Joshua's frustration is clear in his voice. Renard climbs out of the pit and braces himself on the shovel while he studies Joshua.

In the context of what? Renard asks. Of food? Or excursions?

He pauses.

Or something else entirely? he continues.

Joshua huffs but doesn't respond. He drops his shovel, drags the unearthed sack away from the hole, then drops himself down in, where he begins tugging at another sack of gold.

Careful, says Renard looking down at Joshua. Lest you break open that sack and spill the contents of your future into this glorified mud.

They gather four of the sacks in all, leaving two behind, and lug them back to camp, a walk that's even slower going than the earlier one now that it's weighted. Numerous times they must stop to catch their breath. After they gather the horses, they unhobble them, hitch them to a tree, and saddle them. Then they secure the sacks of gold to each of theirs.

Joshua starts toward Free Ray to wake him, but Renard grabs his arm.

Let him sleep, whispers Renard. We will wake him just prior to departing.

Renard cocks his head and stares at Free Ray for a few moments, the same way he might watch his own child sleep. Then he squats, lifts Free Ray's gaucho off of the Black man's stomach, takes off his own hat, and puts Free Ray's on in its stead, an odd and devious gesture Joshua has no idea what to make of.

He and Renard leave the horses and their camp and reenter the woods, tracking a route Joshua assumes is identical to the first when in fact they're walking away from the gold stash. They walk for only a few minutes before Renard stops, squats behind a juniper bush, and pulls Joshua down beside him.

I hear someone coming, Renard says flatly.

Joshua can't hear anything. He starts to speak, but Renard puts a finger to his own lips and then covers his face with his bandana, leaving only his eyes visible. He tucks his ponytail up under Free Ray's hat, pushing the hat so low on his head his earlobes are barely visible. He pulls his mittens out of his trouser pocket and puts them on, then unsheaths his Green River knife.

They wait, the both of them looking out toward the glade until finally Joshua hears footsteps sucking the mud and crunching the stripped and dried hardwood leaves, hears someone stop on the other side of the bush not too far away from them, a rustling around, then the sound of water splattering those leaves. Someone pissing.

Renard stands with his back bent low, the knife held rigidly in front of him like he's been expecting this, like he's known all along these circumstances will play out as they are, and so in fact aren't really circumstances at all but the makings of a cruel, almost cosmic plan. He steps around the bush, and Joshua stands, too confused to move, too scared to look away.

The woman faces away from them. She's still squatted, her loose dress gathered up and held to her waist by her cold-shook hands, her thighs and butt visible even in the dark, so many stars in the sky beyond that burn with their own combusting light, no warmth down here to speak of. Joshua can't see her face, though he knows she has to come from Antioch. He glances toward the camp, as if through those trees he can see something that might tell him who she is, but there's nothing he can see. He can't even see the fires he knows are burning near the half-built structures, or their own campfire. He doesn't remember these woods being so thick during the daytime, but they seem impenetrable now, pairs and pairs of pine symphysied at night into some sort of massive curtain.

Renard approaches the woman with long and delicate strides. He walks so lightly through the dense mud and over brittle winter sticks even Joshua can't hear his footsteps. Neither, of course, does the woman, even when Renard pauses several feet from her and just stands there a voyeur, waiting for her to finish pissing. After the woman shakes herself dry, she stands, her dress still gathered in her hands, and she begins hiking up her undergarments.

Renard lunges, so deft in this style of attack it seems second nature to him. He covers the woman's mouth with one mittened hand, the wool rough on her lips and chin, while the other hand holds the knife's blade to her throat. He whispers in her ear, speaks with a voice Joshua has never heard him use before, speaks like he believes Black men speak.

I ain't afraid to make a white woman bleed.

The woman tries to scream, but Renard clamps his hand even tighter around her mouth, pushes the blade into her throat to cut her just enough that she stifles that scream. She bleeds only a little, and the blood drains across the blade, drips from the handle onto Renard's mitten, where it's absorbed into the thick wool. Renard kicks her feet out from beneath her with his boot heels and then shoves her into the mud, pushing her face down into the ground with his knifed hand while he teeths one mitten off, uses that four-fingered hand to shove her dress up over her butt and undo his trousers. He flattens himself on her back, jolts quick and awkwardly after that, and the woman isn't trying to scream anymore, her lungs burned by the sulfur smell of Renard's body. She seems glued to the mud, entirely unable to move, almost as if she's dead. And which is worse?

Soon, Renard gasps, his limbs going slack, panting satisfactorily into the back of her head.

Joshua is dumbstruck. Half of his mind, in all his virginal ignorance, is telling him he isn't sure what just happened, but the half of him that is, that half that codes into all of us a rudimentary working knowledge of our basest instincts, understands and relays that too perfectly.

Renard pulls his trousers back up, rises to his knees, and leans over the woman while he holds her to the ground with both hands on her back. She still doesn't move, her dress burying itself in the mud. Joshua can hear soft, wounded groans escaping her.

You ain't so bad for a white woman, says Renard still leaning over her.

She doesn't try to roll over. She doesn't try to stand but begins unstraightening and restraightening her bare legs in pain. She's begun to cry now. Renard pushes himself up, wipes his cock with one of the mittens, wipes the knife blade on his trousers.

He says, Free Ray done had his share, and you ain't so bad after all.

Renard sheaths his knife, walks back to Joshua. He pulls the bandana off his face when he reaches the bush and smiles at Joshua.

I will meet you at the horses, he says before calmly walking off through the woods.

Joshua can't speak. All he can do is watch Renard go, like he's transfixed, like he's witnessing in this moment the devil incarnate, until the woman howls, and what just happened tears through him like an electric shock.

Joshua darts around the bush toward the woman. He drops to his knees beside her, puts his hands on her shoulders to try to help her up. She flinches when she feels his touch, drags herself a few feet away from him using only her arms like a paralytic. And for the first time, Joshua sees her face.

Elizabeth.

Her eyes are so wide and so full of fright and full of the hate she has for him, has for all men, and Joshua stays knelt there staring at her for a moment, his body overwhelmed with unspeakable sorrow, that line between perpetrator and victim never having been so clear with the world lost to him now, and the subtle nighttime sounds of those woods shattered by Elizabeth's scream.

CHAPTER SEVENTEEN

Joshua abandons Elizabeth because he has to. That's what he tells himself. He abandons her because if he stayed to help her the others would blame him. And they'll kill me, he thinks. And he's right about both.

How he finds his way back to the camp he'll never know, but he does find it. Renard is seated on his horse, waiting patiently for Joshua with Free Ray still lying on the ground. Joshua runs over to Free Ray and attempts to rouse him.

It is useless, says Renard.

Renard takes off Free Ray's gaucho and tosses it at Free Ray, after which he puts his own back on.

I put the boot to his head. Leave him, and let him atone for any sins committed by our own race. That is the fate of the nigger after all.

Elizabeth still screams, a harrowing sound that carries through the trees and between the hills with miraculous clarity, and already other members of the congregation are awake and frantically trying to ascertain the situation. Renard looks off through the dark woods with his head tilted slightly upwards, basking in that horrific scream, then he turns back to Joshua.

Come on, he says with such plainness it's like nothing at all is happening or has happened.

He turns his horse away from camp and slowly guides it toward the hills.

Joshua mounts his Morgan. He looks at Free Ray, then glances across the glade. Everyone seems to be up, a great commotion of voices punctuating the cold night air. A trail of torches leads into the woods, a kind of earthborne constellation culminating in the same black void all constellations do, and Joshua knows how quickly they'll find Elizabeth, if they haven't found her already, and then how quickly Free Ray will be hanged, if those Christians deem him worthy of a merciful death.

Renard is already riding at a trot, and Joshua kicks his Morgan and sets off toward him, his own hatred for that man so alive and so pure at this moment it's like he is suddenly gifted the sixth sense of prescience, and he sees the death that will be enacted on Renard come sunrise, the firing of his pistol and the bullet that will bury itself in that red-haired, eight-fingered man's finely wrought skull.

CHAPTER EIGHTEEN

No matter how fast Joshua pushes his Morgan he always finds himself ten lengths behind Renard. He chases Renard through the hills and through a grove of black walnut trees and past spindly California oak reaching out with its bare branches a tentacled thing and over beds of dried pine needles that rustle like someone hushing when the horses trod them and through shallow creeks and then deeper creeks that bring the horses into freezing water up to their knees. All the while the stars don't change and the sky never seems to lighten until, after what feels to be hours, a dull gray appears behind them, and then that gray yellows and oranges and here comes the sun. So they are riding west.

Renard's ponytail bounces while the horse gallops. That red strip of hair is redder than blood in this new day, redder than the hate inside Joshua. The sunlight pencils their shadows in the patchy valley before them, and they ride with no camps in sight and surrounded by treeless hills even more barren in the wintertime that begin to shimmer the farther they travel, the longer Joshua reaches for them. The barren faces of those hills darken and narrow as Joshua strains his eyes to keep Renard always in his sight, the shadows the rising sun creates on the hillsides meld together into pits that are the shape and color of dilated pupils, and the blank-broad smile of Renard's that Joshua can't forget, that Renard offered him as he walked away from Elizabeth, is suddenly transposed onto those hills, catenaried from one to the other so that that smile consumes Joshua—body and mind and soul entirely. Joshua can't see Renard anymore. He can't see his own horse anymore. This terrible valley shaped by terrible hills is all there is, and that terrible red-haired man's face hops from hill to hill, always one step ahead of him, absorbing light, absorbing time. The hills boom with Renard's laughter, which cracks Joshua's mind, a canyon carved deeper and deeper as it begins to halve his face, Joshua's eyes drifting further and further apart while he travels on. And on. Joshua is nearly split in two now. The hills swell and gyrate, tectonic revelations that wrench beauty, that render madness, and soon the hills fuse into one giant hill that is Renard's whole body.

And suddenly, they are back in Independence the morning they departed on the trail. Renard leaning against the schooner, listening to Joshua's question about what it's like out there in California. Well, Renard said as he pointed to the other wagons scattered across town. He said, We are all going to see the elephant, where a man is expected to be greedy. The greediest man is the richest man, and the richest man keeps a company of souls no poorer than he is, for the richest man's riches are measured only against those of the poorest man he knows. It is therefore a land where no man is poor. If not rich in gold, then rich in opportunity. If not rich in opportunity, then eternally rich, since the only man in California without opportunity is the man no longer breathing. You simply have to decide what kind of man you are willing to be.

What kind of man am I? asks one half of Joshua's mind as he rides now amongst these possessed hills with each half of his body flapping alongside the Morgan's flanks like the wings of a Pegasus. What kind of man are you? asks the other.

Renard halts his horse, whirls around, and squints in the direction of the sun, that eight-fingered-man's face as clear and definite as the first moment Joshua saw it in Mechner's. Renard is watching him, waiting patiently for Joshua's bisected body, which charges toward him. His laughter booming, Joshua's Morgan picking up speed as if it's being drawn to Renard, as if the weight of Joshua is falling away just like his body is and the Morgan no longer carries him but rather the massless idea of him. You have always been mistaken about me, cries Renard through his laughter while he leans casually against his pommel, cemented in his spot. Then, in a motion so graceful it's almost beautiful, Renard hops from his saddle and the hills collapse around Joshua. Everything goes dark.

Joshua can hear his horse squealing somewhere close to him, the sound erratically crescendoing and decrescendoing and everywhere at once. He inhales the churned earth. His eyes are open, but everything is still dark. He tears at his face with his palms to wipe the dense mud away, pushes himself onto his knees. He is suddenly made whole again. The hills are as dull and lifeless as they have been all winter, the sky so stagnant and clear and it still early in the morning after the assault, a red-tailed hawk shrieking high overhead.

Renard calmly walks toward Joshua, pistol drawn, and Joshua wonders for a second if it's always been this—this place, this moment, this day from the very day of his birth.

Then the pain from his fall hits him. Something unexpected, something new, and he remembers what happened now: He tried to flank his horse to allow a clear shot with the rifle. He planted his gimp foot in the stirrup for balance, which worked against him, and he fell back in the saddle, caught himself with the reins but incidentally threw the Morgan's direction off so that the animal skidded in the mud while attempting to obey him as Renard stepped forward with a fencer's straight thrust and sunk his Green River knife into the Morgan's right shoulder to the handle.

Joshua frantically wipes at his eyes again. The mud brings tears to them. He searches for his pistol or his rifle through those tears. He can't find either. He looks back at Renard's blurry approach.

And then. And then.

Joshua catches sight of Free Ray quickly walking up behind the red-haired man. Renard never turns around. When Free Ray gets to Renard, he wraps a muscular arm around Renard's head and buries that face in his skin before he draws it back in a silent gesture to expose Renard's neck. Free Ray's other hand slips the Bowie knife across Renard's throat, opening a wound so black and wide it's its own kind of vicious smile before the blood rushes out and paints Renard's neck as red as his hair.

Free Ray holds Renard for a moment, bleeds the red-haired man like a stuck pig, short bursts of gargling sounds and weak muscle spasms the only fight Renard puts up. Then, with the front of Renard's coat slick with blood, Free Ray drops Renard's body to the mud, which folds in on itself like a discarded rag doll. No more greater or no more graceful a death than any other death Joshua has seen, perhaps much less so crumpled there in the mud, like Renard's soul is trying to draw that mud into its body, reshape him into the clay mold he was borne out of on some distant, distant, much holier day.

The left side of Free Ray's face is swollen, his eye sealed shut and his cheek bloodied. Nowhere can Joshua see Free Ray's horse. Free Ray cocks his head slightly to the side so that he can use his good eye, and he stares at Renard, the sun having mounted the hills behind him so that he looks mammoth in the enormity of that incipient light. He holds his arms at his side, the Bowie knife's blade shimmering. He stays in that pose for several moments before he looks at Joshua struggling to his feet.

Do you see now? says Free Ray, his voice high and tinged with malice like a catcall. It's never going to be the same again.

CHAPTER NINETEEN

Alone for the first time since he left Independence. But not lonely. Joshua feels freed, though he sees the world and its dark vision through the same pure hate with which he saw Renard. All day he leads the bleeding and limping Morgan on foot over the sparsely wooded hills and through the vales, carting that one sack of gold, a little over five-hundred and fifty ounces, what he has left of the bounty the now-defunct band acquired. Free Ray took his other sack. After Free Ray cut the sack from Joshua's Morgan and tied it to the other two sacks already lashed to Renard's horse, he just stood there silently for a while, his bloodied Bowie knife replaced in his belt, watching Joshua depart before he mounted Renard's horse, turned east, and rode off.

A long line of blood trails the Morgan now, grows thinner with each step. The horse keeps trying to stop, its mouth frothy, pink

foam that cakes its lips. Joshua tugs on it because he has no choice.
The Morgan coughs and whines each time Joshua begrudgingly
jerks the reins. Eventually, he mounts the Morgan, thinking that
riding it will at least endear him to it in some way and make his
insistence less harsh, and they walk into the night.

At what time Joshua nods off atop the horse he doesn't know, but
he is wakened when the Morgan stumbles to the side, then drops to
its front knees. As it rolls onto its side, Joshua jumps from the saddle
to avoid being pinned.

Afterward, the Morgan lies there wheezing. Joshua approaches
its face, crouches, and looks into its eyes for a long time. They are
so glassy, hardly focused. He doesn't know what he expects to find,
he doesn't know what he is looking for. He runs his hand across the
Morgan's cheek and down to its peachy nose, whispers, Shhh. Shhh.
Then he stands, walks over to his duffel bag, and retrieves his pistol.
He barely has the gun aimed before he fires, but he never looks
away from the Morgan. He can give it that, at least. And after the
lingering echo from that piercing *cack* dissipates, silence is dropped
on top of silence, leaving only Joshua beneath a new-mooned sky
and the methodical sounds he makes untying his duffel bag and the
sack of gold, the whole world watching him breathlessly like he is
the only thing left it has to offer.

TWENTY-FIVE MILES AND two sunrises later, he arrives at
Sutter's Fort, the population there having significantly dwindled
since he came over a month ago as more and more workers abandon
it for the gold fields. He buys passage on an old paddle-wheeled
steam dredger that resembles a floating cabin and is departing for
San Francisco along the Sacramento River, takes his place among
the fortunate seekers and the used-to-be sailors and the high-
minded politicians and the conniving businessmen and the lowly

families who ignore the gold rush. Dark gray clouds pile so low there is little difference between river and sky, such that had the world been flipped over like a snow globe the dredger could have kept on running that airy waterway.

A pitiful mist soon commences, and Joshua sits on his duffel bag, back braced against the leeward wall as if he is sitting a porch, and the river the land that would be beckoning before him. He ties the sack of gold to his leg should he fall asleep and a thief see fit to take advantage. Men fight on the huffing boat, fists flying high on drunkenness and pride, and there is a great commotion near the bow while a handful of joyous Mexicans sing along to another strumming a three-stringed inadequate guitar. But Joshua doesn't watch or listen to any of this, for there is nothing in life's gradations he believes he hasn't already experienced.

He speaks to no one, no one speaks to him. Though he hasn't eaten in nearly two days, he isn't hungry now. Hunger is a sensation tethered to a sense of groundedness and normalcy, the body recognizing when it can be hungry the same way it understands when its falling, and he wonders if he'll ever be hungry again. A hoar-haired woman draped in a hodgepodge of tattered rags totters over with one leg a foot smaller than the other, and she offers him a cloth filled with tortillas and pork. He refuses it, turns away from her when she insists with all her motherly instincts, instincts he has no use for because he's never known such a thing.

In the late afternoon, while it is still misting, a young burned-faced girl shuffles past him carting a small round cage that houses a bright green parrot. The parrot is sopping wet, the bird almost as big as the cage, its shoulders wedged between the narrow bars. The girl ignores him, but the sad-looking parrot watches Joshua, its flat eyes shrinking in with the focus of him. With a miniatured voice, it says, I love you!

The dredger clips along in the high river, through the lush and convoluted delta with sloughs as intricate as a man's inner-workings, coming to port in San Francisco Bay in early evening where the masts of abandoned ships like the *Niantic* rise to forgotten prominence and the docks hum with the lives of twenty thousand dreams, broken or yet to be it is hard to tell.

Joshua disembarks. He walks past the clamoring stevedores, their self-soiled clothes crusted and briny. A man by the wharves sells hard candy from a rusted two-wheeled cart to other men with no teeth who ramble about the whisking bay air that tails along with them. Into the densely crowded streets loomed by buildings. Not since St. Louis has Joshua seen so many buildings in one place. A sallow-faced boy with one leg hobbles along using a pine branch for a cane, wears a huge white barrister wig nearly half the size of his body. Bruised and bloodied men stumble past Joshua into fire-heated taverns or raucous banks, disappearing behind closing doors that hush the racket. A group of Ethiopian singers perched outside a gambling house door. Voices chattering at him with rummed breath in languages he's never heard from all manner of races, from shapes and forms that follow on his heels while he clutches his sack of gold (by now enormously heavy) even tighter and does all he can to ignore them.

Everything Joshua has known suddenly seems to mean very little.

He passes restaurants serving seafood and beef, cuisine from all parts of the world. Mexico, Peru, England, France, Italy, China. He passes saloons that appear to have floating eyes the way the fog haloes the lantern light; steep-roofed houses with smoking chimneys and where solitary candles burn in windows; more houses with no windows, no door, and no roof, yet still people celebrate within those walls; not far off the Catholic mission. He passes tents like the ones he saw and slept in in the valley, a church with a great wooden cross mounted to the roof, a thirty-foot flagpole erecting out of the dirt and flaunting an American flag.

Eventually, Joshua comes to a place called Dennison's Exchange. A Chinese man wearing a sedge hat and robes that hide his contours is thrown through the gambling house doors in front of him. The man raves in speech so slurred it's amazing he can talk at all, and Joshua skirts him and the rough-hewn men that threw him, removes his hat, and walks inside where the stale and noxious air is nothing like it was at the bay, the walls hanging with gallant paintings of ancient Greek figures he half-recognizes from books he read as a child, every man in there wearing clothes so polished and so new his own attire is laughable when they turn and regard him as he crosses to the mahogany check-in desk that's adorned with roses carved into the legs. There, he inquires about a room upstairs.

You alone? the attendant asks.

The attend chews a cigar nub between wormy lips, which he removes and holds between thick fingers, eyeing Joshua skeptically.

Joshua slings the sack of gold from his shoulder, drops it onto the counter, opens it. The man smiles all eyes.

Yes sir, the man says. And you prefer a upstairs room of course. Of course. What a view to be had from your balcony, sir. You can see the whole bay from there, when this fog lifts that is.

Joshua agrees: the view is spectacular, even with the fog. Phantomed steamer lights hover along in the bay while invisible sail sheets clap the riggings in the wind, a morbid interlude, so lonely and sourceless in the engulfed city, almost as if everything he sees and hears is alive in only his imagination. Two balconies over, a clean-shaven man leans a chair back on its rear legs and billows a stout pipe.

Joshua looks at him, and the man nods, and he nods in return with the understanding that he, like that man, has now made it. And this is his affirmation.

Joshua leaves his belongings in the room, takes the sack of gold back downstairs. He locks the sack in a safe guarded by a gigantic man with cauliflower ears, then seeks credit against the gold, which, of course, the house is happy to oblige. He turns around and observes the tables after that. Mostly monte, some faro, craps even. The clean and suited gamblers with their top hats and cravats and silver watch chains hooped under their breast pockets are corralled by big-breasted whores, all of them howling when bets are won and howling when bets are lost. Joshua shuffles the chips in his trouser pocket with one hand. The lightness of their weight feels odd given the dense gold he's used to, and he fancies himself a new kind of man, the kind that can keep company with this distinguished crowd and bet against the luxury of bad luck.

He runs a palm across his cheeks and over his paltry beard. He hasn't shaved in months, his face thick and greasy. He walks over to the barber's chair, which is tucked against a corner of the gambling house opposite the bar.

I don't charge by the hair, says the barber.

Joshua climbs into the seat anyway.

The barber hot towels his face and then shaves him slowly. Nothing has felt this good in a long time. The barber cuts the matted curls from Joshua's head and afterward sells him a canister of pomade. Joshua has never known such luxury before, but something turns within in him now, shifts his internal course like the experience of a tragedy where nothing can go back to the way it was (not even a prior memory) and thus remakes the very core of his being.

With the shave and haircut finished, Joshua wants a bath. The attendant has offered to arrange one for him, gesturing lewdly toward the whores in a clear misunderstanding of Joshua's desire. Instead, Joshua cashes out his chips and heads out of Dennison's Exchange.

He leaves behind the acceptable establishments and enters a dark and damp alley where men sleep slouched against brick and other men are dressed in women's clothing and wearing makeup so that it's difficult to tell where the costume ends and the real face begins. Here is a place that will suit him.

In a small and windowless room, one that's musty though surprisingly warm, Joshua undresses. When he gazes at himself in the mirror, he realizes he expected to find another creature staring back at him. Someone (or something) that bears no resemblance to the child he abandoned in St. Louis. And yet, what the glass offers him is merely that same gaunt and still-evolving body.

He turns away from the mirror, wraps himself tightly in a towel, and sits on a stool. He waits for the man who will fetch him when the bath water is prepared. Nothing hangs from the cedar-planked wall.

After a long while, a man who looks to be in his twenties with muscular arms that are swirling with indecipherable tattoos enters through a door opposite that Joshua didn't know exists. The man's thin brown hair is slightly balding on top, makes even thinner his witch-like face, and he wears a large tunic that hangs off one shoulder, his legs, which are ballooned in both thigh and calf and as hairy as a thicket, bare.

He beckons Joshua with one finger. Joshua starts to stand until he realizes he is completely erect, so he sits back down. He can feel his face flushing, and he pushes at the raised towel to hide himself.

The man grins. He walks over to Joshua and removes the towel. He touches Joshua's cock so gently and with hands so surprisingly soft Joshua thinks he might pass out from the rush in his body. These hands are nothing like his own, which are torn and calloused from the digging and the murdering, but he shakes that onslaught of bloody memories from his mind and does what he's grown so adept at doing to be the man he's become: He lets himself forget.

The man pulls him through the doorway, effortless with the strength he harbors in that body. They enter an obscure and darker room with walls covered in red velvet. An oversized white porcelain tub with raptor claws for legs sits in the very center of the room, a layer of steam hovering over the water. A huge gold-framed painting of *The Death of Hyacinthus* hangs on the wall in front of the tub, the laurel-crowned Apollo holding the young and nude Hyacinthus as the latter's body slumps gracefully toward the earth. Never has Joshua seen such a provocative painting before, and it seems only to supplement his arousal, to make him so hard he begins to ache.

Nearly picking Joshua up, the man helps him into the tub. Then he steps back and removes his tunic. Joshua stares at his bulging, dark cock (as wide as Joshua's wrist) that pulsates as he approaches the tub. The man kneels down and begins soaping and scrubbing Joshua's back with a soft washcloth, his arms, his chest. The man's arms work more smoothly than their intensity purports, the tattoos clarifying and mutating in the water, and his body smells sharply sweet with rosewater perfume. He works the washcloth to Joshua's stomach, bends further into the tub to reach Joshua's cock, and Joshua feels himself release, looks down to see the spunk bonding and floating like tiny islands in the milky water. The man smiles at him, rubs Joshua's cock gently as his own body eases into the water.

Knees to knees, the man cleans Joshua's entire body again before Joshua gets hard a second time. This time, Joshua grabs the man's arm and pulls that delicious body onto him. He fumbles around for a moment until the man pushes his hands away.

You lie back now, he says. There you go.

He reaches into the water, grabs ahold of Joshua. Joshua gasps.

How's that now? the man asks coyly.

Then he sits down on him. Joshua loses his breath for the pleasure in it.

That's it, the man says. I'll fuck you nice like.

But Joshua hardly hears him. He watches Hyacinthus's lifeless face come into and out of view behind the man's bobbing shoulders with a great distance between what he sees and the sensations in him, as if he is entirely disassociated from the physical space he occupies while he draws the essence of masculinity from this stranger like a farmer draws the essence of life from a well. So much water spills from the tub that Joshua is shivering by the time they are finished.

The man climbs out and wipes himself clean with the washcloth, then wrings the cloth out into the tub. He puts the tunic back on over still dripping skin, slicks his hair back off his sweaty forehead, pours more hot water into the bathtub, and again begins scrubbing Joshua.

Joshua relaxes, rests his head on the porcelain while the man works, listens to his own heart slowing, closes his eyes; and, far from what he always believed such initiation would reveal, the world and all its exciting possibilities are lost to him now in this culmination.

AFTER THAT, JOSHUA does things to Hardin he never thought possible with a man. Things with his tongue, things with his fingers and thumbs, things with his toes, things with his cock, and then, after his cock turns raw and swells up, things with strings of dark beads Hardin claims to have stolen, straight from the hands of those fawning Celestials.

As long as Hardin will tolerate all of it and keep coming back to Joshua, they keep at it, the two of them secretly secluded now in Joshua's hardly lit room at the 'stalwart and upstanding' Dennison's Exchange (because money can buy you anything except yesterday), the bed sheets so soiled from their escapades they are stiff and plasticky each evening Hardin departs and Joshua attempts to sleep.

When he does manage to sleep, or sleep manages to grace him, Joshua's dreams are filled with unchecked memories of murdered men. He wakes in sweats. He throws the blankets from his body. He opens the door to his balcony. He lies back down on his bed in the nude, shivering and chattering in the cold until his fingers and toes are numb and he can hardly breathe from the shaking, as if such masochism can in some way remedy all the wrongs he's committed, as if he seeks remedy to them anyway.

He takes gambling credit at whim. He buys a bowler hat, a trim-tailored black coat, a black vest, a thin white cravat the shop's owner shows him how to tie, a new shirt and new trousers, black leather boots, pomades his hair into a side part. A whole new being. He gambles downstairs while Hardin isn't around or is occupied by the likes of other men (or women, Joshua refuses to ask), times that make him so jealous he picks fights with the other gamblers just to get his head smashed by metal-ringed knuckles or blunderbuss butts or bare fists so tough they can annihilate stone and surely his consciousness. With the blunt parts of weapons he's never seen before, never even knew existed, weapons that descend on San Francisco from cultures too foreign for his imagination: samurai swords, sabers, bolas, crossbows, tap action pistols, khanjars, battle axes, maces, tomahawks, Dutch grenade launchers. Thus, the whole complex world will go black and simple, tolerable, if even for a matter of seconds.

Midday, on the nineteenth of December, Joshua lies naked in bed, a sheet up to his chest, watching Hardin dress with his head turned toward him. Hardin's cock bounces like a whipped rope while he hikes up his trousers, and then it disappears as he buttons them closed. Being witness to this exact moment in Hardin's dressing is a favorite pastime of Joshua's. There's something inviolable about the trousers closing up that cock, and staring at it openly before it becomes so confined he feels himself privy to a side of Hardin that he wants to believe others can never know.

The late-afternoon sunlight beams on this rarely unfogged and relatively warm day, and behind Hardin through the air toward the open balcony door is drawn a sleek and thin golden ray that swims with detritus. Spontaneously, and without sequence, that light will disappear for a moment, shadowed by an osprey or a great egret or any number of ducks that soar past Joshua's balcony and head toward the Marin Islands, before the light reappears as brilliant as it was before, and the cosmos it houses once again illuminated, the ungoverned patterns of that miniature world's day and night.

You can stay, Joshua says to Hardin.

Hardin has turned away from him and has one foot braced on the desk chair to tie his brogans. He stops tying and looks over his shoulder, sliding his stringy hair, which has begun to fall across his eyes, off his face.

That right?

Joshua pushes himself up against the wall so that he's sitting in bed with the sheet still across his stomach and over his hips and legs. He casually, though conscientiously, slides his hands behind his head.

Of course you can stay, says Joshua.

Hardin chuckles, turns back to tying his shoe.

You don't want to?

It's not about wanting or not wanting, says Hardin.

What's it about then?

Hardin finishes his tying, kicks the chair back under the desk, and turns around. His hair is sloppy and matted with days of unwash. He has this manner of always pushing the sides of it behind his ears, but today, he doesn't do that, and it lingers at his temples impatiently. He displays in his palm the gold Joshua gave him for payment this afternoon before he shoves it in his trouser pocket. Then he pats that pocket contentedly.

That, he says. Nothing else for it to be about except that.

You know I can pay you.

For what?

For staying.

Hardin grins.

And doing what exactly, he says. It doesn't all cost the same. That's no mystery by now.

Being here, says Joshua.

He taps the bed.

And? asks Hardin.

And nothing.

You'd be surprised what people are willing to pay for companionship out here, Hardin says.

He shifts his weight to one leg.

So what then? Hardin asks. You'd pay me for lying there?

Joshua nods.

All afternoon?

And all night, Joshua says. If not for the rest of the day and night, there's no reason to stay in the first place.

Hardin looks out the balcony, absently picking at his teeth with his index finger for a moment. He appears to be mulling possibilities, opportunities, choices in their infinite combinations and outcomes, but when he turns back and looks at Joshua, his expression carries the same apathy it carried before. He swipes at his hair again, crosses his arms.

Anyway, he says, I'm not in a charitable mood today, kid.

Don't call me that, says Joshua.

Hardin laughs.

He says, All right then. I can already tell you every detail of this ceiling, and I don't plan to look at any more than I have to today.

Joshua winces. He collects himself.

The money doesn't matter, he says.

See now? says Hardin. That's why I call you kid. Because you say stupid shit like that from time to time.

Joshua scoots to the edge of the bed and puts his feet on the ground.

It doesn't matter how much, he says. So long as you stay for the whole time, the rest of the day and the night, I'll pay you.

Hardin slowly shakes his head back like he's suddenly exhausted by such desperation. He stands there and looks at Joshua for a minute, his eyes working Joshua's spindly and youthful frame before he turns away without saying anything and picks up his coat, his body shivering slightly once he does like it can finally acknowledge how cold it has gotten in the room.

Will you stay then? Joshua asks.

Hardin still doesn't respond. He walks over to the door, puts his hand on the doorknob. Without turning it, he glances at Joshua, and in that fabricated and propositional voice of his (the one Joshua despises, the one Hardin uses for all the others Joshua believes he isn't), Hardin says, Tomorrow evening, I assume? Same place, same price.

Joshua jumps to his feet, which startles Hardin. Hardin leans back, instinctively grips the doorknob a bit tighter, as if that door and what it has come to signify in all these years working the dreamers that make San Francisco their fetishized and temporal home is his only means of safety. But as soon as he gets his hand securely on the doorknob, his body loosens. He's been in this position before, that much is clear. And whatever reaction he had to Joshua's initial aggression has dissipated in the conscious and pragmatic resolve that he can handle any boy in this burgeoning city that he must.

Joshua recognizes Hardin's changed demeanor, feels uncertain himself. He tries to calm the man by stepping away from him, toward the balcony and into the sunlight. A chill breeze sneaks through the open doors, lights his back into goose bumps, and he remembers in this moment that he is still naked.

The money doesn't matter, Joshua says.

He's forcing the calmness into his voice, cupping his sore cock with his hands to hide it.

He says, I'll pay you whatever you want. Five hundred dollars. A thousand dollars. You can have the gold I have left. It doesn't matter.

Trying to elicit some kind of response from Hardin, anything, he smiles, but that smile manifests with such artificiality Joshua looks possessed. Hardin remains stoic and still.

I like your company is all, Joshua says.

His voice trails off, his body he can feel going limp with regret and hopelessness and whatever other ruinous sensations overwhelm him like a disease, stripping him of energy and cognizance to leave him listless and blank.

For a bit longer, Hardin remains still. Joshua looks so childish and so helpless standing in the room like this, the bay and the distant green islands (Treasure Island and Yerba Buena, we call them now) cast in glory behind him; the sun at his back and so his face shadowed, darkened by his own naked body; his shoulders falling away from him; his face bruised by the beatings other gamblers gifted him; his muscles thin and worn by time, malnourishment, and hardship, by circumstance, by fate, all one in the same, by life immemorial; and he, Hardin, several years Joshua's elder, looking at him the way a disapproving teacher would, before he looks away from Joshua, first to the desk, then at the knobby wood floor as he turns the doorknob.

As he opens the door, Hardin glances back once more, though he only shakes his head.

Tomorrow evening then, Joshua says.

You should put your union suit on so as not to catch a chill, Hardin says and closes the door behind him.

Instead, Joshua bursts into tears.

CHAPTER TWENTY

Into the torment of spirits, wealth the arbiter of disgrace. A coattailed man banging away at a pump organ, a white-faced capuchin bouncing to the jeering melody on the man's shoulder. Joshua, too drunk on whiskey to see the monte cards facedown on the table, bets, and bets again, and bets again, each game losing more than the last. He upends the whiskey glass to his right and takes down nothing, so he yells into the crowd, to no one in particular, and a petite whore in a once-white dress appearing like an apparition through the thickly smoked air arrives with a silver tray holding a crystal decanter. She refills his glass.

He drinks the brown liquor down almost before she finishes pouring, sets the glass back on the baize with a thud, and gestures for another. Outside the sun is long set but Dennison's Exchange hums with the same energy it has all days prior and future, the candelabras lit, the pump organ filling that enormous space with uppity music to liven the men swaying in rhythm or swaying from their own inebriation. Joshua gambles until he has no chips, after which he stands and walks over to an empty chair and puts his head down on the table.

A pistol shot sounds. He throws his head up, reaches for his nonexistent gun belt as the chair tips back and he crashes onto the floor. He scrambles to right himself, frantically searches for aberrations or violence while rubbing the tired out of his eyes. The candelabras are extinguished, the sunlight peers in through the door and the cracks in the gambling house walls, and a wall of men are cheering in front of him. Soon, more pistol shots sound, fresh rods of light bursting through new bullet holes high up on the side walls while the barkeep and attendant plead for the men to stop firing.

God Bless Governor Burnett! a man yells. God Bless California!

December 20, and so begins the fate of this territory so soon to be a state and muddled by the politics of this insatiable nation.

THREE DAYS GONE by. Joshua doesn't leave his room. He waits for Hardin, eating and drinking from room service, each step in the hallway sending his breath and heart into a flurry before the steps grow softer and softer after they pass his door. He can hear the muffled pump organ playing incessantly downstairs, and he wonders if that capuchin still sits the shoulder of the organist and dances the tunes, its own life an oblivious blessing.

To get away from the music, he stands on the balcony wrapped in his fancy black coat and watches the steamers creep in and out of port, scores of people erupting from those boats the way an insect hatch happens in springtime. The days are cloudy, rainy and gray, no distinction between them, the hours clocked by the rich food brought to his door, carried by various half-naked whores he's never seen before or can't recognize from the whiskey drowning his brain, and a steady faint sun that wanes into a night so black and so solid it's like a great blanket dropped across the earth.

Christmas is approaching, festivity in the streets that he hasn't walked since the day he arrived. Goods from all over the world are peddled by merchants from all over the world in a mass of cultural confusion: a Chinaman selling maracas; a Peruvian selling West African tribal masks; a Bostonian selling boned chest plates he claims to have acquired in Texas off the lead-ridden bodies of Apaches he himself gunned down alongside Glanton. And on the afternoon of the numbered day God created the sun and the moon and the stars, the seasons, the passage of time, Joshua ties his cravat, buttons his fancy coat, puts on his gloves, and walks through his door and down the staircase.

At the bottom of the stairs, a bloated whore with her neck festooned by vivid flowers steps in front of him. She wears a bland-colored woolen dress that unsuccessfully conceals her pregnant belly. She brushes her long-nailed hand across Joshua's chest up to his shoulder.

He pushes her hand away, shoves past her. She spits at his feet, calls him some name in some language he's never heard before that sounds like a snakebite might feel. He walks on past the faro tables where gamblers pound glasses of whiskey and pound their fists on the baize, the banker calling the turn. He keeps on past other men and their accommodate whores, the organ piping shrilly to his right, as he tries to hide the limp he visibly and forever carries, but his knees and ankles are stiff from walking so much more now than he has in three days and thus make that limp all the more visible.

He steps out the front door into a rush of bay air and cold, a dank smell that creeps out of the bay and is transported to him on the westerly wind, and he rounds Dennison's, progresses through the dimly lit streets of San Francisco and the moral lassitude those dim lights foster. Into the green hills west of the bay, where deer track out in front of him and crows balk from the tops of pines. He walks for over two hours, cutting his way across the hills through the overgrowth.

When he breaks through the trees and the winter-green into a world much flatter and colorless, the wind is at his face, an instantaneous, environmental shift that would be impossible to imagine were he not experiencing it. The salty air feels heavy in his lungs, and he stares out at the Pacific, the immensity of which he can hardly believe even with it unfurling before him.

He walks onto the cold, hard sand. Small pale crabs no bigger than his palm skitter away, disappear into the surf. He expects the crabs to be revealed when the waves withdraw, like nature itself will lay bare their tenuous hiding places, but there is nothing to see but the washed sand smooth and ridged as bunched silk, as an elderly man's skin. Here is the end of the world, or the end of the world as it is known to him, and beyond where the sky goes on unchecked forever seems to reside the greatest freedom of all, for there is nothing of definition there, no history or remembrance, and what magnificent possibility can be had on such a blank canvas.

Joshua takes off his gloves and takes off his socks and boots, rolls up his trousers and union suit and steps into the frigid water. His clothes still get wet in the waves, which come in now at a greater height and a greater ferocity. The water is so cold it numbs his feet and turns the skin bright red, a cold just like that one that took his toes so many years ago, though this water is less dense, less like it wants to pull him to the dark depths of it and hold him there forever.

He looks down at the gnarled foot and the tiny white bits of shell tumbling over it, and his father returns to him for the first time since he arrived in San Francisco. The pain of his father's death, the absence it creates is so viscerally a part of him in this moment that his chest constricts and he thinks his heart might simply stop beating, his body dropping into the ocean and floating into the giant unknown where his father will be waiting for him with open arms. His mother and other father alongside the doctor, the three of them filled with so much love and warmth for Joshua that he will only know pleasure and happiness from that point forward, his fortune the depth of their forgiveness.

He leaves the water when his feet stop hurting, because he knows soon after this is the trouble. He returns to his boots and socks, sits in the sand and rubs each foot with his hands to warm it before he puts his boots and gloves back on. Then he leans back, waiting for the sky to darken, waiting for what inglorious and insignificant sunset can be had on this day with the rest of the nation at his back. Just the wind and the waves he faces, the white gulls that soar in the distance, diving chaotically. Sounds so rhythmic and so monotonous nature has become fed up with its own diversity, stages here the kind of consistency it would always maintain if not for humanity's penchant for boredom.

Lord Lord Lord, says a man behind him suddenly. Haven't you never seen anything so beautiful as that great body of water stretched out from here like some kind of field that just don't have any end? Going on and on into tomorrow, and perhaps the day after that if what they say about time and the lands beyond is true after all.

The man is young, younger than Joshua even, healthily round with his hair pasted to his head in thin wet strands, as he wears no hat, a left ear that hangs slightly lower than his right. He has sharp eyes, the kind of eyes that seem to see everything a few seconds before it's truly visible. He keeps those eyes on the ocean when Joshua turns around to look at him, and he takes a deep breath, sucks the ocean air into his nose and then exhales emphatically before speaking again.

It hits you when you see it for the first time, in the exact way they all warn you it will.

The man looks down at Joshua.

He says, It hits you like waking up from a nightmare with all that thankfulness and relief washing over you.

The man screws his eyes, noticing perhaps the bruises and cuts on Joshua's face he's suffered in the fights he's waged with the other gamblers at Dennison's the last several days. But if that is the source of that look, the man gives no other indication. His right ear drops even lower down his cheek with a smile to make it look like his head is tilting even though it isn't. His coat and other clothes are dirty and tattered, rags of blue, remnants of a once-pristine U.S. Army uniform, though the man's complexion and stoutness belie a tragic story those clothes appear destined to tell.

The man introduces himself (Aaron P. Cowl is his name) and shakes Joshua's hand vigorously before he takes a seat beside him, says he's from Laurel County, Mississippi.

Mighty pleased to meet you, William Tallow, says Aaron P. Cowl.

Joshua heard that fake name sliding out of his mouth before he fully registered the intention behind it. But as soon as it reached his ears, he felt a newfound calmness and confidence, his second past life disintegrating with each fresh iterance of that new name in his mind: Tallow, because he should pay homage to the doctor he and his father once were; William, because it is the most stately, venerated name he can think of right now.

Aaron P. Cowl points at his own clothes and says, I came straight from Fort Hall, courtesy of that Yank-run West Point Academy. And wouldn't you believe the poverty of Army life is an intolerable burden when stationed not more than a Herculean stone's throw from the richest valley in the world.

He pauses, kicks some of the wet sand with his heels. A nail jutting out the back of his left heel carves a deep rut into the sand. He sniffs the air around Joshua a couple of times.

You smell good, he says.

Joshua leans away in a nervous manner.

I apologize, says Aaron P. Cowl. I've not been around others in a little while, and I haven't been around others that didn't smell like the undersides of a sow during a Mississippi summer in an even longer while. I always did say things without fully thinking about how they'd sound outside my mind. Course, even if I do think about them, they don't sound much like I imagine they would. The peculiarities of speech, I suppose.

Joshua nods.

And you, William, he says. Are you a gold seeker?

Joshua nods again.

Of course you are. Why, I believe we all are here, if not yet then certainly soon to be. We live on the cusp of a new world.

Aaron P. Cowl rubs his bare hands together.

I left the Army for the gold, he says. Though leaving is a bit of a misnomer. The Army refers to it kindly as desertion. But I would desert any day for the chance at a bit of color versus one dollar killing Indians. I don't much like killing, so I didn't much like the Army.

I've never been in the Army.

You are a better man than me then.

Joshua doesn't say anything for a few moments. Then he asks, What are you doing on this beach if you're here for gold? There's no gold out here. You've got to go much farther inland.

I wanted to see the ocean, says Aaron P. Cowl. I've never seen it before, and a man who travels this far from his family and home must see every phenomenon, natural and otherwise, that he can before his inevitable departure.

It is beautiful, Joshua says.

He looks back out at the ocean.

He says, I don't think I've ever seen a thing like it.

Not even gold? the man asks.

Not even gold.

Aaron P. Cowl laughs.

On the day that gold is no longer beautiful, he says, you'll find me face down in the mud, or face up in a coffin, if I should be so lucky to have a death worthy of ceremony.

The sun has fallen beneath a lid of clouds and shoots that thin sky hovering just over the water with a brilliant and deep orange. The gulls that soar inside that color are dense black outlines of themselves, and Joshua stares at those depthless creatures.

So tell me, says Aaron P. Cowl. Have you found any gold?

Joshua nods. There's no point to dissemblance anymore. He's made and unmade and remade himself so many times that what he has left to hide is a conflation of lives and memories and objects that belong only to the actions that wrought them, which are themselves nonexistent now that he refuses to give them credence in his mind.

A rich man I imagine you are now, says Aaron P. Cowl. But of course you are. For what other kind of man would I find clean-shaven and sitting on the beach in such a nice suit with complete disregard for the saltwater and the sand. That is the kind of man I hope to one day be.

Joshua looks down at his clothes while he digs the sand with his foot, as if seeing them in a new light since Aaron P. Cowl noticed them. They are nice clothes after all, and he hadn't considered that lately. Aaron P. Cowl draws tight his ragged coat against the wind. He tucks his hands underneath his armpits to warm them, brings his knees to his chest.

It's mighty cold out here, he says. There's no kind of sun for warmth, not like a Mississippi Christmas, that's for certain.

Soon it will be dark, and with the clouds still so thick, that dark will bloom moonless and heavy. Aaron P. Cowl shivers. Joshua removes his gloves and offers them to the ex-soldier. It isn't that he feels sorry for Aaron P. Cowl or pities this ill-dressed man, but he feels, at this moment, some vague sense of compulsion. Like he has to give the man his gloves. Like the day can't proceed without him doing so, life itself depending on this one trivial act. A kind of hubris. A kind of lie we tell ourselves given the selfishness such generosity is often borne of. But Joshua believes in this gesture, convinces himself of its goodness. Because this is the first gesture in nearly a year that he's done in spite of himself, that he's done because everything inside of him told him not to do it.

I'm all right, says Aaron P. Cowl. Believe me, William, I've suffered worse in the winters at West Point. And Fort Hall.

Take them, insists Joshua. Like you said, I'm a rich man. I can buy new ones.

Aaron P. Cowl takes the gloves and thanks him. He puts them on with great satisfaction, then shoves his hands back under his armpits. Joshua clamps his hands under his armpits, too, for the cold that bites them is even sharper than he thought it would be.

The both of them sit there for a minute, Aaron P. Cowl kicking the sand with his boot heels while Joshua watches the sky going colorless, before Aaron P. Cowl stands.

I'm going to San Francisco tonight, then off to Sacramento City in the morning. I've got a horse I borrowed that's tethered to a tree over yonder. Well, borrowed is a tad of a misdirection, I suppose, but nobody is looking for her anymore.

Aaron P. Cowl pauses, tries to pull his coat even tighter though it's already pulled as tight as it can be.

Let me ask you, he says. Is it what they say?

Is what what they say? Joshua asks.

The gold digging. Those boys in the Army talk about it as if gold is as common to the ground as meanness is to a possum. That true?

Joshua thinks about that question for a minute.

I don't really know, he says finally.

I thought you said you were gold digging before.

It seems harder to find for some than for others.

So it's not like finding rocks then.

Aaron P. Cowl sighs.

He says, I figured as much. People say a lot about a lot of things, and from my experience, only about one tenth of it proves to be something other than a fabrication.

He turns and looks in the direction where his horse was left, then looks back at Joshua.

I don't know your state and all, William, he says, but you're welcome to a ride.

That's all right.

Lord knows I'm more than obliged, given that you offered up your only pair of gloves.

Consider them an early Christmas gift, says Joshua.

My one and only.

Aaron P. Cowl laughs.

He says, So you going to stay on this beach then?

For a little while.

This cold can kill you.

Joshua nods and looks back out at the dark water.

A few moments later, he hears Aaron P. Cowl's footsteps muffled by the damp sand as the man retreats, then hears only the lapping waves after that.

JOSHUA WAKES TO a shock of cold several hours later. The tide has come in and splashes his legs. It's after midnight, Christmas Eve morning. The clouds have cleared and directly above him, in a sky sprent with stars, hangs a half moon so bright it casts Joshua's indefinite blob of shadow on the sand behind him.

He pushes himself to his feet, stumbles awkwardly across the sand led by his own bumbling shadow. He takes the woods back toward San Francisco, walking more fluidly once the blood begins to loosen his muscles, his wet trousers heavy and uncomfortable and cold. The trek back seems hours longer than it was for him to get to the ocean, like he's been walking for days, although, in actuality, it only takes him a little over two hours before he reaches the city again. Even in that time-bridge of late night into early morning, the streets buzz with gamblers, miners, whores, sailors, and venture capitalists, and Joshua makes his way to Dennison's Exchange.

He stops outside the front doors, the thin windows of that great gambling hall before him lit yellow from the candelabras and the sounds of men yelling and cheering and the organ piping coming at him each time the door opens. He stands out there for a long time, still shivering though there's no wind, his jaw sore from so much chattering and his head pained with cold, before he turns, walks alongside Dennison's, goes around it toward the hills north of the city. He keeps his head to the ground, ignores those who mill around him until he no longer hears the myriad languages or smells that fishy, foul smell of the streets and people and looks up and there are no more buildings. Just juniper bushes and all manner of trees.

He finds himself climbing for a long time. When finally he stops in a small clearing out of exhaustion and turns around, he can see the entire city beneath him, the pale yellow light that sneaks through the buildings' wavy-glassed windows mashed together like a single star fell and landed on that island, a thing out of place, no more belonging here, he thinks, than perhaps any city belongs anywhere it's been settled, and that is the story of civilization, springing as if from nothing before the land on which it sprung is the nothing civilization once was. In that small clearing, Joshua collapses into sleep, his body exhausted from the climb and the cold.

He wakes having slept more soundly than he slept in months, thinking it's the sun rising that wakes him. The sky is a deep, pre-dawn blue, a rich and dense hue, but to the south it's lightened by a growing body of yellow and orange, where no sun will rise at all.

Joshua stands up and stares back at the city, half of it consumed by raging fire and Dennison's Exchange nothing but a wall of flames on its way to ashes, that fire rising so angrily and spewing from its tips such dense black smoke it's like a true and final reckoning. The rancid smoke is nearly unbearable even this far away. Still, he stares at that fire for as long as he can, wiping tears from his eyes, his hand clapped over his mouth, his breathing slow and measured. Gone is his gold, his guns, everything he once owned save for the clothes he wears. Gone is Hardin, and the organist, and the capuchin that sat that man's shoulder. Gone is the bed he rarely slept in, the bath-tub in which he was inaugurated. Men small as ants cluster around the fire, frantically throwing buckets of water at the unmitigated flames. But that fire coughs on and on until, finally, sudden flashes of light erupt east of it, the direction the flames run, and soon after, the boom from those explosions reaches him while he watches the buildings in its helpless path being demolished to stem its spread, and much of that great city on the bay leveled to the state it once was not so long ago.

When Joshua can't stand the smoke anymore, he turns his back to it. He faces off to the bay, to the east. The just-waking horizon unveils a gentle undulation of indistinct features where the right and actual sun will rise in due time. Standing here, thinking noth-ing, for his mind is now and finally clear, Joshua yawns the fatigue of a thousand days gone by and a thousand days to come. He scratches his chin. The budding hair on it seems bristlier to him, and one day it will make for a fine beard. One day, in a future too distant for imagination, too transformative for memory, where he hopes good and precious moments can be found.

LAND ACKNOWLEDGMENT

This work of fiction spans nearly half of the continental United States. Land that was mined, settled, commercialized, and developed through the displacement and forced removal of its Indigenous inhabitants. I would like to acknowledge the tribal nations and peoples whose traditional lands are both the backdrop of this story and the stage for our country's difficult and violent history in this wide region: the Osage, Quapaw, Kickapoo, Kaskaskia, Kaw, Otoe and Missouria, Oceti Sakowin, Pawnee, Cheyenne, Arapaho, Crow, Shoshone, Goshute, Ute, Bannock, Northern Paiute, Washoe, Nisenan, and Ohlone. I also recognize that despite my best efforts, this list may not be exhaustive.

ADDITIONAL ACKNOWLEDGMENTS

Many thanks to:

Kirby Kim, agent extraordinaire and a brilliant reader, along with Eloy Bleifuss and the rest of the team at Janklow & Nesbit Associates.

Meg Reid and Kate McMullen, stewards of Hub City Press, pioneers in publishing, and just all-around good people; and the amazing party of proofreaders, artists, and more who support Hub City.

Charles Frazier, for the vision, passion, and commitment that make the Cold Mountain Series possible.

Early readers, enduring supporters, and community builders: Michael Nye, LaTanya McQueen, Rachel Hanson, Dai George, Lauren Howard, Anne Barngrover, Vedran Husi, J.D. Smith, Heather McGuire, Alexander Landfair, Tana Wojczuk, Glenn Michael Gordon, Jeffrey French, Austin Segrest, Melissa Range, Can Kantarci.

Those who have given their gift of craft: Ben Marcus, Pam Houston, Stacey D'Erasmo, Susan Steinberg.

The organizations who helped me get these words down on the page: Columbia University in the City of New York, the University of Missouri, the Vermont Studio Center, the State Historical Society of Missouri.

The ranger at the Marshall Gold Discovery State Historic Park, whose name I can't remember but who humored me when I wanted to take a gold panning class alongside a bunch of elementary kids.

Mary Ann and O.D. Smith & Mary Louise and Gordon C. Sauer, for giving me the stories of my own history while making certain I see beyond myself.

My incredibly supportive family (Mom, Dad, Adam, Kinzie, Rebecca, Kyle).

Carli and Edith, my gold, my heart.

The COLD MOUNTAIN *Fund*
S E R I E S

NATIONAL BOOK AWARD WINNER Charles Frazier generously supports publication of a series of Hub City Press books through the Cold Mountain Fund at the Community Foundation of Western North Carolina. The Cold Mountain Series spotlights works of fiction by new and extraordinary writers from the American South. Books published in this series have been reviewed in outlets like *Wall Street Journal, San Francisco Chronicle, Garden & Gun, Entertainment Weekly*, and *O, the Oprah Magazine*; included on Best Books lists from NPR, *Kirkus*, and the American Library Association; and have won or been nominated for awards like the Southern Book Prize, Crooks Corner Book Prize, and the Langum Prize for Historical Fiction.

The Parted Earth • Anjali Enjeti

You Want More: The Selected Stories of George Singleton

The Prettiest Star • Carter Sickels

Watershed • Mark Barr

The Magnetic Girl • Jessica Handler

PUBLISHING
New & Extraordinary
VOICES FROM THE
AMERICAN SOUTH

FOUNDED IN SPARTANBURG, South Carolina in 1995, Hub City Press has emerged as the South's premier independent literary press. Hub City is interested in books with a strong sense of place and is committed to finding and spotlighting extraordinary new and unsung writers from the American South. Our curated list champions diverse authors and books that don't fit into the commercial or academic publishing landscape.

Janson Text LT Pro 10.8/15.9